A Spring
Retreat

Margaret Amatt

LEANNAN
PRESS
INDEPENDENT PUBLISHER

LEANNAN PRESS

SCOTTISH ISLAND ESCAPES

Book Two

First published in 2021 by Leannan Press

Second edition published 2023

© Margaret Amatt 2020

The right of Margaret Amatt to be identified as the author of this work has been asserted in accordance with the Copyright, Designs and Patents Act 1988.

Cover designs Margaret Amatt 2021

eBook ISBN: 978-1-914575-99-0

Paperback ISBN: 978-1-914575-72-3

For Ian and Ossian

CHAPTER ONE

Beth

Beth McGregor ran across the rocky beach and scrambled over the seaweed-covered boulders. Her wellies didn't give much grip, they slid on the kelp and she threw out her arms to balance. On her sharp whistle, two collies stopped and waited, ears pricked high, eyes alert. Beth slowed as she made her way to the shore edge. Bobbing up and down in the sea was a black shape; the round head of a sheep, gasping for air. Pulling some stray hairs from her face, Beth pinned them to the top of her head. Her heart thumped. Now what? The sound of a lamb bleating from a rocky ledge throbbed in her ears. Checking to her left, she saw it some feet up a sharp, rocky cliff face.

'Ok, how am I going to get you out?' she muttered, looking around, shielding her eyes from the low, bright spring sun. The lamb was safe for the present. In the sea, the sheep bobbed and spluttered. If she hadn't seen it jump, she might have thought it a seal. Approaching too soon might spook it. Sheep were flighty.

Ducking down, she crept across the rocks. If she had to go in, she'd freeze and she wasn't a great swimmer, certainly not if dragging a struggling ewe with her, but did she have a choice? It might drown, leaving a perfectly healthy orphaned lamb. Throwing her waxed jacket, heavy with mud, to the ground, she slid off her boots. She didn't fancy shedding anything else. A chill wind snapped, despite the blue sky. But she'd need dry clothes when she came out.

Before removing her overalls, she crept to the edge of an enormous boulder; the exact spot the animal had jumped from moments before. Loosening her zip, she watched. The sheep swam closer to the shore. Was this a chance? Moving too quickly could cause all sorts of problems. Behind, the two dogs, Mac and Rab, sat alert, waiting for the command.

Then with serene indifference, the sheep strolled out of the sea and hopped onto the rocks, shaking its sopping wet fleece. After a few kicks, it ambled up the ledge towards its lamb.

Beth breathed slowly until mother and baby were safely together. Adjusting her ponytail, she blinked towards the sea. What was that about? With a sharp headshake, she grabbed her jacket. No time to dwell. So many other animals needed to be checked. The warmth in the spring sun would dry the sheep better than any man-made device Beth could imagine and thank goodness because she was out of ideas. Lambing anywhere had its challenges; lambing on an island had its own special problems. Beth had lived on the Isle of Mull all her life, but every year the lambing brought something new. A diving ewe was a first and hopefully a last.

After retrieving her boots, Beth jumped on the quad and whistled the dogs. They trotted obediently and jumped on the back as she pulled off. 'Let's hope that's the only drama for today.' As they whizzed off, the wind whisked her ponytail. No chance to kick back and rest on her laurels. No. The perpetual fizz in her brain drove her to a blithering wreck every spring. Still so many long days to go, and who knew what dramas. She'd witnessed many birthing horrors in her time.

Once she and her dad had tried to rescue a ewe on a precipice in the middle of a birth. Beth still had nightmares about it. Thank goodness Dad had been there to keep her calm as she scaled the slippery cliffside. They hadn't been able to save the ewe or lamb. Then her world had been flipped upside down when Dad died shortly after, not because of the lambing, but a heart attack. Beth inhaled the fresh sea air. If only he were still here, how different things might have been.

A typical day in the lambing season could be traumatic. Some births were enough to put her off wanting children of her own. Another matter entirely. Beth stopped examining a ewe and stood up. At almost thirty-one, she was aware of her biological clock and had a lot of catch-up to play. Maybe too much. An unsettling twitch wriggled in her chest. Stretching and cracking her fingers above her head, she yawned. She'd devoted her life to this and dwelling on what might have been didn't help.

Gazing into the distance, she surveyed the familiar landscape. Rocky ledges and ridges circled a bracken-tangled incline towards the sea. The main road snaked through their land. A long, sloped bend marked the centre where Beth had parked the quad. On the upper side of the road, the scrubby grazing areas rolled higher towards the West Mull Wood. She stroked her throat, scanning for the other sheep and frowning at the vast countryside. No fences and fields here or the luxury of a lambing shed. 'Imagine that.' She raised her eyebrows at the dogs.

After locating all the ewes, she gave a brief sigh of relief. 'Well, they're all here and we haven't lost any lambs. Yet. So far so good.' It was the end of March, early days. All it would take was a short cold snap and that could be that. Lambs out here were susceptible to many things as well as the weather, attacks from birds: gulls, ravens or golden eagles. Even rabbit holes could be fatal; once in, they couldn't escape.

After an hour, she was satisfied and returned to the farmhouse for a quick breakfast and nap before round two. The warmth on her back was pleasant as she trundled up the track to the family farm, *Creagach*. She parked the quad and looked back down the path lined with large wooden sculptures of wildlife. These carvings were a tribute to what she could achieve given a rare moment of free time. Lasers of sunlight beamed through the clouds into the sea. A car stopped at the track end, and a woman got out to take a picture. The tourist season had started.

'Right, have a rest, boys.' Beth opened the barn door for Mac and Rab. Checking her phone as she crossed the courtyard, a message flashed. She swiped it open and grinned.

FIANCÉ FRANK: You still sheeping? Got any baaabies yet? (Haha, get it?) Why do you do it, you head-case? I'm coming back end of April, think you can still beat me at welly chucking?

'Yeah, no sweat.' She thumbed out a reply.

ME: Got a few lambs, they get a good price, island lamb is highly sought after, that's why I do it! Duh! And you even need to ask about the wellies? You've always had a pathetic action. Look forward to seeing you. Beth the Betrothed.

Kicking off her mud-caked boots, she entered the traditional farmhouse through the side door that led into a small porch off the kitchen. The smell of bacon and toast filled her lungs as she stepped onto the paisley rug which separated the room and acted as a passageway to the main corridor and the stairs. To the right of the rug was a lounge area with a view to the sea, Beth dropped her jumper over the sofa back, then turned to lean on the kitchen island.

'What are you reading?' she asked her sister, Kirsten, who was sitting opposite, engrossed on her phone.

'Just stuff.' Kirsten didn't look up.

Beth edged around the large island to the sink, inhaling the delicious cooking smells. Her mother, Gillian, stood at the range, turning the sizzling bacon.

'Everything ok?' Gillian asked, lifting the bacon from the pan to the plate. 'No problems?'

'Well, not now.' Beth threw her hands under the running water. Despite having removed her boots and overalls, she still had a mucky feeling that never quite disappeared. Oh, for a long lazy bath, but when? Freeing her hair from its ponytail, it caught and tugged. She needed to wash it and soak it in conditioner for about three days, but it wasn't going to happen. Not until around May.

'What happened?'

'A ewe jumped from a boulder into the sea. I've never seen the like,' said Beth, 'I don't know what possessed it.'

'Suicidal?' Kirsten ventured. 'But it got out?' She looked up.

'Yes, just strolled out like it had been swimming in the lido. I couldn't believe it.'

Beth settled at the island beside Kirsten, and Gillian served the delicious breakfast of bacon, fresh eggs, toast and Beth's favourite, cheese.

'Thank goodness, it survived,' Gillian said.

Kirsten resumed looking at her phone as Beth tucked in. The familiar twinge in her chest had nothing to do with how quickly she was eating and everything to do with how silly she felt having her mum cook her meals. But right now, she just needed to eat then get some sleep. Life in its raw state. Worrying about how pathetic her existence was could wait.

'Have you heard about this?' Kirsten spun her phone around for Beth to read. 'It's the newsletter from the Island Community Woodland Group. They've hired a new manager.'

'Yes,' Gillian said. 'Donald Laird told me they'd employed someone from off the island.'

'Read this.' Kirsten nudged Beth. 'On the agenda for the next meeting, the new manager wants to discuss plans to build a path and a logging route from the West Mull Woods to the main road. Isn't that straight through our farm?'

Beth looked at the tiny PDF on Kirsten's screen and squinted to read. If she tried to enlarge it, it would jump all over the place. 'It is. Has anyone spoken to you about this?' she asked Gillian.

'No, first I've heard.'

Beth scrolled down. 'Murray Henderson? Is that him?' Frowning, she read the summary of his career.

'Are you reading the bit at the end?' said Kirsten. 'It sounds like his full CV. It's as long and convoluted as the road to Fionnphort. He's been everywhere and done everything by the looks of it.'

Beth rolled her eyes. 'Yes. But I don't care if he's been to Timbuktu and back. No one's building anything over this land. I can't believe they put it on the agenda before consulting us.'

Gillian sat with a coffee. Beth slid the phone to her.

'No point, I can't read it without my glasses. Whoever this person is, I hope he doesn't come in all guns blazing. A path was mooted ages ago and your father approved of the idea in principle, but it was so long ago, must be at least ten years. This man can't just barge in here and think he runs the place.'

'One of us needs to go to that meeting,' Beth said. 'I don't want them deciding something and showing up here with big plans like it's a done deal.'

'Sounds like a job for you,' said Kirsten.

'No. You should do it, Mum. I'm hopeless at that kind of thing and I'll still be lambing.'

Gillian shook her head. 'Oh no. You better do it. I don't like to get involved in politics.'

Beth frowned and gave her breakfast a glassy stare. Gillian *did* like to get involved in both politics and everyone else's business, just not until she knew the winning team.

Another job for me, thought Beth. As Gillian sipped her coffee and Kirsten carried on reading her phone, a prick of irritation needled Beth's chest. *Like I don't have enough to do already?*

Yes, she got free board and lodging for her pain, but at thirty years old, was that anything to be pleased about? Gillian ran the B&B and the holiday cottages during the season, and Kirsten worked for an island tour company. They both had jobs, but of their own choice. Beth downed her coffee. In her back pocket, her phone vibrated. Pulling it out, she glanced at the message.

FIANCÉ FRANK: My biceps have developed since last we met! You're too devoted for your own good. Why not spread those wings? Fly like me!

'No chance,' she muttered into her coffee. Stuck in the grind, several days could pass when she saw no one except her mother and Kirsten, unless she counted Sandy, their farmhand, but as he worked on a couple of other farms in the area, she didn't even always see him. What other options did she have? Most thirty-year-olds had travelled, owned their own house, had partners and children, they didn't live with their mothers and have their breakfast cooked and served on a plate every day. The question always came back to who'd run the farm, if not her? It was her legacy. She couldn't just walk away.

Beth took off upstairs for an hour of shut-eye before the next check-up. She'd barely closed her eyes when Gillian called her from downstairs.

'I've got Sandy on the phone. He says it's urgent.'

No rest for wicked farmers. Not even for perfectly angelic ones who never put a foot wrong or did anything unexpected. Beth hauled herself up. Sometimes she wished for some excitement, a bit of something different, though hopefully not in the shape of another suicidal sheep.

CHAPTER TWO

Murray

Murray Henderson's trainers slapped the ground in a steady rhythm as he jogged along the road. A light breeze cooled his face. Was this really happening? If he hadn't been so intent on taking in every bit of the stunning seascape, he might have pinched himself. Mull had to be the most beautiful place he'd ever been, and he was here to live. He grinned, almost whooped. If anyone drove past, they would probably think him unhinged, running along looking so cheerful.

He rounded a bend. A winding section of road descended into the distance. Parked on the verge, a dirty Jeep was the first vehicle he'd seen for ages. Scattered sheep and a few lambs grazed on the scrubby hillside above the road. He sped down the hill, coming to an abrupt halt as he heard a gruff voice from below.

'Hey, you there! Give us a hand, will you?'

Murray's chest leapt in surprise. He looked around, scanning the verge beside the road. It dropped into a sharp incline. 'Hello?'

'Over here.'

Approaching the roadside, Murray adjusted the band in his hair. He hated hair on his face when he was running. Tightening it into a knot high on the back of his scalp, he peered over the road edge. The verge sloped into a hillside of scrubby wilderness and low bushes leading to the sea at the bottom, a mile or so from the road. Some bushes moved and an older man in a flat cap heaved himself up. He held his leg, struggling. Murray jumped off the road and waded through the bushes until he reached him. Taking him under the elbow, he helped him up.

'What happened?' Murray asked, pulling the buff from his neck. The man's trousers were torn, he held a nasty gash on his thigh. Sitting on a boulder near the roadside, he inspected it. 'Here.' Murray pressed the buff on the gash to stem the bleeding.

'Down there, laddie. In the gully.' The man nodded, his bushy grey eyebrows pointed the way.

Murray followed his gaze. At the hill foot, in a flat area, a herd of highland cows advanced on some sheep with lambs. The lambs frolicked around the shaggy cows, winding them up. One angry-looking beast shook its colossal head in warning. A stray hair fell across Murray's forehead and hung close to his mouth. He shoved it behind his ear, observing the scene with horrified fascination.

Before he could ask what the worst case scenario might be the man said, 'The coos are no' happy about the sheep. If they get too close, they'll skewer the lambs. I tried to warn them off, but one got me. Normally they don't bother, but when they're riled, you don't want to get too close.'

Lamb kebabs took on a whole new meaning. Murray turned away, squinting. This wasn't something he wanted to watch, and he most definitely wasn't going down. 'Ok, you sit tight. I'll try to get help. Is there someone I can call?' Murray asked.

'No need, laddie. I've already called the farmer.'

Murray covered his mouth to hide his relief. Thank goodness, someone who knew what they were doing. He glanced back into the gully. It would take someone a lot braver than him to approach those cows. His eyes widened as another one tossed its giant head alarmingly close to a lamb. 'Jeez.' Running his hand over his mouth, and onto his close-trimmed beard, he held his breath. The sound of an engine drew his gaze. A silver, mud-spattered Land Rover pulled up. 'He's here.' Murray vaulted on to the road, ready to explain. A young woman in dark green overalls jumped out of the driver's seat and Murray's shoulders dropped. Where was the farmer? He looked into the passenger seat, but it was empty.

Before he spoke, the woman crossed the road, jumped onto the verge and crouched beside the man. 'Oh, Sandy,' she said. 'Let me see'

'Naw, it's fine.' He furrowed his thick grey eyebrows. 'This young laddie helped stop the bleeding.'

'He should probably go to the hospital.' Murray placed his hands on his hips and surveyed Sandy's leg. 'Can you take him? I'll wait for the farmer and explain what happened.'

The woman frowned at him; her hazel eyes narrowed. Murray waited for a reply, peering out from under the stray hair as it sprung across his face again. He tucked it away.

'The hospital's on the other side of the island,' said Sandy. 'We need to rescue those lambs. The coos are nae giving up.'

'I thought you said the farmer was coming.'

Sandy's look implied Murray was a bit slow in the head. Murray turned to the woman and caught the end of an eye roll.

'You stay put, Sandy,' she said. 'I'll get them. Then we should get that seen to. It'll be worse if you leave it. And we can't afford to have you out of action.' Getting to her feet, she scanned the scene below.

Murray stepped up beside her. He was six foot two, but she wasn't far off being level with him. 'Excuse me,' he said, 'I'm not being funny, but did you just say you're going down there.'

'Yes.' She didn't look at him but whistled. Two black and white collies bolted across the road.

'I don't think that's a good idea.' Murray glanced back at the cows. They'd backed off, but still. 'Look what happened to him.'

The woman's keen eyes roamed over Murray's hair, then his neon running gear. Her left eyebrow piqued slightly. Murray's jaw snapped rigid. What did she mean by looking him up and down like that? She was the idiot proposing to waltz into the midst of a herd of angry beasts, not him.

'I'm going to move the lambs. Whoever you are, you can stay with Sandy.'

'But you can't do that on your own.'

'Why not?' She folded her arms, challenging him to reply.

'Well, because it isn't sensible.'

'And how would you know?' With a dismissive headshake, she flicked a bug from her sleeve. 'It's a lot more sensible than leaving them. I can't afford to waste any more time. Stay here. I don't want to risk anyone else getting hurt.'

Murray took a step back and held up his hands. 'It just seems a bit foolhardy to me.'

She didn't hide her eye roll as she trotted down the hill, through the bushes on the embankment and into the gully.

'She'll have them out in a jiffy.' Sandy nursed his leg as the woman crossed to the flat, tufty grassland where the lambs were now frolicking about still perilously close to the highland cows.

'Is she crazy?' Murray scratched his finely-trimmed beard. His mouth fell slightly open as the woman whistled the dogs, manoeuvring them into action. They scampered around, following the commands.

'Naw.' Sandy dabbed at his leg. 'She's no' crazy. She's a rare lass. No' many like that one.'

'Who is she? The farmer's wife?'

Sandy chuckled. 'Naw, that's Beth McGregor from Creagach Farm just up the track. She's from good stock so she is.'

That cleared everything up then, thought Murray, watching as the woman tramped along with the dogs, herding the sheep to safety. Clapping her hands, she warded off the cows. After checking over the lambs, she made her way deftly back to the roadside. The dogs trotted alongside.

'Right, let's get this leg sorted.' She approached Sandy and looked him over. 'Do you need a hand to get to the Land Rover?'

Murray gaped. After facing off a herd of highland cows, she was chatting as if she'd done nothing more exciting than take a stroll in the glen.

'Naw, course not. I'm fine.' Sandy pulled himself to his feet and limped onto the road.

'Well, I'm still taking you to the hospital,' said the woman.

'Yeah, he should go,' agreed Murray.

Her eyes flashed with irritation, and he mentally backed down. She was a bristly one. Ushering Sandy into the silver Land Rover, she whizzed off. Not even a wave.

Murray sat at the roadside with a sigh, resting his arms on his knee. What drama for only his third day on the island. To see it now, you'd never have known anything had ever been amiss. If that was the biggest problem he had to deal with, he was sailing. How hard could it be?

A two-year contract in a place that felt like a holiday island. One long vacation. He picked at a tuft of grass and threw it into the wind. Wonderful remoteness. Untouchable serenity. He was in control, finally. What could go wrong?

CHAPTER THREE

Beth

B eth stared at her nails. They hadn't been so clean for about a month. She adjusted her black t-shirt over her skinny jeans for about the hundredth time. Was it ok?

'You look fine.' Kirsten rolled her eyes as she passed, seeing Beth turning sideways in the hall mirror. 'In fact, you're blooming lucky. Lots of women would kill for a figure like yours. I'm stuck being tiny. It's not fair you were the one to inherit Dad's tall gene.'

'Yeah, well.' Beth sighed, not particularly enamoured by what she saw in the mirror. How did that thirty-year-old get there? She still felt like she was eighteen and ready to challenge the world, but the world wasn't her oyster any more.

'How about I put some make-up on for you? I've been watching some YouTube tutorials, you can be my guinea pig,' Kirsten said. After some indecision, Beth agreed, though it set her running late.

'Here you go.' Gillian stepped into the bedroom and passed Beth a black blazer before Beth could check what her face looked like. She hoisted on the blazer, now feeling ready to attend a Dynasty themed cocktail party. As her wardrobe contained nothing other than jeans, t-shirts, hoodies and one black dress, at least ten years old (that only got dragged out at Christmas), she didn't have much choice.

Pulling on Gillian's smart leather boots, Beth's toes curled as she dragged up the zip. They were a size too small and quite agonising.

Would anyone notice if she sneaked her trainers in with her? Before she got into the Land Rover, she removed the blazer. Resembling a 1980s film star wasn't going to give her a professional edge. Checking her make-up in the rear-view mirror, she almost jumped back. *Who is that?* Kirsten's newfound skill with the make-up brushes had made her look pretty good. Wow, she moved her face around the narrow mirror, *I actually look like a girl.* Her light-brown hair felt weightless as it rested on her shoulders. She wanted to flick it like that "just walked out of a salon" advert. The clean feel was beyond amazing after the weeks of lambing and having the tangled mess permanently scraped into a ponytail. She rolled down the window slightly to move the strands around in the wind and put on the music, rocking away to her version of "Eye of the Tiger", oh so glad the roads were quiet.

The village hall at Dervaig was filling up when she arrived. She recognised some old family friends, Neil and Joyce Paterson, sitting at the long table which had been cobbled together from various trestle-tables and was a bizarre jumble of heights. Pulling up a chair, Beth slipped in beside them.

'Good turn out.' Joyce Paterson smiled at Beth. 'I reckon there might not be enough seats. I've never seen it this busy.'

'Curiosity, I expect.' Beth placed a paper cup of coffee on their wobbly section of the table.

'I expect so.' Joyce shuffled her large bottom round to face Beth. 'Is that why you're here? To see how this new manager gets on?'

'Not exactly.' Beth tried to ease down her left boot with her other foot to stop it chafing her heel. 'We saw plans noted on the agenda for a logging road over our land. First we'd heard. I'm here to make sure nothing is decided without my permission.'

'Quite right too.' Neil Paterson looked round his wife. 'I met the new manager the other day. Not sure about him.' He looked around checking no one was listening and continued even though lots of people were. 'He's very young.' His voice was little more than a whisper, but he enunciated every word.

'Is he?' said Beth.

'And trendy,' Neil said in the same over-enunciated way, rolling his eyes.

Beth raised an eyebrow. 'Really?' Not the impression the CV-style career-summary had given. 'From his résumé in the newsletter, you'd think he must be about fifty, the amount of stuff he's done.'

'I never trust people like that,' said Joyce. 'The ones who've seen everything, done everything and got the t-shirt.'

'I expect he'd only have the t-shirt if it had a designer label on it,' muttered Neil.

'Well,' Joyce continued, 'I also heard he's taken one of the Westview cottages on short-term let and he's living there alone.' With a pronounced wink, she nodded and tapped the side of her nose. 'That'll please some ladies around here.'

'Yeah, my sister and my friend, Georgia,' Beth said into her paper coffee cup. Because who wasn't on the lookout for young, trendy, single men on the island? *Me, that's who.*

'Exactly,' said Joyce.

'Steer clear is my advice,' Neil added. 'Never trust these slick types.'

Joyce rolled her bulging blue eyes.

'That's him there,' Neil mouthed, cocking his head at a man who'd just entered the room.

Beth's gaze widened. A jolt hit her in the stomach, and even more stupidly, she felt hot. He was the jogger who'd helped Sandy. She'd assumed he was a nosey tourist and had been rather short with him. Flattening her lips, she remembered his flashy running clothes, the ones that left little to the imagination. She blushed at the recollection, how unlike her. Having worked with numerous male animals, very little surprised her, or so she'd thought. She tugged at the neck of her t-shirt, feeling dull, shabby and far too warm.

Murray Henderson caressed a neatly trimmed beard and laughed with a man beside him, before slipping his phone from his back pocket and checking the time. Beth toyed with a lock of hair, noting how effectively his jeans displayed a pair of well-toned thighs. He approached the table, revealing an eyeful of masculine chest under a crisp, pale blue shirt. Beth drew the strand of hair towards her lip.

'Oh, my.' Fanning her face in an over the top manner, Joyce turned to Beth, who quickly swept her hair behind her ear. Joyce waggled her eyebrows, making her eyes bulge. 'He's a bit of a tasty turnip. Not what I expected at all.'

'Me neither,' Beth agreed.

'And I like his hair. He could be a model for John Frieda.'

Beth sized him up as he ran his long fingers through said hair. It was a subtle mix of dark undertones with a lighter top layer, and although it was longer than average, it fell effortlessly around his face and didn't look straggly or unkempt. Even when it was tugged back into the band, it had looked stylishly windswept rather than just a mess, like hers. She smirked at the agenda in front of her. So, this was who they'd been landed with. An overdressed mainlander who'd been known to wear a man-bun. They were doomed, all right.

Adjusting his watch, Murray took a seat beside Donald Laird, the group chairperson. Beth's eyes darted to the man on Donald's other side. His son, Will. She gave him a wave and Will returned it with a grin. Once they'd been best pals, but he was married now. Things were different. He'd moved on.

Donald coughed in a fake little gesture, unnecessary as the chatter had died out. All eyes fixed unashamedly on the new manager, perhaps trying to suss him out by telepathy. Murray had a serious smile and kept his eyes down as Donald opened the meeting. With another cough, Donald said, 'Without further ado, I'll hand you over to the man on my right. This is Murray Henderson, and as I'm sure you're aware, he's taken over the position as Island Community Woodland Group manager. I think we'd all like to welcome him with a round of applause.'

Beth barely raised her hands off the table as she brought them together a couple of times. Pulling a side pout as Murray nodded and smiled with even and sparkly teeth, she half expected a twinkling star to gleam at the corner of his mouth. His pearly whites were toothpaste-ad perfect. In fact, everything about him looked as if he'd been cut out of a fashion magazine and pinned together to make the ideal man.

Putting up his palms to acknowledge the applause, Murray looked around, not making eye contact with anyone. 'Thank you,' he said, 'for making me so welcome. It's great to see so many people here.'

'He'll be lucky if there's more than one the next time,' whispered Joyce.

'This is just my first week in the job and I'm already getting stuck in and finding out about the land and the countryside. I can honestly say it's one of the most special places I've ever had the pleasure to work.'

Beth rolled her eyes as he gave a short résumé of his jobs so far. As she'd been awake since four-thirty, she had to stifle several yawns. When he concluded, he handed over to the secretary, Anna Maxwell, to give updates on previous actions. This was worse than parliament. Beth leaned her chin on her hand. Maybe a man with a black stick would come knocking on the door. At least that would wake her up.

Joyce looked at her and rolled her bulgy eyes into the back of her head, empathising with her boredom. Beth smirked, trying again to focus her weary gaze on Anna; a forty-something with a long narrow face and a husband she seemed to have forgotten about as she repeatedly swished her hair and flicked her eyes at Murray.

Feeling the desire to rub her eyes, Beth remembered just in time she was wearing mascara. Sitting for the next hour, or however long, with panda eyes was an alarming concept, especially if she had to speak at some point. Hopefully, she wouldn't. She sipped at the disgusting, now cold, coffee, hoping it might revive her.

'Next item, toilets,' Anna said, in a serious tone.

Beth groaned. *Really?* An agenda item on toilets?

'Yes, toilets.' Anna frowned towards Beth, 'There hasn't been any movement on these for weeks.'

Beth almost spat the dregs of her coffee back into the cup. Seriously? To put it like that. Hadn't anyone else noticed? Joyce smirked. Will Laird covered his mouth, but didn't look at Beth. Beth thought if she caught his eye they might burst into a fit of childish giggles. As if sensing a disturbance, Murray glanced down the table. The flutter in Beth's stomach was hunger that was all, though he was handsome, so most women would think. Not her, well, maybe a little. Clasping his hands on the table, Murray sat upright, hanging on every word Anna was saying or at least doing a first-rate impression.

Beth picked up a pen and doodled on the agenda. How long could she keep her eyes open? Anna coughed and Beth checked up, hoping Anna wasn't looking at her because she'd lost the plot. As Anna ploughed on with the next item, Beth caught Murray zeroing in on her. She made vague eye contact, though she focused more on his angular jaw, and the blondish brown beard covering it, the same colour as his perfectly shaped man-brows. Yeah, good-looking, sure, but also a pompous dick going by his résumé. He narrowed his eyes slightly, and his brow creased. Was that a flicker of recognition? No, it died. He looked away, shifting his striking pale grey eyes back to Anna. Maybe he was wracking his brains as to where he'd seen her before. *Yup, same scruffy girl, hiding behind some make-up and the wonders of a hairbrush,* thought Beth as she scrawled random shapes on the bottom of the agenda.

Finally, Anna concluded her round-up, but that was just the beginning. Beth was longing to go home and curl up in a snug, warm bed. At least for a few hours. It was getting late, and she had another early start the next day. She groaned as Murray laid out some papers and sent handouts winging round the table.

'Take one and pass it on,' Joyce intoned, pulling her lips down to indicate her utter boredom.

Beth straightened as she laid her handouts flat. A map. She stared at it. Printed in red, a road ran straight through her farmland. Shaking off the tiredness, she pulled on her invisible boxing gloves. She was ready.

Murray spoke again and began explaining the plans. It was an appealing voice, of course. He was a well-bred, well-dressed man who sounded well-educated and sure of himself. His low certainty would suit a TV voice-over. Beth bristled with every syllable coming from his honeyed lips. A few people nodded in agreement, as if under a spell.

'A good logging road is a necessity to minimise the damage to the environment,' he continued. 'Everybody here knows the benefit of—'

'I have to stop you there.' Heat fired in Beth's cheeks, but she had to say something. All the faces turned to her. Will looked directly at her, shaking his head as if to stop her. Looking away from him, she met Murray's eyes. Her body temperature spiked. She must resemble someone running a fever.

Murray granted her his full attention, pinching his bottom lip and tilting his head to the side. The cogs of his brain almost visibly ticked around trying to place her. 'You have a question? Fire away.' He smiled and oh, it was a beautiful smile, designed to put her at ease. But it had the opposite effect.

She shook her head as she laid the plans across the table one by one. 'I'm sure these plans are great, in theory, but have you consulted the landowners?'

'Well.' Murray briefly pressed his lips together. 'The fact is, Mrs? Miss?' He glanced at Donald for help and clasped his hands in front of him. His face took on such a patronising air Beth felt her teeth grinding.

'Beth,' she furnished.

'Well, Beth. We own the land in question, it's a community-owned woodland.'

Folding her arms, she stared at him; her left eyebrow almost left her forehead. If he was going to patronise her, she wouldn't be taking prisoners. 'Yes, I'm aware of that, since I happen to be part of this community. But these plans show a road stretching over land that doesn't belong to the community.'

'That's correct.' Murray's eyes flickered. 'And we've started negotiations with local landowners to ensure the plans can go forward.'

'Have you? When did you do that?' Beth rested back, keeping her arms crossed.

'We're doing it right now,' Murray said with an irritatingly calm voice. 'It's an ongoing process.'

'I didn't know a thing about it.' Beth blinked. His staring was unnerving. Was his brain working overtime to remember where he'd seen her? Or was he annoyed at her interruptions? Maybe both?

'The committee and the landowners involved are the people that need to know about this just now. There's no reason why anyone else should. That's what this meeting is about.'

Donald coughed as if to get Murray's attention, but it didn't work. Murray zeroed in on Beth.

Tilting her head, she pulled a fake smile. 'Exactly. And as I happen to be one of those landowners, I repeat, I don't know a thing about it. Nobody has negotiated anything with me.'

Murray shifted slightly, but his smile didn't flinch. 'Perhaps we spoke to someone else in your family?'

Joyce sniggered beside her, but Beth didn't find it funny. She trained her eyes on Murray. A hush settled in the room. 'No. No one has spoken to me or my family. In fact, in the plans, my farm seems the most affected. I should have been asked before anyone else.'

Murray had a steely look now. She sensed he'd worked out where they'd met before. His expression took on a new under-standing, and his roaming gaze was calculating. 'A thoughtless oversight, I assure you. You will be consulted.' He stopped and flicked through a notebook. 'Within the week, I have you on my list, and I apologise you weren't spoken to sooner.'

Beth wasn't ready to back down. She doubted he even had a list. He was probably reading his notes on his puffed-up CV. 'And what if I don't consent to this?' She cocked her head at him.

Murray's smile returned. 'We can discuss that during our negotiation. I'm sure everyone in the community wants what's best. Now, if you don't mind, perhaps we can move on to another point. We have a lot still to get through.'

It was Beth's instinct to get up and walk out, but she forced herself to stay put.

Joyce looked around and whispered. 'He really has a high conceit of himself.'

'He certainly does.' Beth's eyes still fixed on Murray. He looked everywhere else. *Trying to avoid me?* 'Well, if he comes knocking on my door, I'm going to knock him right off that high horse of his.'

CHAPTER FOUR

Murray

Laying his dumbbells in the corner, Murray stretched, flexing his hands in front as he looked out of his window at the view of the woods. So beautiful, like being in a holiday cottage. But the dream was already unravelling. Murray's plans had taken a dramatic turn after yesterday's meeting. A little damage limitation was needed. It shouldn't take long to smooth things over, then straight back to the timetable.

He showered and put on a soft grey shirt, not too formal, not too casual. He had to strike a balance and tread carefully here. His hair fell into position, and he ran his fingers through it.

Donald Laird had filled him in on the woman who'd chucked the spanner at the meeting. He pulled on his navy wool jacket and checked back the notes he'd scribbled.

Beth McGregor, daughter of farmer, died some years back.
Works on farm
Mother possibly landowner, not her?

Shutting the notebook, he kept the last fact upfront. He might need to play that card if she was going to be bolshie, and that seemed likely. It had taken a while, but he'd finally worked out where he'd seen her before. Murray had wrestled with the idea and concluded she was the same scruffy woman he'd met on his run. The intrepid lamb rescuer – either bold or crazy – but if she was willing to take on a highland cow, he'd have to tread carefully. She had balls, the figurative variety. He face-palmed, *stupid thought*.

Through force of habit, he switched on the Sat Nav, but he remembered where to go. The farmhouse was distinct, set back from the road with two neat little bothies at the track end. He'd noticed it on his run as a striking two-story building with smartly painted green trims at the windows. Driving south on the main road, Murray considered what tack to take. Tread extra-lightly or be firm? He smirked, she'd looked ready for a fight, but he wanted to play heavily on the community card. It would be hard for a local to come up against the entire neighbourhood.

The old stone building levelled into view from some way off. As Murray rolled up the track, he saw various outbuildings and a tourist office sign with four stars under the name Creagach Farm, Bed and Breakfast, no vacancies. Pretty planters offset a mix of old trailers, diesel drums, straw bales and various spare parts outside the door. Green daffodil shoots poked out among the snowdrops and crocuses, not quite ready to bloom. Most unusual were the large wooden wildlife sculptures, first on the track, then two more in the yard. Who made them? They looked bespoke. As a lover of woodcraft, he'd enjoy meeting the carver for a masterclass. A pleasant way to spend some free time.

With a deep breath and a quick collar adjustment, he knocked on the door. An older woman opened it and folded her arms. Beth's mother? She must be. Her eyes and the shape of her face said so. Frowning slightly, she pushed her glasses on to the top of her head to hold back her iron-grey hair. 'Can I help you?' Despite her sharp look, her tone was pleasant.

'Yes. I'm Murray Henderson, manager of the Island Community Woodland Group. I've come to talk to you about an ongoing project which may include some work taking place on your land.'

'Oh.' The woman looked around. 'You'll need Beth for that.'

He flashed her a smile. No, he definitely didn't need Beth for anything. In fact, if he could clear it up with the mother, he'd be content never to see Beth again. 'Is she the owner?'

'We all are, but she's the one to talk to.'

'I'm sure I can explain it just as well to you as it's your name on the title deeds, I believe.'

She placed a hand on the doorframe. 'I don't get involved in that side of things. Beth manages all that. I doubt it's your name on the land ownership certificate for the community woodland, but you're the manager. I'm sure you see the similarity of the positions.' She smiled. So benign. Murray made a quick mental reassessment. If he'd imagined the mother agreeing if Beth refused, he was wrong. This woman was equally intimidating. Her meaning rang loud and clear. He'd get nothing from her.

'Ok. So, Mrs McGregor? Is it? That was the name Donald gave me.'

'Ah, good old Donald. Yes. I'm Gillian McGregor.'

'So, is Beth here?' Murray raised his eyebrows and smiled as though he sincerely hoped so. The exact opposite of how he felt.

'She's out doing the sheep rounds. She'll be back soon, assuming nothing goes wrong. Come in and wait.'

'Thank you.' Rubbing his feet on the mat, he proceeded inside the warm room. 'This is lovely.' Exactly the kind of place he was working towards. Once he'd sorted the work stuff, he could get back to personal goals. Placing his hands on the back of a grey tweed sofa, he admired the cosy living set-up.

'I can't guarantee Beth will want to discuss anything just now. She's exhausted from the lambing. She might just want to lie down, but I'm sure she'll arrange a time with you.' Gillian stepped into the gorgeous farmhouse kitchen. The epitome of highland living with its thick oak worktops and the shiny black range. Murray ran his eyes around; he could see himself here, cooking something special on the range.

'Take a seat. Tea or coffee?'

'Tea, please. Thank you.'

Gillian gestured him to the tea table by the window in the lounge section. He hung his coat on the wooden chair back but didn't sit. The views both inside and out captivated him. The house was special, but outside, wow. His little cottage was just too far inland for a sea view. This, however, was perfect. The land rolled out over a neat garden with a rustic stone wall. Beyond the wall, the path split, one section veered in front of the garden towards a barn and some outbuildings, the other ran to the road and the two little bothies. The backdrop to it was the wide expanse of sea, some distance off but so dramatically present.

'So, how's life on the island suiting you?' Gillian brought over a tray of mugs and cakes. She sat at the table, and he followed suit.

'Good, thank you,' he said. 'Such a beautiful place.'

'What made you choose here? Out of all the places? I read your résumé on the Woodland newsletter. You've been around a bit. What's so special about Mull?'

'What isn't? Islands have always fascinated me.' His hair swung across his mug as he checked out the cake plate. 'There's something so intangible about them.'

'I see. But it seems like you've travelled a lot. You must enjoy it.' Gillian cradled her mug as she smiled at him.

Murray almost laughed, tucking his hair behind his ear and picking a slab of shortbread. It wasn't his fault he'd spent the last few years travelling, covering people here and there, never settling. He'd had very little choice.

'I like travelling, yeah.' That part was true. Though not from job to job. His career had been on track to be something special until Naomi had happened. And when Naomi happened, things went pear-shaped.

Gillian nodded and sipped her tea. 'Island life isn't for every-one. It's tough. Visitors see the bits they want to see but don't understand the day-to-day struggles.'

'Yeah.' He slid his fingers through his hair. 'I guess time will tell. My contract is for two years. That'll give me a good idea if it's somewhere I want to stay long term.'

'Indeed, it will.' With a glance at the clock on the mantelpiece, Gillian said, 'I think I'll give Beth a call and let her know you're here. If she's run into a problem, she might be a while.' She took the phone into another room, claiming she didn't get a good signal in here, but Murray suspected she wanted to talk in private. It'd be rude to listen in, especially when he guessed what they were talking about. It didn't take a master's degree to work it out. Him.

He'd finished his tea and was onto a piece of carrot cake by the time she returned. So much for his usual healthy eating routine. This didn't bode well. Where was his discipline?

'Beth's having trouble with a ewe, so she won't be back for a while. If you want to pop back tomorrow afternoon, she'll talk to you then, assuming there aren't any complications.'

He restrained his eye roll. This smacked of a tactic. Perhaps Beth wanted to make him sweat. 'No bother, thanks for all this. I've got some other things to do so I'll call back tomorrow.'

At the track end, he turned the opposite way from home and proceeded along the road, the sea to his right was a beautiful wide expanse of turquoise, shimmering in the bright spring sun.

Winding down the window, he put on the music. This was the life. Barely a mile along, Beth's Land Rover was parked by the roadside. He slowed, surveying the vehicle. Was the troubled ewe just a story? Maybe Beth was inside having a flask of tea and reading the paper. He wouldn't put it past her. His eyes travelled over the hill beyond. Just off the road, he spotted someone wrestling with a sheep. Was that her? He stopped the car and jumped out. Ok, so it was a genuine problem. He adjusted his cuffs, toying with the idea of getting back in the car and driving away. Why had he got out? What useful help could he give? His knowledge of farming was zilch.

Letting out a little cough, he announced himself. Beth glowered, her face, red with exertion, turned a deeper hue as she stared. He waved. How pathetic. She couldn't exactly wave back. 'Are you ok?'

'Do I look ok?' She gripped the struggling animal.

'Can I help?' Why had he said that? He was useless when it came to animals. She looked him up and down. He glanced to the side. *Yup, I'm not dressed for farming and I don't have a clue.*

'I don't need help.' She pinned the sheep to the ground. 'Is this some excuse to talk to me about the road? I just told my mum, I can't talk right now.'

'No. I was passing. Are you sure I can't do anything?' The animal flailed about. 'What are you trying to do?'

'I need to check her. Ok, fine. You can hold her still.' Beth waited, not looking at him.

Now he'd done it. With a curled lip, he rolled up his sleeves, approaching cautiously. He didn't have a clue where to start. Animals could smell fear. He must reek. 'Ok, so where do I hold it?'

'Just like I'm doing, take her and don't let go.'

Placing his hands on top of Beth's, he dug his fingertips into the oily fleece. Beth withdrew quickly and knelt to examine the ewe from behind.

It flailed and kicked. His instinct was to let go, he could hardly hold it, but he clung on for dear life. Dodging its frantic shuffling without getting his head butted was near impossible. He let out a groan like an angry bear.

Beth, totally unconcerned, put her arm out to restrain the kicks. Fluid seeped from the sheep's rear. Murray looked away. His stomach turned over.

Half closing his eyes, a crushing blow landed on his chest. He fell onto his back and let go. The ewe hopped off, wincing around, looking skittish. Murray rocked into a sitting position and massaged his ribs. Mud patches stained his shirt. The greasy sensation of lanolin clung to his jeans. Screwing up his face, he dusted off his arms. What a state. The shirt was going straight in the bin.

'Shouldn't wear your Sunday best when you're on a farm.' Beth rubbed her palms clean on her overalls, towering over him.

'Thanks for the tip.' Murray raised his eyes to her.

She put out her hand; he reached up. Gripping him tight around the wrist, she hauled him to his feet. As soon as his soles hit the ground, she released him.

'Sorry, I had to let go. It got me right in the chest.'

'Never mind,' Beth said. 'I saw everything I needed.'

'Thanks,' Murray muttered, still rubbing his bruised ribcage. Beth took no notice. 'What was wrong with her?'

'She's a young hogget and an inexperienced birther. I think I need to call the vet for this one. It doesn't look right.' She fiddled with the end of her ponytail.

'Oh,' said Murray. 'Is there a vet nearby?'

Beth rubbed her shoulder. 'Let's just say, it'll take him a while to get here. I'll stick around. Things can change quickly, for better or worse.'

'Should I wait with you?'

'I'm not some helpless child. I do this myself, all the time. You can go and do whatever you have to do.'

Murray backed off. 'Sure, no problem.' She really was touchy. His eyes lingered on hers. She had a striking face, though most of it was spattered in mud or worse. And she also had a point. She knew what she was doing. He was considerably out of his depth and he didn't fancy another close encounter with that ewe. 'If I stayed, we could chat about the land. We could use it as the ideal opportunity.' Cocking his head, he smiled, hoping it was an appealing look.

Beth's hazel eyes flashed, and she stepped closer. He thought for a second she was going to lamp him. She was so tall. He didn't back down. *Maybe I shouldn't have said it.* Truly terrible timing. Her face twisted with pure rage. Why couldn't he take his eyes off her? Energised, his chest tingled, and he clenched his fingers, maintaining his ground before releasing them. She halted a few feet from him. He held his breath, staring, his mouth fixed in a half-smile.

'Seriously?' She folded her arms. 'Didn't you understand my message? Tomorrow afternoon. I'm not talking about anything out here. I have work to do.'

Resigned, he backed off. 'I hear you.' He could also see her, and the sight was interfering with his ability to act rationally. His breathing had gone haywire, but he didn't dare push his luck any further. 'I'll see you tomorrow afternoon then.'

'I can't wait.' Beth turned away, her voice laden with sarcasm.

'Me neither.' Murray got into his car and sped off, flexing his fingers on the wheel. She was one hot girl. Wow! Where had that thought come from? He loosened his collar. *Control Murray. Control.* He had to behave himself and make her sweet. So far, he was doing a terrible job.

CHAPTER FIVE

Beth

L eaning on the table at the window, arms rigid, Beth bowed her head and stared at her hands. A heavy weight pressed on her hollow chest. She'd lost their first ewe and lamb of the season yesterday, and it hurt. 'It was my own stupid fault,' she said.

'The vet said it wouldn't have made any difference if he'd been there,' soothed Gillian, placing a steaming mug of tea on the table.

'I interfered too soon. Maybe I should have let nature take its course. I thought something was wrong.'

'And you were right,' said Gillian. 'Try not to dwell. These things happen.'

Dismayed, Beth rubbed her hand across her forehead, succumbing to unwelcome reflection. How could she not dwell? Two animals had perished under her care. A testament to her failure. The struggle to crawl out of the pit of imposter syndrome increased tenfold. What gave her the right to do this job? Other than what she'd learned from her father – how she missed him – everything else was just muddling along, pretending she knew what she was doing. If the pretext failed, so did the farm. 'We should cancel the meeting this afternoon. I'm in no state for discussions.' She moved away from the window and tied up her hair. What would she say? Country girl Beth didn't know how to work with managers and businesspeople. 'I'm bound to say something stupid.'

'You'll be fine, Beth. Stop running yourself down. I don't want to lose any land unless we know the ins and outs of it.'

'Then why don't you talk to him. I'm happy to tell him to shove his road somewhere the sun don't shine, but I don't have the energy for negotiating right now.'

Gillian rubbed her back. 'You're a strong girl and you always know what's best for the farm. I'll let you decide.'

No choice then. Was there ever? She downed the tea and left. A powerful temptation to get carried away and "forget" the meeting burned in her chest. When Sandy pulled up mid-morning, it left her only the thread of an excuse.

'You get back. I'll sort everything here, lass, and keep an eye open for anything this afternoon.'

With a deep sigh, Beth returned home, making the most of her time. A long shower. What a luxury, being clean at last. Once she was in fresh clothes, she pulled on a comfy pair of slippers. Oh, for just a few hours lounging in these. Not the most professional footwear, but she didn't care. Her feet needed a break from wellies.

Pinching her cheeks in the mirror, she squinted and pulled a pout. Too late for make-up. She was terrible at doing it anyway. Arriving like the pantomime dame wouldn't help her cause. Turning sideways, she pouted and waggled her eyebrows. Not too bad? Was it? Oh crap. She dropped her head in her hands. Who was this person? Beth McGregor, thirty, still living at home with her mum. Sad in anyone's book. Calling herself a farmer and hiding behind that was fine, but there was no escape from the truth. She rarely left the island, and she'd never had a boyfriend.

Boys had always been her friends. She'd hung around with them ever since she was a child. Even now, her best friend was a guy, Fiancé Frank. She grinned at the silliness of the name. The reality wasn't even close. Their childhood pact, to get married if they were both still single at thirty, had been a joke since the day they hatched the plan. It had brought tears of hilarity at the time and still invoked similar feelings. Beth looked back at her reflection. 'I'm ok being single,' she insisted to whoever was listening. Their ginger cat, Jellicle, opened one lazy eye from atop her bedspread. 'The farm is my life.' McGregors had farmed here for almost two hundred years, she was damned if she would let it fail because of her. Straightening her top, she stood tall and took a deep breath. Now she had to act professional, or Murray would trample all over her. He looked like a suave city-guy who was used to Friday night cocktails with a girl on each arm. She was bound to get tongue-tied and drop her size sevens right in the middle of everything.

'Get a grip.' She slapped her forehead. It was just the sheep, if she hadn't lost the ewe and lamb yesterday, she wouldn't be thinking any of these things. Nipping down the semi-carpeted stairs, she stopped at the bottom for a further adjustment. Nothing could change the plain Jane farmer. Waiting in the kitchen, she paced around with a knot in her stomach.

Gillian came in carrying a plastic box filled with white bed linen. 'I've accepted a booking for the holiday cottages. I didn't mean to start this early in the season, but why not? The people sounded desperate.'

'Right.' Beth checked out the front window for any sign of a vehicle.

'Would you rather I stayed? I'm sure everything will be fine, but I can leave this until later if you want.'

'No.' Beth put her hands on her hips and threw back her neck. 'You go. I just wish he'd get a move on.' She glanced at the window again.

'Ok dokey,' said Gillian. The door clicked and a few seconds later, Gillian passed the front window, heading towards the holiday cottage beside the barn.

It was better this way, without an audience, in case she made some ridiculous goof. Leaving the window, she moved into the kitchen. Should she boil the kettle? Put biscuits on a plate? This kind of thing wasn't her. Hosting afternoon teas and morning coffees was Gillian's domain. As Beth raked through the cupboard looking for something appetising, she heard the knock. Bracing herself on the worktop, she took a deep breath before shouting, 'Come in.'

Murray stepped over the threshold, his hair swept back in the high band. He raised his golden eyebrows and flashed a smile. Beth was suddenly aware of her heartbeat. It pounded in her chest and rang in her ears. She tapped her cheek; it had gone into spasm. She tried to allow a smile, but her face twitched.

Shutting the door, Murray wiped his black Chelsea boots. They looked cleaner than clean already. How could anyone keep their shoes that shiny? Beth blinked, biting her lip. He oozed super-smart, even in his casual grey sweater and trim jeans. The man version of the iconic woman who turned heads even in a bin bag. Here he was, man-bun and all, looking like he'd just strolled off the catwalk. Beth folded her arms, feeling like a grungy kid with a hygiene problem.

'Hi.' Murray pushed a leather folio under his arm and extended his hand.

Beth raised her eyebrow. Seriously? He wanted to shake hands? 'Good afternoon.' She put on a plummy accent. His answering smile made her want to laugh. When their hands met, a jolt of electricity ran up her arm. She tried to get free, but he held on longer than she expected. Did she have sweaty palms? *Let go!* Talk about embarrassing. She wrenched out her fingers.

Murray cleared his throat. 'How are you? How did it go with the sheep yesterday?'

He couldn't know it was the worst question possible. Beth's hackles rose. 'The sheep died, so did the lamb.'

'Oh no.' He looked genuinely concerned. 'That's awful. How?'

'Just one of those things that happen at lambing time.' She shoved her hands in her pockets, hoping she sounded aloof. She sure didn't feel it. 'It wasn't the first and it won't be the last.'

'I'm really sorry.' His tone was gentle. He gave an understanding nod and stepped forward. Panicking he might hug or try to console her, Beth nipped behind the kitchen island and retrieved two mugs from the rack. She slapped them down beside the kettle, harder than she meant to. 'Sit down,' she said. 'I'll get some tea.'

Noticing the tin full of Gillian's home baking in the corner, Beth beelined for it. She expected Murray to take a seat at the table by the window at the far end, sensibly putting as much distance between them as possible. The biscuit tin slipped as she turned to get a load of him lounging on a wooden-backed barstool on the opposite side of the island. Inhaling a lungful of air, she marched forward and clanged the tin in front of him.

'Wow.' He peered into it. 'Did you make these?'

'Of course.' She thumped a mug before him and leaned on the opposing side. 'Not.' Cradling her mug, she glared at him. Waiting.

He bit into a piece of Malteser cake, flicking a tiny crumb into his mouth from the edge of his neat honey-coloured beard. What a delectably sensuous mouth. Beth's jaw fell slack. Grabbing her cup, she took a quick sip of tea in case she'd drooled.

'So.' Murray placed his cake on the plate. 'I have the plans here. You saw them a couple of nights ago and I hope you've had time to review them and check they meet your satisfaction.'

Beth started to laugh. She couldn't help it. Maybe it was nerves or sleep deprivation. Whatever. It released some tension. Straightening up, she folded her arms. Murray had his stoically cheerful face on like he'd sported at the meeting, preceding one of his patronising remarks. He waited for her to stop, rubbing the short golden-brown hairs above his top lip with his thumb.

'Why don't we just cut out the crap? If you think I'm going to smile sweetly and sign your consent forms, then you've picked the wrong girl.'

Maintaining steady eye contact, Murray ran his thumb across his bottom lip. Beth nipped at her wrist. What was he thinking? He looked calculating; she shifted her feet.

'I'm sorry you think that. My predecessor left a file of notes about the logging road and path. The idea has been put forward before, as I expect you know, but the route was disputed, and the idea thrown out. According to his notes, preliminary discussions had taken place with...' Murray flicked some papers from his folio and read, 'The McGregors from Creagach Farm. They are in agreement that a logging road is a necessity and are strong supporters of this. They back the idea of it either partly or wholly crossing their land.'

'Let me see that.' Beth snatched the paper from him and read it. He looked up and continued rubbing his lip. 'This changes nothing. This could be ten, twenty years old.' She threw the paper. It drifted in front of him. 'Or someone could have made it up.' She scrutinised him. 'You, for example. It's hardly a document of any importance. It looks like something you wrote to cover your back.'

Murray's stare was unnerving. Beth gripped her mug, trying to look back, but her insides turned to jelly every time she did. Even if her father had agreed to plans in the distant past, he'd been dead seven years, things had changed. No way was she climbing down. Murray nodded and leaned back. 'What's this really about? The land or me?'

'Meaning what?' She really hoped she wasn't blushing. Fever rushed in her face, travelling downwards. Couldn't they settle it with an arm wrestle and move on?

'You seem to have it in for me, but I don't know why? It's unreasonable to obstruct what's clearly a sensible move for the community, and something you gave your support for at some point.' He pointed at the paper. 'I didn't make it up. What a ludicrous suggestion. Why would I? I'm a business manager, not an amateur.' He looked at his folder and shook his head.

'Excuse me?' He was asking for a face slap and if he opened his mouth again, she'd oblige. How dare he? 'Are you calling me an amateur?'

'That's not what I said. But the benefits are clear. I don't understand this U-turn.'

'Stop right there. Before you make a speech.' Beth straightened up tall. 'If you ever refer to me as an amateur or anything else along those lines, you'll never set foot in this house again. Your road will never see the light of day and you can flush your job down those non-existent toilets. I'll complain to whoever I need to, to get you sacked. I don't know who you think you are, but I have many, many friends and connections on this island. Name-calling respected people like us isn't a smart move.'

Murray's smile faltered. 'Look, let's not get upset. I didn't say you were an amateur, or that's not what I meant. I know you're not.' He side-eyed the door and blinked. 'It's your stance, it doesn't make sense.'

'Really? Maybe where you come from, you're used to steam-rolling over people, but it isn't going to happen here.'

'I'm used to no such thing.' For the first time, a twinge of anger clouded his voice. 'You don't seem to have grasped what we're trying to do—'

'No, you're right. How could an amateur like me possibly grasp something as complicated as that?' Crossing to the door, she held the handle. 'Leave. I am sick of you talking to me like this. It was the same at the meeting. Of course, I've grasped what you're trying to do. A five-year-old could grasp it. I don't need you patronising me every time you open your mouth. You're the one that hasn't grasped what's going on.'

'Then tell me.' He reclined in the chair. His calmness was beyond infuriating. Blood pounded in Beth's ears.

'Principles. That's what.' She advanced closer, wishing she hadn't. A waft of expensive fragrance drifted up her nostrils. 'It's... irrelevant what these plans look like, whether or not they benefit the community. It's the plain fact you did all this without mentioning to the people it concerned *before* putting it out there like it was a done deal.'

Murray leaned casually on the barstool's wooden back. She mustn't let him distract her. Why did he make her feel like a dim-witted child?

'That's what I'm doing now,' he said. 'No one said it was a done deal. This is the consultation. I saw the notes and acted. This way, we have the maps and plans ready. It's easier for everyone to see rather than having several discussions before we go anywhere, speculating about this and that. This way we can view things objectively.'

Beth shook her head. Could any more drivel flow from those peachy lips? 'You should be a politician, you're so good at twisting the facts to suit yourself, but it changes nothing. I don't care if we need a hundred and one discussions before any plans are drawn up. We should still have them. These are not community plans, they're not my plans, they're yours and yours alone.'

'So, what would you have me do?' A loop of stray hair swayed free from his band. He casually flipped it away.

Beth crossed her arms. 'Do what you want. Anything except build that road.'

Pushing the plans back into the folio, Murray got to his feet. Their eyes met. A surge resonated low down, an urge to rip off his clothes fizzed through Beth. She almost laughed. *How desperate am I?* Murray's smile vanished. Eye contact lingered. A tingle of fear-ridden excitement quivered up Beth's spine. Was he contemplating similar things? She looked away. That was stupid, of course he wasn't. Men like him didn't look at women like her, even to wipe their boots clean. It was obvious he would only settle for a well-groomed girlfriend with long acrylic nails and perfectly straight hair. He was probably just thinking how naïve and backwards she was.

'So, if I rip up these plans and start again from scratch, necessitating months of consultations just to come up with the same thing, then will you be happy?'

Without looking at him, she shrugged like a moody teenager. 'Who knows?'

'This is impossible,' he said. 'Why are you making this personal?'

'I'm not.'

'Yes, you are. What have you got against me?'

She smirked. *Well, I don't like man-buns; they look ridiculous.* Continuing to stare forward, she tapped her finger on the work surface. 'Nothing,' she said. 'I'm just protecting my rights and my land.'

'But you're hindering the community.'

'I think you'll find everyone here will fully understand my position. If I give in, who will you browbeat next?'

Murray shook his head. Beth's heart rate increased two-fold as he took a step forward. The intoxicating smell filtered into her lungs. 'I'm not browbeating anyone. You've got this all wrong. This is business.'

'Well, you can take your business elsewhere.' She shuffled back. 'I don't deal with shady traders.'

'Fine.' Murray slipped his folio under his arm. 'I wish I could say it was nice talking.' He stared for a second, dropped his head, then moved into the porch, slamming the door behind him.

Beth supported herself on the worktop, resting her face in her hands. God, she must have sounded like a boorish peasant. She knew it, but she couldn't simply allow him to march in and trample all over them. Beth McGregor didn't give in that easily. This was war. No matter which way she looked at it, she was right. He should have consulted her first. So why did she feel so irked?

Exhausted from her early mornings, she headed upstairs for a rest, but her eyes wouldn't shut. Thoughts pummelled her brain. Clinging to her forehead, she tried to shut down her mind. What if she'd done something really stupid? Did everyone want that road? Maybe Murray was right. And if he was, what else was he right about? Was she just a stupid amateur playing at farming? Just as he'd said. Probably. Because in the real world, she didn't have a clue about anything, especially men.

CHAPTER SIX

Murray

Throwing logs onto the fire, Murray not only relished the sharp crack as they walloped into the grate but the excuse to hurl something. 'That bloody woman,' he muttered through gritted teeth. Another log hit the pile.

Spring may allegedly have sprung, but the cottage hadn't noticed; it was freezing, especially in the evenings and at night. It had less insulation than his North Face jacket, but it would do to tide him over. He'd only taken it on a short-term let. Eventually, he wanted to buy a house. It was part of the master plan, the one he'd been working on for eight years and wasn't any closer to achieving, thanks to another bloody woman. With his contract fixed for two years, he would have time enough to figure out if this was the forever place.

He slumped onto his sofa and stretched his legs out in front. If he lay down and extended his arms above his head, he could probably touch his fingertips on one wall and his toes on the other side, but with so much furniture crammed into the room, he couldn't test the idea. Cute for a holiday cottage, but too small for him, especially as he banged his head every time he went through the bedroom door.

Rubbing his hands together, he craned his neck and checked out the view from the window. A chill in the air threatened snow. Even towards the end of March, it was possible, but nothing yet. From the cottage's lofty position, the view stretched across the forest that eventually met the West Mull Woods. If he needed a reminder of why he'd moved here, there it was. He stood to admire the trees silhouetted against the backdrop of a crimson sunset. Resting his hands on his back pockets, he savoured the remote location, relishing his cocooned position at the edge of the world. For several minutes, he remained quite still, looking and not thinking about anything. Yoga for the brain, beauty for the eyes.

As the sun dipped, and the sky darkened, he returned to the sofa. His eyes zoned towards a chat-head open on his phone. He didn't get mobile reception, but thank goodness for Wi-Fi. The stunning blonde woman in the little round icon was instantly recognisable. His jaw tensed. Flicking it open, he read.

NAOMI WALSH: Hey, Gorgeous. How's it going, handsome? I miss you. You don't have to do this to impress me. Come back, babes, please. We can pick things up again. The island idea just doesn't appeal. It's too remote for me. Come home and we'll find

*something. Please, babes. Sorry about the other thing, you know I
didn't mean it. Love you forever. Naomi XXX*

Dropping the phone beside him, he ran his fingertips across
his forehead. A message like that should have given him the warm
fuzzies and made him desperate to get back to her arms, but he
was stone cold. He leaned forward and grabbed a log to fling onto
the smouldering grate; sparks hissed at him.

You don't have to do this to impress me. She had the nerve to say
that. Seriously? Didn't he? Hadn't that been all their relationship
had ever been about? Both trying to impress and outdo the other.
*And she misses me! Ha, she has the nerve to say that. And she will
love me forever?*

Despite everything they'd been through, she still clung on like
a limpet. Snatching the phone, he discarded the message. Even
analysing it would make him sick. Sorry? Sorry! She expected
him to believe she was sorry. As if that one word atoned for
everything. She'd got him sacked, for Christ's sake. It didn't get
much worse, though it almost had. He could have ended up in
jail. And all because of her lies. Storming to the front door, he
opened it and let rip a yell into the glorious dark. Several birds
flapped out of a nearby tree with an eerie cry.

As he turned to go back in, the leather folder propped against
the wall caught his eye. He wanted to grab it and fling it into the
stream. From one pig-headed woman to another.

'I need a plan. This is just a hiccup,' he told himself. But when
did his plans ever go right? Should he burn the damn plans and

go back to the drawing board? No way would he grovel back to Beth with apologies, asking her to change her mind. Oh no. She'd made this personal and taken a dislike to him. How could he change that? Did he have to? He could just agree to hate her back. Sure, he could do that. What was there to like about her anyway? Annoying, stubborn woman. Strong, determined, hard-working, intelligent, and crazy-damned gorgeous woman. Exactly. Nothing.

Murray double face-palmed and threw his head back. No. No. No. He didn't need this kind of thing. His phone flashed again. He really, really didn't need this. He switched it off without reading the message.

After a disturbed sleep, full of crazy dreams, Murray woke, fearing for his sanity. If he visited a therapist, they'd have a thing or two to say about the bizarre nocturnal occurrences his brain produced. Opening his phone, he swore. The previous night's message wasn't from Naomi but Donald Laird.

With racing thumbs, he messaged back agreeing to meet at Donald's house that morning at, crap! Half-past nine, twenty minutes from now.

Ten minutes later, Murray was on the road, his wet hair pulled into a band. Feeling unkempt, he rolled his shoulders. Going out dishevelled made his skin crawl, but he didn't want to keep Donald waiting, especially as it had taken him all night to reply to his message. The whole OCD thing about being perfectly groomed had intensified during his years with Naomi. They both liked to look their best. Not *for* each other, but to be better than each other. So, who was it he was trying to impress now? Himself? Maybe. He just hated the idea of appearing at someone's door looking untidy.

The village of Dervaig was about a fifteen-minute drive from Murray's cottage, assuming no floods, stray cows or lost tourists blocked the way. As he followed the road around the edge of a low, curved bay, he admired the peaceful beauty. Winding down the window, he listened to the curlews and watched a heron wading through the reed beds.

Donald's cottage was along a side road close to the village hall. Checking his Apple Watch, Murray rocked-up twenty minutes late. Rapping on Donald's door, he waited, adjusting his cuffs, and smoothing his hair, which thankfully felt dry.

'Come in.' Donald pulled open the door with a smile. He was a well-built man in his sixties, casually dressed in a sweater and thick knitted socks.

'Sorry, I'm late. Should I take my shoes off?' Murray observed the spotless carpet.

'Aye, son, take them off if you don't mind. And there's no rush. This isn't anything urgent, pressing maybe, but not urgent.'

Murray leaned on the patterned wallpaper as he pulled off his Timberland boots and placed them on the doormat. A pressing matter sounded as serious as an urgent one. Donald led the way into the kitchen, Murray ducked under the doorway.

'This is my wife, Ida.'

Murray shook hands with the dainty woman. She smiled and patted the top of his hand before letting go. 'I'll put the kettle on while the two of you talk.'

Murray and Donald sat at the kitchen table in front of a square window with brightly patterned floral curtains. Donald shuffled some papers about. The map for the proposed logging road bobbed in and out of view.

'Is this about Creagach Farm?' Murray's nose wrinkled.

'Actually, yes.' Donald looked up. 'I had a call from Beth McGregor yesterday.'

Creasing his brow, Murray gritted his teeth. 'Complaining about me, I suppose?'

'Aye, son,' he said, 'pretty much that.'

'I might have known.' Murray raised his hand to his forehead. 'What am I supposed to have done?'

'Nothing really. I think you just came across a bit too full of yourself.'

Murray opened his mouth, dumbfounded by Donald's bluntness. Was that how people saw him? He wanted to reply, but he couldn't.

'Your plans are grand. And you're correct in thinking that's the best and least invasive route. You're aware the previous plans were kicked out because of several issues. It was part of the reason we couldn't get any sensible islanders to take on your job. There's a history.'

'I know that.' Murray had done his research, made new plans in a different location using the notes his predecessor had left. Sure, there might be difficulties. Nothing he couldn't handle. After the stress of life with Naomi, how hard could this be? She'd tried to talk him out of coming to the island right to the last, but he was determined. He'd let her rule him for too long. Murray slowly closed his eyes. He was still doing it, competing. He didn't need to, not now. Naomi was gone, they were finished. Why was he so quick to take up the gauntlet against Beth?

'The McGregors are reasonable people.' Donald gave the table a stoic pat. 'You talked about the note which stated they were behind the road and they are. Or at least they will be. They know what's at stake here, they've always been staunch community folks, they'll do what's right. They've farmed that land for a long time. When Malcolm died, it was a tremendous shock for all of us. He wasn't an old man, but one heart attack and boom. That was him. We all thought the farm would collapse, but Beth stepped in. And my goodness, she's a hard-working girl.'

'Aye, she works far too hard.' Ida placed mugs in front of them, making no secret she'd been listening. Opening a box of biscuits, she set it on the table. 'I feel sorry for that poor girl. She's young, she should be out enjoying herself. Married to that farm, so she is.'

'You wouldn't say that if she was a man, would you?' said Donald. 'And you'd be the first to accuse me of sexism.'

'But it's not the same. A man could get married, have a family and keep on running the farm. She can't do that, if she has a family, she'll have to be away from it for some time at least. Pregnant mothers, for a start, can't go near the lambs because of infection risks. So, unless she's lucky enough to meet a farmer, she's stuck. That's my point. And not only that, it was a terribly young age to have that responsibility thrust on her. Man or woman, no one deserves that. She was only twenty-three when Malcolm died. I don't think she's had a day off since then.'

Murray dropped his chin to his chest and rubbed his eyelids. Hearing it laid bare made him feel sick. He'd charged in like a highland bull and smashed the china on the dresser. Not so much as a second thought as to how Beth really felt. 'So, what should I do?' He tapped his fingers on the table. 'Throw out the plans and start from scratch?'

Donald sipped his tea thoughtfully. 'Aye, son, you might have to.'

'Or you could try the old-fashioned way,' Ida said.

'Which is?' Murray asked, taking a biscuit.

'Apologising.'

'Yes,' Donald said, 'that might work, but you might be a bit late.'

'It's never too late,' said Ida. 'First impressions can be changed. I'm not saying it'll be easy, mind.'

Tail firmly wedged between his legs, Murray left. Maybe Naomi was the sensible one after all. She didn't want this kind of life.

Now, he wasn't so sure it was for him either. Barely a fortnight in, and he was going to have to grovel. With a downcast expression, he sat in the car for a few moments. This could go either way, but south seemed most probable. His heart hammered as he approached Creagach Farm, almost as loud as it had when he'd stood in his manager's office not so long ago, facing questions about allegations that made his blood boil and his stomach churn. He was innocent, but the fiery heat of fury in his face was misread as guilt. His manager had been unconvinced. Murray's job had been effectively over from the second Naomi opened her candy-gloss lips.

But why now? What was he afraid of? Beth? He'd been afraid of Naomi. Her lies were dangerous. Was this any different? Beth wasn't lying but her stubbornness could cause all number of problems and now he was in the hot seat. All he needed to find was one word, five letters, starting with s and ending with y. If he got it out without choking, they might be friends and start over.

The Land Rover and quad loomed in the yard, a strong indication Beth was in. He bit the inside of his lip and rapped on the door. Waiting inside the porch, he looked around at the muddy boots and jackets. Gillian McGregor answered. Her smile morphed into a frown as she realised who it was. Murray summoned his most charming smile, but he suspected it wouldn't work.

'And how can I help you?' The cold nip in her tone told him Beth had given her side of the story very vividly.

'Can I speak to Beth, please?'

'Well.' Gillian's eyes darted sideways as she tried to look behind without turning around.

'It's all right, Mum. I'm here.' Beth advanced into the space behind her mother. She towered a head higher than her. Her hazel eyes flickered with irritation as they latched onto Murray. Folding her arms, she tilted her head, her expression closed.

As Gillian swapped places with Beth, Murray held eye contact. Beth's hair was loose and hung at her shoulders. A surge of heat coursed through Murray like he'd swallowed a naked flame. The embers crackled low, burning and gnawing deep. She was affecting him, but he had to stay cool.

Casually leaning on the doorframe, Beth pulled her arms tight across her flat chest. 'So? What do you want?'

Murray looked into the orbs of hazel. Hundreds of inappropriate ideas flashed through his mind, fuelled by the fiery embers chafing inside. His creative brain, usually restricted to nocturnal insanity, fired out all sorts of wild scenarios.

'Well.' He shuffled his feet and looked down, not wanting to open any kind of connection to his thoughts. They were not for her. But her face was too magnetic not to look back. His core temperature soared dangerously high. He had to get these words out before he said something stupid. 'I've come to say sorry.'

Her eyes darted skyward, and she shook her head. 'So, you think if you say a nice sorry, I'll smile sweetly and sign the consent?'

The corner of his mouth quirked up. 'Will you?' What a look. If eyes could kill, he was a goner. 'No, and that's fine. I spoke to Donald this morning and I'm going to hang fire on the road and the path.' He looked around, collecting himself and employing his most diplomatic tone. 'It was too much, too soon. I see that now. The plans are in the backburner and if we come to it at a later date, we'll go through the proper channels, starting with you and any other affected landowners.'

She leaned her head on the door. 'Good.'

'Good,' he repeated. His eyes dropped to her lips. Not a hint of gloss, but still perfectly pink. Her upper lip had the cutest little dip in the middle. Why the hell did he want to kiss her so much? *So inappropriate, Murray, so inappropriate*. 'Good. So we're all good.' Too many goods. And he really wasn't feeling good. He needed to go for a ten-mile run, or a cold shower, or both.

'Yup. All good.' Keeping her arms folded, Beth faced him down.

'Ok.' He shuffled for a few more seconds, then left. Back in the car, he knocked his forehead against the steering wheel. Damn it. He'd hoped maybe if he said he was giving up on the idea, she'd relent. Now, he had to give it up for real. But that wasn't what was bothering him. It was *her!* And what she did to him. Why? She wasn't his type, not in a million years. 'No, no,' he said in a grave voice, starting the engine. 'We are not going down that road.' No complications. Moving here was for time out, his retreat from mainland-life, Naomi, and the dating game in general. Beth was strictly business.

But business wasn't going well. He had no choice now but to return to the drawing board and slip back to square one.

CHAPTER SEVEN

Beth

B eth threw herself onto a grassy mound and sat back, enjoying the sun on her face. Sensing their work was done, the dogs flopped at her feet. 'Three more lambs and it's not even ten o'clock,' Beth told them. Mac gave a wide yawn and lowered his head to the ground. 'I agree.' The urge to follow suit almost overpowered her. Since the disappointment of losing the ewe last week, things had gone ok, but she couldn't afford to be complacent. Lying back, she admired the eruption of green spreading across the hills and along the banks. The mountain stream trickled towards the road, under a small bridge, and onwards to the sea. So tame. Come a few showers and it would be a raging torrent. She'd have to be mindful and move the sheep if a storm hit. It was a death trap if the burn flooded.

A cloud rolled over the sun, and the temperature dropped enough for her to want an extra layer. Opening one eye, she peered at the quad bike. Her jacket was slung over the seat and she couldn't be bothered getting to her feet. Her gaze rolled over the distant green to the woods, to the proposed log road's location.

'Ugh.' She threw back her head and covered her eyes. It just wouldn't go away. The most annoying part of it was she liked the idea. What she didn't like was Murray. Ok, not true either. Nothing personal. Though his lack of basic manners was unfortunate. As a man, he was, well, never mind. She had no business thinking about him.

'Come on.' She sat up and ruffled Mac's neck, then tickled Rab. 'Let's go and check the others.'

After an uneventful round, she returned home for lunch and found the kitchen table occupied. Kirsten cradled a hot mug, staring into the distance. Opposite was Georgia Rose, a friend of them both. Georgia smiled at Beth with a meaningful look at Kirsten.

'Nice hair.' Beth removed her jacket, making a beeline for the sink.

Georgia flicked the ends of her shoulder-length blonde hair to show off the newly dyed pink ends. 'Thanks. I thought I'd try something new.'

'Are you ok, Kirsten?' Beth eased off the tap, pulling her brows together. Sisterly concern she knew she'd regret. Cue a lamentation.

'Well, obviously not. You'd be the same if you'd had your heart broken.'

'Right.' Beth let out a sigh and dried her hands. 'I'm not really the heartbreak type.'

'Only because you never go out with anyone.'

Whatever. Beth kept the word in her head. No use reminding Kirsten she didn't exactly have time. It would just start a fight. Wallowing and mooning over guys wasn't Beth's style. How she and Kirsten had been raised in the same house, with the same family, and ended up so different was a puzzle Beth occasionally pulled out of the box and tried to solve. Not frequently though. And right now, her energy was channelled elsewhere.

'You'll get over him.' Georgia smiled at Kirsten, but winked at Beth. The sooner the better. Kirsten had mooned over island lad, Carl Hansen, for months, sometimes it felt like years. He was kind, handsome, and an altogether good guy. Except he'd never been interested. A month ago, he began dating Robyn Sherratt, the daughter of Gillian's friend, Maureen.

'Is Mum at Maureen's?' Beth asked, clocking on to why Kirsten was so down in the mouth.

Kirsten nodded and sipped her tea.

Beth sliced some bread and a mountain of cheese. When Gillian visited Maureen in the past, Kirsten had always wanted to go along hoping to see Carl. This was new. A deliberate protest. Staying home to let everyone know how upset she was.

'So,' said Georgia brightly. 'How are the sheep?'

'Fine.' Beth poured herself a cup of tea. 'All good this week.'

'Are there still a lot to go?'

'Oh, yes, a few weeks yet. Even though we have had a lot considering how early it is.'

'You'll be glad when it's done.' Georgia smiled with her broad pink lips. A mainlander by birth, Georgia had adapted comfortably to island life despite not having lived there for long, a sharp contrast to Murray, who still stuck to his city boy ways. Beth put down her mug with an irritable sigh. Why was she thinking about him?

'What brings you here, anyway? Come to commiserate with poor Kirsten?' Beth ruffled her sister's shoulders. Kirsten shrugged her off.

'No, well, yes. I mean, I understand how upset you are about Carl, but there are lots of fish in the sea.'

'Not here,' said Kirsten.

'Ok, true.' Georgia grinned. 'Maybe we should go for a man-hunt on the mainland.'

'No thanks.' Beth sat beside Kirsten. 'There's no way I could leave the farm for that long. And for what? The chance to hook up with someone I'll never meet again.'

'You never know.' Georgia winked.

'I think we do.' Kirsten flicked her long hair over her shoulders. 'I couldn't anyway. The season starts again in two weeks and I'm taking over the business this summer. I'll be solid with tours, plus all the extra paperwork. Not to mention my move.'

'What move?' Beth dropped her sandwich before it had even crossed her lips.

'Oh, yeah. I forgot to tell you. I never see you these days. I'm moving into the bothy. I need a place of my own. I'm too old to be living at home. Mum says I can have it rent-free for a month or so until the money starts coming in.'

Beth bit back several responses she didn't consider appropriate in front of Georgia, perhaps at all. Kirsten was going to be rent-free while they lost income. The bothy was a decent little earner. And all so she could have her own place. Well, lucky her. Pinching her lips together, Beth sparred with resentment. Sometimes things were so unfair.

At least once, Kirsten had hooked up with someone she met on one of her tours. Being tactful, Beth never let on she knew. Perhaps it would be easier for Kirsten if she had her own place. Maybe that would help her find a man. And wasn't that just dandy? Glaring at her uneaten sandwich, a sharp pain needled Beth in the ribs. The fact her life didn't revolve around dating was a relief if Kirsten was anything to go by. Being that cut up about a man didn't seem healthy. Beth was the older sister and there was no possibility of her moving on anywhere. Not unless they gave up the farm. And though she enjoyed it, for the most part, it was also a chain.

'You look tired.' Georgia pulled Beth's musings back to the table. 'I get up early sometimes to get the best photographs, but to *have* to get up every day. I don't know how you do it.'

Beth shrugged. 'You get used to it. So, are you two heading out somewhere?'

'No,' said Georgia. 'I just dropped in on my way past. I'm doing a photography session in the West Mull Woods behind the farm.'

'Oh. Is it a wedding?'

'No, thank goodness. I'm not fond of doing weddings, and can you imagine trailing the bride up there all dressed in white? Anyway, it's the...' She pulled out a piece of paper from her pocket. 'Island Community Woodland Group, a Mr Murray Henderson. He wants some pictures of him and his committee in the woods. For a website, I think.'

Beth's eyes rolled heavenward. 'You are kidding? He hired a photographer for that? No offence to your photography, but seriously, couldn't one of them just have done it with their phone? He really loves himself.'

Georgia smirked. 'Do you know him? I've never heard of him.'

'Yes, I know him.'

'Oh dear. Is he awful?'

'You'll probably love him,' said Beth to her sandwich.

'Why?' Fiddling with the pink ends of her hair, Georgia looked intrigued.

'He has a pulse, and he's single,' Beth suggested.

'Oh, Beth,' smirked Georgia, 'you are funny. What age is he?'

'No idea. Thirties, I guess. I don't know.'

Georgia waggled her eyebrows at Kirsten. 'Sounds promising.'

Beth sighed and took a sip of tea. 'Don't get your hopes up. He's an arrogant prat. Maybe I should come along and photo-bomb, I'd like to see his reaction.'

'Haha, feel free. You've got me worried now. What have I let myself in for?'

'Mum said he was quite a dish,' Kirsten said into her mug. 'Is he?'

'Depends on your taste, I suppose. He's not my cup of tea, far too slick. But I could introduce you if you like,' said Beth. 'Not sure he'd get on with the in-laws, though.'

Georgia shook her head, bemused. 'Well, I'm heading off in about twenty minutes.' She checked her Fitbit. 'All photo-bombers welcome.'

It was too delicious an offer to refuse. An excited wave of something new formed in Beth's stomach. The idea of bumping into Murray gave her a triumphant sensation like having the upper hand in a game. Though she wasn't sure what game it was they were playing. 'I'll drive up on the quad later,' she said. 'And innocently drop by.'

Georgia left with a broad smile. 'I'm so intrigued,' she said.

'Want to come too?' Beth asked Kirsten.

'No. I want to pack some stuff for moving.'

The pang in Beth's chest struck again. Kirsten maybe felt simi-lar things about being stuck, but she could go if she wanted. And here she was doing just that. Beth couldn't. 'Ok, see you later.'

After parking the quad at the wood edge, Beth vaulted the
fence and waded through the mass of branches and trees until
she reached the path. The dogs scrambled about, enjoying the
fresh smells. This was where the proposed logging track would
join, and she saw the sense in it. An easy track from the road,
rather than the convoluted way Georgia and the committee must
be walking just now. It was also unsuitable for log trucks, which
proved a great difficulty in using the timber viably. She knew that;
she knew it too well, yet here she was standing in opposition to
the community wishes because she didn't want to give in. A nice
little hole she'd dug for herself.

She strode down the hill for about twenty minutes until chattering voices came into earshot. As she rounded a bend, she spied
a group gathered by the trees. Georgia snapped happily, nipping
around to capture the best angles. Beth held back. What was she
going to say? Why was she even here? To cause some disruption.
She didn't want to do that. A fun notion, but...

Murray stood tall, stroking back his perfectly shaped hair. His
bright blue jacket looked brand new and designer. White teeth
flashed as he smiled. Holy crap! He wasn't just a dish, he was
a banquet. Gaping from behind a clump of trees, Beth forced
her mouth shut. Stupidly, childishly, ridiculously, against every
rational theory in her brain, she knew this was why she was here.
To see him. Even if they ended up fighting again, it didn't matter,
she just wanted to ogle him with a good excuse. Or even with a
terribly flimsy one, like this.

With a deep breath, she carried on walking. Georgia spotted her. 'Oh, hello.' Her voice was bright and chipper. Her lips, sparkly pink, matched the ends of her hair. 'Fancy meeting you here. Are you having a nice walk?'

'Yeah, it's great, thanks.' Beth scratched her neck as she moved her eyes to Murray and the group. 'A pleasant break from lambing.'

Murray trained his sight on her, burning into her like he could see right through her. He didn't waver. Did he guess what she was up to? It must look totally random, her wandering around these woods when she was so busy at the farm. A slight smirk played on his lips, but his eyes sparked with irritation.

Donald gave her a wave. She nodded in return. Will followed suit. Oh no, he was here too. So many spectators to her stupidity. She had to bury her true reason for being here. Her insides cringed. Murray was still looking.

Beth was on the verge of making a quick excuse and zipping on, but Georgia beat her to it. 'I'm photographing this group,' she said. 'Would it be ok if we nip onto your farm? There's a lovely spot there where the woods curve round. I can get them in and the sea as well.'

'Sure,' said Beth. 'I'll walk with you. I should get back.'

'Let's go this way, folks.' Georgia called to the chattering group as she caught up with Beth. Seconds later, Murray fell in step with them.

'Why are you here?' he muttered. The words landed close to Beth's ear. His exquisitely pitched accent wasn't rough or broad, just a perfect well-bred Scottish tone. Her insides froze.

'I can walk where I like.'

'Hmm,' said Murray, 'an interesting coincidence.'

'Isn't it?' Georgia smirked.

'Very,' Murray said. 'I hope you're not here to heckle me.'

'Like I even knew you were here?' Beth kept her head high. Georgia's grin was so vast it threatened to give the game away. If she opened her mouth, Beth would murder her.

'So, are you two friends?' Murray glanced between them.

'We are,' Georgia said.

'It's an island,' said Beth. 'Most people are friends. If they play nicely together.'

Murray's eyes glinted and he edged closer. 'I can play very nicely if I want to. What about you?'

She pulled a fake smile in his far-too-close face. Did he have no respect for personal boundaries? But holy cow, it was such a sight to behold, she'd given up caring.

'I mean, are you sure it's ok for us to have our picture taken on your land? I know how precious you are about it.'

Beth rolled her tongue inside her mouth, then smirked at him. 'Unlike you, Georgia asked politely.'

'And is that all it takes?'

'Maybe.' She dared him with her eyes. 'After all, you can play nicely when you want to, apparently.'

The corners of his lip curled. 'Oh, I can be very persuasive.' His voice was so low, it tickled in her ears and sent shock waves into her tummy. What other persuasive powers did he have?

Facing him eye to eye, she inhaled a waft of his cologne. Every golden-brown hair on his upper lip came into sharp relief and she wanted to get closer, maybe touch them. Clearing her throat, she said, 'Well, there's no need. You've scrapped those plans, haven't you?'

He looked around at the committee as if to check if they'd heard. Why? Had he not actually given them up? Was it just his big talk? 'I told you, they're on the back burner for now.'

'Best place for them,' Beth muttered.

Georgia giggled, and Beth jumped. She'd forgotten Georgia. 'Am I missing something here?' Georgia's eyes bored into Beth. Adjusting her collar, Beth looked away.

'Just a local disagreement.' Murray looked ahead, clasping his hands behind his back.

'Caused by you,' Beth added.

Tipping his head back, Murray set his gaze on the sky, and let out a low grunt. Georgia looked on with a slight frown as they clambered through the fallen trees and over the fence back onto Beth's land.

'You see how much easier this would be if we had a proper path.' Murray beat away some dead plants with a stick.

'Then you should have consulted with the person who owned the land and tried persuading them nicely. Oh, wait, that would have been me.' She flicked him another fake smile.

They approached the fence into the field. Murray jerked his head to indicate Beth should go first. Without hesitating, she sprang forward, clamped her hand on the post and jumped over. Murray vaulted over behind her. His heavy boots crunched into the thick undergrowth. Without touching her, he steered her forward, like one of her dogs herding a sheep. As they emerged from the overhanging trees, she stopped. They stared at each other. Behind, the others struggled over the fence, but she only had eyes for Murray. He stepped closer until barely a centimetre remained between them. Clenching her fists, she was ready for whatever he threw at her.

His brow furrowed, and his head cocked to one side. 'You have the most beautiful eyes.'

Ok. Everything except that. 'What?'

'Nothing.' He snapped his fingers as if to dismiss the notion and turned back to help someone in the committee who was struggling over the fence.

Beth swallowed and looked around. Had anyone else heard? Maybe she'd imagined it. Will grinned and waved. He wasn't the most astute observer, so nothing to worry about there. But Georgia. Her impassive face was glued to her camera. She flicked through some pictures. A tiny curl at the side of her lips indicated she'd heard something. Or at least suspected.

Cheeks flaming, Beth bid the others goodbye, claiming it essential to return to the sheep. No, it wasn't a claim. She did need to return to the sheep. They didn't say things that sent her head spinning into all sorts of confusing places. Struggling not to glance back at Murray, she descended the hill with a niggling sense he was watching her every move.

CHAPTER EIGHT

Murray

Leaning over the desk in his office, Murray clicked open an email from Georgia Rose on his laptop, ignoring the chair's creak. Flicking through the attached photos, he rubbed his chin. Very good. A professional take on the committee members out in the wilds, rather than in front of a clinical wall. No need for the committee to find out how much a professional photographer cost to hire for an hour. He was determined for the website to look first class.

People chatting below the window distracted him. Murray glanced into the street. His office being on the first floor above the village shop gave him an excellent vantage point. Well, if he was interested in what Mrs A said to Mr B. It could hardly be described as a hive of activity, a sea view would be nicer. Technically, he could do his job at home, but there was mobile reception here and a printer, not to mention the ready availability of snacks from the store downstairs.

The noise became distracting and Murray leaned over and closed the window before returning to his browsing. 'Oh my god,' he exclaimed, pulling back and almost toppling the flimsy office chair. Plastered across the screen was an extreme close-up of his profile and on the other side, Beth. Every detail magnified. The freckles on her perfectly straight nose. Stray hairs whispering over her forehead. And was that a grey hair in his beard? He squinted and frowned. Why in hell's name had Georgia put this in? Screwing up his face, he remembered what he'd said to Beth straight after that picture. Beautiful eyes. So corny. What had he been thinking? The truth. Oh, boy! He gaped forward, staring at the picture. She looked very serious. They both did. It was an expression highly charged with a mysterious force. He leant back and rubbed his thigh. Beth was a beautiful cocktail of explosives. She had the power to send him to all sorts of places he really didn't want to go.

Minimising the picture, he returned to the email. The temptation to pull it up again burned deep. With a determined sigh, he scrolled further to the message.

I included a nice photo of you with Beth, locally disagreeing about something! Maybe better keep it off the website, though, unless you have her express permission.

Three emojis crying with laughter followed. Murray snapped his brows together. He wasn't crying with laughter. No way was he going to try to get her permission for anything. He valued the shape of his nose too much. If they could just make friends, think of the progress. He could pull the plans from the back burner, get started straight away, work together, get to know each other properly, and show her he wasn't an awful guy. Yeah, friends would be good. Putting his hands behind his head, he reclined on the creaky chair, picturing himself down the pub with Beth. She looked like she could take him on in a drinking contest and probably win. Since he'd passed thirty, he'd become such a lightweight.

Donald had given him Beth's number. Picking up his phone, he brushed his thumb over the screen, then put it down, repeating this action several times before hitting the call button. It didn't connect. He wasn't surprised. She probably had no reception. Maybe she'd see a missed call later and call back. Was that hoping a bit too much? Especially as she wouldn't recognise his number.

Manoeuvring pictures into position, he continued tweaking blocks on the website, lining up text, trying to get everything perfect, while also avoiding looking at the one photo he most wanted to. After about forty minutes, the phone rang. Beth. His fingers twitched as he reached for it.

'Hello.' He attempted to strike a balance between professionalism and cheer all in one word.

'Someone called me on this number. Can I help you?'

'It's Murray.'

'Murray? Oh. What do you want? How did you get my number?'

'Donald.'

'He shouldn't be giving out private numbers. Isn't that against the data protection act?'

Murray leaned back in the seat with a grin. Her indignation was funny. 'Yeah, I think you're right, but I begged him.' He flattened the phone to his ear.

'You expect me to believe that. Didn't you just take it when he wasn't looking? That sounds more likely.'

'I'm not that bad,' he insisted. 'Listen. I really need to talk to you.'

'About what?'

Your eyes? If he said it out loud, she'd probably drive over to slap him. 'The road.'

'Again? What now?'

'It would be easier face to face. Can we meet? I can explain it better in person.'

'Fine, but you know how busy I am.'

'I do. So name your time and place. I'm available all day or tomorrow. I can drive over anytime.'

The line crackled and fizzed like she was walking. 'Well, I should be done here by six. Assuming there are no problems. We have guests in the annex, Mum's cooking for them. It'll be noisy in the house, so I could swing by yours if you like.'

'Wow, perfect.' He almost fell off the seat. 'Do you know where the house is?'

'Yes. The Westview Cottages.'

'The one at the top of the track.' Still in a daze as he ended the call, he smiled at the now blank screen. How easy was that? No arguing, nothing. His house was always immaculate, so he had no problem with her seeing it. An unexpected tension spread over his shoulders, the desire to do something flashy and impressive. Just like the Naomi days. Date nights were a big thing, each one had to be more spectacular than the last. Right, but this wasn't a date. Just a chat. Still, pressure. Should he cook? Rocking his head from side to side, he weighed the idea. He was a talented enough chef. Pulling a speciality out of the bag wouldn't be a problem; a spicy curry, an extra-cheesy lasagne or one of his legendary pizzas? But would she have eaten already? Maybe he could open some wine. Or was that just an insult because she'd be driving? Sticking to tea and coffee was the best plan, but with what? Everywhere he went on the island people served him home baking and goodies, but he was no baker. Especially not in – he checked the time – three and a half hours. It would mean a trip to Tobermory to buy ingredients, and the cake may still flop. A plan sprang into action. If he nipped to Tobermory, he could drop into a coffee shop and get something ready-made. Inspired, he grabbed his coat and left the office. Buying a box of Mr Kipling from the village store on the way out would have been simplest, but Murray Henderson liked to do things properly.

Stuck behind a tractor on the serpentine-like road between Dervaig and Tobermory, he tapped his finger on the steering wheel, almost abandoning the plan. Eventually, he arrived and headed straight for the bakery. Claiming the cakes as his own was a tactic he'd reserve for Naomi, Beth deserved the truth. At least he'd made an effort.

'Do you know Beth McGregor?' he asked the woman serving him. 'She's the farmer at Creagach near Calgary.'

'The name sounds familiar. Why?'

'I just wondered if you knew what kind of thing she likes.'

'No, sorry. These are very popular, though.' She pointed at some pretty cupcakes and smiled.

'I'm not sure pink cupcakes are the thing.' Beth was the least girly person he knew. Or was that just his assumption? Who was he to say she wasn't fed-up being a tomboy and would welcome a bit of pink? 'Actually, I'll take one, just in case.'

'Lucky lady, getting all these treats.'

'Ah, just business.' Murray pulled his wallet from his inside pocket. Yes, that was all it was, a business incentive, though she might call it a bribe. He could live with that.

Cutting a neat dash in his electric-blue Audi, Murray drove back, determined to be on his best behaviour. He would let her lead and go along with whatever she wanted. Hopefully, the right result would follow. A feverish bolt struck him between the ribs. Business, yes. Nothing else. What was he thinking? He needed to keep on the straight and narrow. Business was the only thing going down tonight. Changing into casual jeans and a loose shirt, he resisted the urge to light candles. *Seriously, Murray!*

Six-thirty came and went. Seven-thirty. Murray waited. Eight-thirty, the sun was setting, and an ambient red hue filled the window like a giant painting. He checked his phone. Nothing. Where was Beth? At nine-thirty, he gave up and put on the TV. But he couldn't concentrate. Where the hell was she? Should he call? He knew how busy she was.

Bitter thoughts needled him as he stared blankly at the TV screen. How much he'd given up in his life for women. One woman in particular, Naomi. He didn't want his fragile truce with Beth to evolve into another competition. Who would win the battle of the road? With Naomi, it had been: Who earned the most? Who had the toughest job? Who dressed the best? When Naomi had thought she couldn't win, she'd filed a sexual harassment complaint at their work. Despite it being false, Murray had been advised to leave. A quiet way to avoid unwanted attention. Naomi had been oh-so-sorry. She didn't think they'd take it so far. Yeah, right? Like he believed that. She'd got what she wanted, his downfall. He was sick to the back teeth of it.

By quarter to eleven, he was ready for bed. He cleared the kitchen and switched off the light. His phone flashed. Finally.

BETH: Trouble with lambs, sorry.

He smacked it down. Nice of her to tell him four and a half hours after she was meant to be there. It was so typical of women. Every ruddy time. He rubbed his forehead, massaging calm into his tired brain. Ok, that wasn't fair. Beth was busy. She'd had a tough time in the past couple of weeks and deserved some slack.

Beth wasn't Naomi. She was different, wasn't she? She wouldn't make up a story like that. Jeez, she didn't have to. Being stuck there on her own must be a living hell. How did she do it? He lay back on his pillow and stared into the darkness. A rustle of wind played with the trees beyond the window. Beth ran the farm on her own, so admirable. What a disappointment it would be if she turned out to be just like all the rest. Fickle and unreliable. Was he crazy to think differently? He closed his eyes, but sleep was a long way off. He was a bear with a sore head, confused and disgruntled.

CHAPTER NINE

Beth

Sleep eluded Beth. Despite not having gone to bed until after midnight and exhaustion crawling through every pore in her body, her brain wouldn't shut off. If she'd annoyed Murray by not turning up, did it matter? She couldn't help how busy she was. Time had run away. All her justifying wouldn't wholly remove the qualm in her chest. When her alarm buzzed at four-thirty, she almost launched it through the window. It took all her self-control not to hammer on her mother or Kirsten's doors and suggest they go out and do the rounds for a change. Honestly, Kirsten had a lie in every bloody day and got annoyed if anyone woke her before seven. She didn't know her luck.

Beth's mashed brain zigzagged between hyperactivity and crushing lethargy. The lambs were coming thick and fast and she couldn't let up for a second. Twinges of guilt poked her midriff when she recalled the night before. *Bad Beth.* She hadn't meant to miss the meeting, but things had gone crazy in the evening and she didn't have a second to call it off. Was Murray furious? She pulled her hair into a messy ponytail and grabbed her jacket. Obviously, it was a manic time, but she wouldn't be surprised if he came storming round in a foul mood. Which was just great. A face-off round about now was precisely what she needed. Like she didn't have anything else to do.

Racing over the scrubby hills on the quad, she stopped at ewe after ewe, helping when she could or if necessary, and constantly observing and checking for difficulties.

It was after twelve-thirty when she returned to the house for lunch. Utterly exhausted, she could hardly take another step, but a long afternoon loomed ahead. Gillian had made an enormous pot of soup. The smell was heavenly. Beth was so hungry, she dropped onto a chair and put her head in her hands.

'Everything ok?' said Gillian.

With a barely audible response, Beth checked her phone. No acknowledgement from Murray, she didn't expect it. The reception was dire. Messages sometimes got through several hours late, if ever. Mobile phone calls rarely connected. She imagined him seething in a cloud of steam. Maybe she should call, but she felt too frazzled. 'Has Murray called?' she asked Gillian.

'No. Not unless I was in the garden and didn't hear the phone. Why? Are you expecting him?'

Beth shook her head as she wolfed her soup. It burned her throat. 'I was meant to meet him yesterday about this bloody road, but things kicked off in the afternoon and I didn't have time. I bet he's really hacked off.' She slapped her forehead with her palm. 'It was silly of me.'

Gillian sat down and clasped her hands. 'What exactly is going on with the road? A couple of people have asked me. I just play dumb, but are we agreeing or not?'

'At the moment, no. He was underhand about it, but he wants to negotiate something, so I'm going to listen.'

'And then refuse?' Gillian raised her eyebrows in an all-knowing way.

'I don't know. I need to hear what it is first. But before I do any of that, I need to lie down. I am so tired, I can hardly think straight.'

Stripping off her clothes, she didn't bother putting anything on but jumped under the covers, enjoying the blissful warmth of the bed. Another perk of living with Mother, fresh sheets every day. She rolled over, but something was missing. Something she wanted. There had been no one in this bed other than her. Ever. Her eyes closed. Was it normal for a woman of her age to be so delayed? Behind? Backward? She didn't know what she was; she didn't feel any of those things, but something wasn't right. These days, if she met someone she fancied, she'd be embarrassed to do anything in case they found out about her complete inexperience. As the years ticked on, it was getting less and less likely. Who wanted a boring farm girl who'd never even visited the block, never mind been around it?

Hours later, she woke, unsure if she felt rested or disorientated. Her phone told her it was three-thirty. She leapt out of bed. Time for the afternoon checks.

Back in her old clothes, she whistled the dogs and jumped on the quad. She'd circled the lower area when a car pulled up. A man jumped out, and she recognised Donald Laird. He waved and headed towards her. 'All going well?' he asked. 'Looks like you're doing a fine job.'

'Yeah, not too bad.' She brushed herself down and joined him. 'Where are you off to today? Are you on woodland business?'

'Sort of, well, not exactly. I came to see you. Gillian said you'd be out and about somewhere.'

'And what do you want me for?'

'Well, it's about the plans for the logging road.'

Beth folded her arms. 'I see. Did Murray send you?'

'No, I haven't seen him. We talked about it last week, but I wanted to chat about your stance on it.'

'I stand by what I said.'

'But you do realise the plan has merits, for everyone, you included.'

She knew it. She wasn't stupid, better access, more productivity. Even on the tourism side of things, B&B guests could reach the walks directly from the house without trudging across a mucky field and scaling a fence. 'Of course, I do.' She threw her hands into her pockets and looked around.

'It wouldn't be invasive. The path will be done sensitively. Logging trucks will be infrequent users. I can't see it being a huge inconvenience.'

'I know that, but it's the way Murray went about it. That's what I disagree with. I don't appreciate his methods. And if I give in, what's next? Who's to say he won't do the same thing to someone else, only worse?'

Donald frowned, bobbing his head. 'I understand, but he's actually a pleasant chap. He just doesn't get how we work around here. He wants everything to move quickly, he just needs to slow down a bit. I'll have a chat with him.'

Beth rubbed her forehead with her oily palm. 'I was supposed to talk to him yesterday, but with everything else, I didn't have the chance.'

'His last job was on a huge forestry project in Perthshire, he's used to deadlines and quick work. When he gets used to the pace here, he'll get on a lot better.' Donald patted Beth's arm and nodded reassuringly.

After he'd gone, Beth slumped onto the quad bike. Should she phone him right now and have it out? She had no energy for arguing or even thinking. The raw part of her brain wanted to see him and tell him where to stuff it. Images popped up at random times and she found herself rehearsing conversations in the field, telling the sheep everything she wished she had the nerve to say to Murray's face, usually they ended with her snapping at him to piss off, though occasionally, rather alarmingly, they ended with them ravishing each other. Sleep deprivation was a killer.

With so much going on, she'd lost track of what day it was. And as weekends were just another working day for her, when Saturday came, she didn't even click. A brief lull in the lambing that morning set up the moment. It was now or never, and if she thought about it too hard, it really would be never. Leaping into the Land Rover, she drove a couple of miles northwards towards Calgary.

Letting out a yawn as the Land Rover jostled up the Westview Cottages' track, she passed the first two houses before seeing Murray's. Very quaint. Nestled amongst trees and invisible from the road, it had a cosy remoteness about it. The curtains were still drawn. Beth jerked her head back with an incredulous stare. What a lazy sod. It was almost nine-thirty. To her, it felt like midday, she'd been up so early.

Standing on the doorstep, she hesitated. Maybe she should leave it. What if he was ill? Or maybe he had someone with him. Her cheeks warmed. Murray may be pig-headed, but he was handsome, fit and sizzling hot. Anyone could see that, even a total neophyte like her. Adjusting her top, she held back. Who might be in there? A girlfriend? Maybe Georgia. She was trendy, single, and bound to fancy Murray. What if they were inside together? Burning acid fizzed in Beth's stomach.

Her fist hovered over the grey paintwork on the door. She pulled back, steeled herself, then rapped on it. Her heart thumped. This could backfire spectacularly.

Birds twittered in the trees surrounding the cottage, the only sounds for a moment until she heard some shuffling. Maybe Murray was throwing his woman into a cupboard and hiding her before he opened the door, but why bother? Experienced guys like him took things like that in their stride. Beth flattened her lips and looked around. What was she doing here, butting in on his privacy? She should go, and fast.

The door clicked open to reveal a bare chest under an open pyjama shirt. Beth reeled back, her pulse rocketing. Raising her eyes to his face, she swallowed. Murray squinted at her and raked his fingers through his hair. The bedhead gave his usually immaculate appearance an interesting twist. One that suited him, just the hint of ruggedness.

'Yes?' He frowned, leaning his arm on the door frame. The seductive nature of his body sent Beth's heart thumping a tattoo. 'What are you doing here at this time in the morning?'

'It's after nine.' She held her gaze fixed on his eyes, preventing them from straying down, but it was so tempting. Just a little peek.

'It's Saturday.'

She glanced sideways. Oops. 'Well, I had time, so I thought I'd come for that chat, but if you're busy...'

'Only three and a half days late.' He dropped his arm and sighed.

'I'm a busy girl. Unlike some people,' she muttered.

'Excuse me? I waited several hours for you the other night. I'm a busy man too. And it happens to be the weekend. I was having a lie in, but fine. Come in. Why not?' He stood back to let her pass.

'Thanks,' she muttered, taking the step up, so she was level with him. The urge to touch his chest was almost impossible to restrain.

'You can wait in there until I get ready.' He pointed to the door on the left.

She ducked into the little living room. 'Are you... alone?' she said.

'Well, I was until you showed up.' His sullen tone dripped with sarcasm.

Pinching her lips, she nodded and looked around. 'Shall I open the curtains?'

'Yeah, whatever. Watch TV or something. I'm going for a shower.'

I'd rather watch that, thought her lecherous brain as he left the room. Drawing back the curtains, she checked around as the room brightened. Obviously, he'd rented the cottage fully furnished. It didn't quite marry with his style. The sofas looked a little tired and the dining table-for-two slightly worn. Still, for the lack of space and modernity, it was immaculate. As she sat flicking through a golfing magazine, she worked out the layout. It was similar to one of the farm cottages they let to holidaymakers. Four rooms; living area, bedroom, kitchen and bathroom. The bathroom must adjoin the living room. Pipes clanked into action, and the shower started gushing. If only she could see through walls. What a vision. She cast her eyes around, trying to force a stop to the mental images. This was what happened to repressed thirty-year-olds who didn't get out enough. Ridiculous fantasies about people they didn't even like. Behind the two-seater sofa on the little dining table were several papers and notes, stacked neatly on top of Murray's leather folio, including the offensive plans. Funny how a few bits of paper could cause so much trouble.

The shower stopped. Some thumping about. The door clicked open. Footsteps and another door closed. Murray didn't seem in any rush. It was annoying and most probably on purpose. Revenge for her keeping him waiting the other night.

Beth jumped at a sudden thud followed by a series of thumps and Murray swearing.

'Are you all right?' She got up and edged into the corridor and peered towards the end door she assumed was his room.

Tip-toeing forward, Beth chapped the door and peeked around, trying to push it. It jammed.

'Jesus.' Murray jumped back, fastening a towel around his waist.

Beth's jaw almost hit the floor and she abandoned her attempt to force the door. Holy shit. Murray was incredibly fit, like a god. His muscles! Jeez. An actual, real-life six-pack. Hercules had nothing on this. Loosening her neckline, Beth felt dazed. *Pull yourself together!* Where had this silly girl sprung from? Hanging around with guys all her life, she'd seen topless blokes before, but not like this. 'Are you ok?' Why the husky voice? For Christ's sake, this was getting worse. With a deep conscious breath, she steadied her mind. It was just a body. They all had one.

'Yeah, fine.' He exhaled a brief laugh. A pink tinge appeared on his cheeks just above his beard line. Beth raised her eyebrow. He blinked, composed himself, and continued. 'I, eh, opened the airing cupboard, and the shelf fell out. I think the landlord has booby-trapped it.'

Beth realised the reason she couldn't get any further was the pile of towels blocking the entrance. A bifold door lay ajar.

'Seriously, it does my head in.' Murray moved forward and waggled the askew shelf. 'I opened the hatch to the attic the other day and a dead bat fell out.'

Beth's eyes dropped unintentionally to his bare torso. 'That's old houses for you, isn't it?' She pouted, considering. 'I could fix that shelf.'

Murray smiled, his light-grey eyes sparkling as they roamed over her face. Suddenly, she felt even more exposed than him despite having her clothes firmly in place. He turned towards her. The movement filled the air with a powerful scent of masculine body wash. Beth didn't flinch, but a stream of crazy fantasies burst into her head. Murray's gaze dropped to her lips and back. He gripped his towel until his knuckles blanched. 'Go ahead.'

'Not right now, obviously.' Swallowing hard, Beth pressed her lips together. A tremor fizzled through her. Murray grinned his perfectly even smile, and the urge to grab hold of him almost overpowered her. Deeper down, the desperation to escape held her back. 'Eh, no, after you, er...' She wished her voice didn't smack like someone in need of Strepsils. Clearing her throat, she continued, 'Get your clothes on.'

'Well, you better get out then,' he said. 'Unless there's something else you want to see.'

She folded her arms and tilted her head. Murray's lips curled up, and he scratched the top of his towel with his index finger. If he let go of it, she might actually die. 'I'll give that a miss.' She backed out.

He gave a wry nod, suggesting she didn't know what she was missing. And he was right. Before reaching the safety of the living room, she let out a deep sigh. Wow. He was hot. Scorching hot. She fanned her cheeks. He wasn't for her. No. If he knew what she was, he wouldn't touch her with a barge pole. He was a man who'd been around the block, while she hadn't even peeked around the corner, making her incompatible with the walking six-pack in the bedroom.

Her eyes closed. God, if Murray found out, he'd laugh her out of the house. He'd appreciate exactly what kind of idiot he was dealing with. Some blind infatuation had struck. She had to keep her crazy hormones in check. It boiled down to her lack of sleep and total mental exhaustion. She wasn't thinking straight.

When Murray came into the room in a full set of clothes, the random surges in Beth's lower stomach increased as she observed how tight his jeans were. His grey check shirt draped open just enough to make the heat rise in her cheeks.

'So.' He ruffled his slightly damp hair as though trying to coax sense back into his brain. 'What did you want to discuss?'

'The road, I assume. You're the one that invited me. I've just been caught up in the lambing.'

'Well, nothing much has changed regarding the road. I've left it on the back burner as we agreed.'

'Actually, the plans are sitting on the table,' she said, 'which kind of tells me, you haven't put it to rest.'

Murray shuffled his feet and placed his hand over his mouth before replying. 'What I really want is for us to work together.' He lowered his hand and drummed his fingers on his elbow. 'I wanted to talk about how we could best do that. The road is important to me, but I haven't acted on it or done anything with it since we last spoke, apart from telling the committee it's unlikely to go ahead in the next year.'

'And how did they take that?'

He shrugged. 'If you want the truth, I think they were annoyed.'

'With me?'

'Not really. More with me. I handled it badly. I know I did, and I can't go back and change it. So, I have to work with what we've got.' Murray let out a sigh. His usually confident shoulders sagged a little.

Beth steeled herself. It hurt seeing him so crestfallen. Why? Wasn't this what she'd wanted? No. Hurting people wasn't her. What was the point in stooping as low as him when she had the chance to make it better? 'How about we make a deal?'

Murray folded his arms. 'I'm listening.'

'If I grant the access rights and the permission to build the road, we get something in return.'

'Such as?' He scanned her face.

'I don't know yet.'

'I have a three-day-old pink cupcake I bought especially for you,' he said.

'Seriously. You did?'

'Most certainly, I did.'

'Well, I'll take it as security, but I'm not that easy.'

His smile widened. 'I'm happy to hear it. That would have spoiled all the fun.'

She narrowed her eyes but couldn't help smiling. Returning it with a slight headshake, he disappeared into the kitchen. When he came back, he flipped open the lid of a white cardboard box to present the cake.

'Very me.' She lifted it out carefully. 'I can see you chose it with me in mind.'

'Actually, I did.' Murray closed the box. 'I realise you're a tough girl, but it doesn't mean you can't appreciate the finer things in life.'

'Like glitter icing. How cultured am I? Though I prefer chocolate and cheese.'

'Noted.' He smirked.

Rolling her eyes, she bit into the cake. 'Now, in the meantime, while I decide what we get out of this deal, I have some conditions.'

'Oh yes?' Murray arched his eyebrows.

'There is to be no gloating, no smugness, no rubbing my nose in it and no repeat of this, ever again. You are to consult me on every single bit of this project, or I will withdraw my consent. You understand?'

'Loud and clear. But you are saying yes?'

'If you follow my conditions.' She took another bite of the cake. Pink or not, it was delicious.

'Then, I swear.' He smiled again.

His mouth was gorgeous, so bloody flirtatious and kissable. If only she had the nerve. 'I said no gloating.'

'This is a smile.' He pointed at his lips. 'Not a gloat.'

She ignored him and carried on. 'If you bring the papers round sometime, we'll sign them. You'll need my mother's signature. She's on the documents.' Beth polished off the cake. 'Ok. So that's sorted. Do you want me to fix that shelf? Why are you still smirking? I said no smugness.'

He raised his hand as if pointing. 'You've got...' Reaching forward with the most delicate touch, he rubbed the corner of her lip with his thumb. 'Glitter icing.'

Her shoulders froze, closely followed by the rest of her. Unable to move, she stared at those iron-grey eyes.

'Don't worry about the shelf. I can do it. Listen, stay if you like, I'll make you tea.'

Shaking herself from the body bind, she looked away. 'That counts as celebrating, so no. And if I walk out of here and look back in a few minutes to see you doing any kind of dancing, the deal's off.'

'Ok, no dancing. Though I think you'd like my moves.' He raised his arms above his head, gave a mischievous pout that emphasised his strong cheekbones, and thrust out his hip.

'Oh, bugger off,' she said, though she couldn't help a smirk, especially as his grin had split his face. Yes, she liked his moves; very smooth, very seductive, but wasted on boring Beth.

'Hey. Take care.' He clapped her on the shoulder as he opened the front door and peered out. 'It's got a bit wet.'

'Understatement of the year.' Beth drew back from the deluge.

'You're welcome to stay for a while.'

'No, thanks. I have to get back. Rain doesn't stop lambs. See you.'

Murray gave a quick wave. Beth caught it before she darted to the Land Rover. So, she'd given in, but finding the common ground with Murray didn't feel too awful. In fact, as she bumped the Land Rover down the path, peering into the onset of gloom, a giddy sensation spread over her, like being a bit tipsy. Her finger traced across the corner of her lip where he'd brushed off the icing. Everything about him sent her heart racing at breakneck speed, it thrilled and terrified her in equal measure.

CHAPTER TEN

Murray

Murray stood behind the window watching the Land Rover's rear lights blurring down the track before he fist-pumped the air.

'Whoa.' He steadied himself and blew out a long breath. Hottest meeting ever. Running his fingers through his hair, he smoothed it flat against his scalp. Beth wasn't his type, but the buzz when she was in the room. *Wow.* His skin prickled all over at the thought. The way she looked at him. He had to be careful. This was not a safe road. Her appearing in his bedroom had sent him spiralling.

He didn't remember feeling anything like that with anyone, even Naomi, but hey, there was no comparison. Beth had a hundred thousand more things going for her. She was a smart thinker. And so natural. Naomi put on more make-up in a minute than Beth probably put on all year. She wore tight-fitting dresses and heels that made your eyes water, while Beth was happy in her overalls and still looked hot AF. Murray rubbed his beard. Beth had a stunning figure too, but Naomi was aesthetically perfect with curves in all the right places. Beth was straight up and down. Not that he objected. Why would he? She was gorgeous. And why was he still thinking about her? *Business, Murray! Be professional.*

Sitting down, he rested his head on his hand. Because, despite the differences, Beth and Naomi shared something oh so similar. That competitive edge. The need to beat him. Naomi was only satisfied if she won. And if she lost, she made him pay. Their relationship had been nothing but a constant war. Beth was like that. He saw it in her eyes, the fire and determination.

At least he wasn't in a relationship with Beth and he wasn't going to be. The spark came from the competition, exactly how it had started with Naomi. Only this time, he knew better. Naomi, he could beat at everything if he dared tackle the fallout. Until her last move. The lowest in a catalogue of toxic and sneaky mind games. He'd lost, or so she'd thought. But she'd shown just how stupid she really was. How could she possibly think he'd go back to her after her behaving like that? Her intelligence was misapplied, and he was free.

But Beth, he clapped his hands together. She was a completely different challenge. Hard to gauge, but she seemed trustworthy. And if that was round one, he had it in the bag. Still, he didn't want to run the risk of her regretting her decision and changing her mind. Time to strike while the iron was hot.

On Monday morning it was chucking it down. The downpour hadn't stopped all weekend, and the wind gusted with angry groans. Next to the cottage, the stream raged down the hill, a grey torrent rather than the little trickle bubbling over the stones he'd grown used to.

Gathering the papers together, Murray headed to Creagach Farm. Rain lashed the windows, and the car shuddered from side to side. As he crawled along beside the sea, his windscreen wipers slashed at top-speed. Naomi would hate this. She couldn't have handled it. *I win again.* He steadied the car round a bend. Stormy blasts pummelled the sparse trees, and the sea rose in great swells to his right; distracting and terrifying, but stunning.

Relieved to get to the farmhouse, he knocked three times on the door. No answer. Pulling his hood tight around his face, he tried one more time as squally rain slapped his back. The Land Rover wasn't there. Should he wait? He returned to the car and tapped the steering wheel. All he needed was a couple of signatures. Beth was usually close by. She didn't go far from the lambs. If he drove down the road, he could have a look. Even if she didn't sign today, they could arrange another time.

It didn't take him long to spot the Land Rover, parked beside Beth's quad bike and an old Jeep. He halted, slamming on the brakes. The road was awash. A mountain stream had burst its banks and water gushed over the bridge sides and down the incline towards the sea. A group huddled together in a sharp dip. Murray opened his door and jumped out. All three people were clad in saturated jackets, undistinguishable from the back. Two of them stood not far off. Further down, the third bent over a sheep. Beth, he could tell. His heart pulsed, and he put his fingertips to his mouth. The sheep was either dead or in a bad way. Leaping down the embankment, he joined the group. 'Hey, can I help?'

Gillian McGregor turned around, her face soaked, straggly hair stuck to her forehead. Beside her, Murray recognised Sandy, the man he'd helped with the gashed leg.

'It's too late,' said Gillian. 'We've lost two ewes.' She ran her hand across her brow. 'It's terrible to lose any, we can't even save the lambs.'

Beth hunched over the sheep. Murray couldn't see her face for her hood, but he had the impression she was crying. Her shoulders seemed to shake.

'Is she ok?' Without meaning to, Murray took a step forward to go to her, but Gillian grabbed his arm and held him back.

'Leave her a minute,' said Gillian. 'She thought we might try a caesarean, it's risky at the best of times, but the mother's been gone too long. The lamb won't have survived.'

'I'm sorry,' said Murray. He felt like they were crowded around a coffin at a funeral. The desire to go to Beth burned. She shouldn't have to deal with this alone. 'What happens now? Can I do anything?'

'Naw, laddie. I'll deal with them,' said Sandy, 'the lass should go home and warm up. She's done the best she can. None of us could have done any better. This was an act of God, and a cruel one.' He moved towards Beth and knelt beside her.

Beth got up. Cautious, Murray squinted through the rain. Beth looked composed. Pale and drawn, but no tears or evidence of upset. Perhaps he'd been wrong, or maybe she was just skilled at hiding it.

Barely looking at him or Gillian, she said, 'I've moved the other sheep to safety. Sandy will deal with the bodies.' The robotic nature of her voice betrayed her pain. Pulling down her hood, she smoothed her sodden hair flat against her head then put it up again. She reached the quad, whistled the dogs, and whizzed off before the others were at the road.

'Poor Beth.' Gillian stepped onto the roadside. 'She's very hard on herself. I know it's business and losing any animal is terrible, but she always blames herself. I better get back. Were you here to see us?'

'I was, but it's a bad time. I'll leave you in peace.'

'Come in for a cuppa,' said Gillian. 'If Beth isn't up to talking just now, you can at least enjoy the warmth for a bit.'

'Thank you.' Murray followed the procession back to the farmhouse. A sense of unease lingered. This was a private thing. He didn't want to intrude. 'Are you sure this is ok?'

'Let me just check Beth,' said Gillian. 'You dry out.' She left into the corridor through the door opposite the one they'd come in. Murray paced the rug between the kitchen and the seating area.

'No Beth, just us.' Gillian returned to the room and headed straight to the kettle. 'She's taking a bath and she might be some time. I don't think she's in the mood for a chat.'

'That's fine,' said Murray. 'I completely understand. I should go, I don't want to trouble you.'

'Stay for a cuppa.' Gillian set the kettle to boil. 'Beth told me you'd come to an agreement about the road. I'm glad to hear it. She said she'd imposed some conditions.'

Murray gave a brief grin. He wasn't sure if Beth had told her mother what they were. Perhaps even talking about them counted as a breach of contract. And he wasn't sure Gillian would appreciate the joke. For all she came over as friendly, she had a discerning eye and didn't look like someone to cross.

'Well, I've met the conditions so far.' Beth couldn't have seen him fist-pumping. 'We'll give you something in return for the access rights, but we haven't decided what that is yet. So, all I need is your signature.'

'Mine?'

'Well, yes. Beth isn't listed as the owner on the title deeds. It's you. That's why I'm here.'

'Hand it over then.'

'Don't you want to wait for her?' Murray stroked his beard.

'Not if she said it was ok,' said Gillian. 'I think it's a good idea. Though I don't agree with your methods either.'

He looked at the floor. 'Yeah, sorry about that. It was an honest mistake. I had a note saying your family supported the development. I just didn't back it up myself.'

'What's done is done and we don't want to stand in the way of progress. Let's see those documents.'

Gillian put on her glasses and read through every page before signing and handing them to Murray.

He tucked them away safely, holding off the urge to jump in the air and click his heels together. This wasn't the time or place. He had to go, but he wanted to talk to Beth first. After half an hour listening to Gillian's stories about people on the island, he decided enough was enough. He'd have to make it another day.

Inside his leather folio, he had exactly what he needed, but something didn't feel right. He had an unsettled blip in his stomach. Beth must be feeling dreadful. He couldn't change that, but he wanted to say something. He pulled into a passing place and typed a message. No reception, but he sent it anyway, hoping it might find a hotspot somewhere and take his condolences with it.

MURRAY: Hope you're ok. Sorry about the sheep. X

'Duh.' He swiped at it, but it sent before he could do anything about the fact he'd signed it with a kiss.

CHAPTER ELEVEN

Beth

Nothing could wash away the smell of failure. Beth had scrubbed herself within an inch of her life. The skin on her arms was chafed red where she'd rubbed so hard. The sheep weren't her fault. Just nature. So people kept telling her. But it was unacceptable. She'd botched the job. The forecast had warned of heavy rain. She knew the dangers of flooding. Why hadn't she remembered sooner and acted faster? A more experienced farmer would have prioritised better, moved the sheep beforehand. Some imperceptible distraction had forced her eye off the ball.

'I'm an imposter,' she told the dogs, trudging across the muddy hill, rain dripping down her face, wind flapping her jacket. But she had to keep marching blindly into the abyss. Other farmers nearby would help in a second if she asked. She could have their good, wholesome advice on tap. Wouldn't they just love that? Time to show the silly girl how to do it properly. Their respect was based on her father, not her own merit. If only he were still alive. Times like this she missed him more than ever. Fighting away unbidden tears, she continued her rounds.

The weather didn't let up for two more days. Beth was beyond exhausted, her body weary with toil and grief. Yes, she grieved the lost sheep. Four living beings had died in her care, two unborn. How could she reconcile it?

Gillian's eyes filled with concern as Beth pulled on her jacket, ready for round three hundred and ninety-eight. 'Can I help?'

'No, I'm fine,' Beth said. Gillian had never been a farmer. She was ok in an emergency, but this was just normal farming.

'You look like you're struggling. I didn't realise how bad it was.'

'I told you, I'm fine.' Beth left for her rounds. Appalled by herself, Beth knew her mum was just being kind. Her lingering irritation was from Gillian signing Murray's papers. Yes, Beth had agreed, but why the rush to do it without her? Curse Murray's silver tongue. He'd obviously charmed Gillian into signing. Like a few more hours would have hurt? Oh no, he had to get one over on her. Adding insult to injury, he'd sent her a crawling text signed with a kiss! Seriously, how slick was he? Negative energy fizzled and simmered in her stomach. Exhaustion like she'd never known clawed at her. Previous years hadn't been *this* gruelling. Had they? Or had she just blanked it out?

After more sleepless nights and interminable days that rolled into one, an adrenaline crazed monster had woken in Beth. Gillian tiptoed around her on eggshells. Beth was ready to bite off heads before breakfast. Downing a glass of cold orange juice in one, she bashed the tumbler on the worktop. 'I've had enough,' she said. Without explaining herself, she stormed out, leaving Gillian standing stock still and bemused.

Barely aware of what she was doing, Beth strode up to Murray's cottage, with no recollection of the journey once she got there. One minute she'd stormed out of the kitchen, now she was pounding her fist on the door.

Murray snapped it open, his eyes wide, brows drawn together. 'Jeez, it's you. I thought it was a hit squad. What's wrong? Do you need help with a sheep or something?'

'Like I'd ask you for help with that? You know nothing about sheep.'

'True, but I'd still help.' He slid his fingers through his hair. Beth squinted at him. On the doorstep, he towered several inches taller than her and she didn't like it. Her hands squeezed into fists, she glowered upwards. Murray searched her face. 'Are you ok?'

'It's about the papers.' Why did she sound like a snarling dog? She felt like one too.

He frowned and examined her eyes. 'They're signed. It's sorted.'

'No, it isn't. You did exactly what you said you wouldn't do.' She knew she was shouting, she couldn't help it.

He put up his hands. 'Hang on. I didn't. What do you mean? I've been good as gold. No dancing, nothing, I swear.'

She folded her arms. 'I don't believe that either, but that's not what I meant. You agreed you'd do nothing without consulting me. Yet, the minute I'm not there, you sneak in and get my mother to sign it.'

'Look, Beth, calm down.'

'Don't you dare tell me to calm down,' she said through gritted teeth. He had a nerve. She shoved her hair aggressively behind her ear.

'I'm sorry. I suggested we wait, but your mother said if you'd agreed, she would sign. That was it. It's only a preliminary document. We have to do it officially with solicitors and witnesses. I just need consent to get the ball rolling. I'll do nothing without you. Cross my heart. I'll sign in blood if you like.'

Scrunching up her face, Beth felt her hackles prickle. Why was she so volatile? She could cry. Where to look now? What to say? She'd made a complete fool of herself.

'Listen, why not come in? I'll get you a coffee. You look like you need one.'

'No, really. I can't. I have work to do.'

'Come on. Ten minutes won't hurt.' Murray leant his head on the doorframe. He was almost irresistible. Who could say no? Beth McGregor, that was who.

'I should get back.' She looked away, levelling her breathing as she watched the mountain stream bubbling. Soothed by the rushing sound and the twittering birds, her shoulders relaxed, but it was a fake calm. A few miles away, the demanding bleats of hundreds of sheep and lambs clamoured for her. A silent scream battled to escape its inner cage. Beth reined it in.

Murray hopped off the doorstep and drew level with her, holding her gaze. Her pulse rate spiked; she pulled her lips tight. The freshly showered smell of him mingled with the clear spring air and burst into her befuddled mind. Move back, get away, said her brain, but her feet wouldn't budge.

'Ok, but why don't we go for a drink sometime?' His pale grey eyes gleamed with promise, scanning her face.

Beth's shoulders froze. Was he asking her on a date? No. It was a friend thing. Or frenemies at the very best. 'What for?' She briefly raised her eyebrows. What kind of idiotic reply was that?

He flicked his head to the side. 'Fun? You know, to chat, chill out. We got off on a bad foot. We could drink beer, play pool or darts. You could use me as target practice.' He held out his arms, inviting her to use his body as the bullseye.

'Right,' she swallowed. Like mates, yes, she could do that. 'When the lambs are done. In about a hundred years from now.'

'Well, something to look forward to.' His smile returned; it revived her exhausted insides just admiring those smooth lips, forcing a dent into his fuzzy cheeks.

'I don't know. It's not been a great season.'

'Oh, come on, Beth.' He gave her a playful nudge with his elbow.

She pitched back and frowned. What did he mean? Shrugging, she indicated she didn't get it.

'You had a few losses, and it hurts, I get that, but what about all the healthy lambs? You've worked miracles. I take my hat off to you. I really do. No matter what differences we've had, I admire what you do. Totally impressive. I bow to the mighty Beth.' He grinned and tipped his head.

She returned it with a weak smile.

'I stand in awe, and you can probably guess that doesn't happen often.'

Raising one eyebrow, she muttered, 'Thanks.'

'Well, if my company's not good enough, you better get back to the sheep. Go on.' He gave her a nudge, and she smacked back his hand. He laughed. 'Don't forget that drink. I mean it. My treat.'

The oddest sensation bubbled in her tummy, burst to her chest, and spilt into a smile. Whatever it was; it erased her foul mood.

Back in the Land Rover, she opened the window and whistled along to "Shut Up and Dance with Me" all the way to the farm.

Gillian backed off when she returned from her rounds, but Beth hugged her. 'Sorry, Mum. I'm just tired.' The pleasant mood stuck around. She had an almost unbroken sleep, even though Murray-related images cropped up as she lay in bed. That smile, those eyes, the chest, his hands, even the man-bun was growing on her. If anyone suited it, it was him.

After dinner the following evening, she headed out to do the rounds as usual. She'd reached the farm gate when a pink van pulled up. Everyone on the island knew that wacky vehicle with the floral decals. Georgia wound down the passenger window and beamed with her glossy lips. She leaned over her photography equipment bundled on the seat. 'I've got a proposition for you.'

'Oh?' Beth folded her arms.

'Don't panic. I've come to rescue you from the lambs. I'm off to the pub. Come with me. I'd ask Kirsten, but I'm meeting Carl and Robyn and I don't think she'll want to see them.'

She wouldn't. Kirsten couldn't forgive Carl for breaking her heart by doing nothing more than finding the love of his life.

'I suppose I should.' Beth wavered. She'd promised Robyn, her old classmate, a drink last month, but time hadn't allowed. Socialising and lambs didn't go together.

Georgia smiled, her eyes pleading.

'All right, but I need to do these checks and get changed first. I can't go like this.' Her gaze roamed over her ancient overalls.

Nobody in the local pub in Dervaig would have batted an eyelid. They were used to all sorts; locals and holidaymakers alike trailed in with muddy boots every day, but clean clothes and brushed hair were always preferable. At least Beth would feel vaguely human.

The pub was quiet. Sometimes you couldn't move in here, but plenty of tables and seats were free at the old-fashioned bar. Georgia looked round. 'They're not here yet. You sit, I'll buy this one.'

'Thanks,' said Beth, 'and for driving.' It wasn't even the fact she could drink. Just the relief at getting to chill for a few moments, with no drama.

'No probs, it doesn't matter to me.' Georgia beamed. 'I can be just as crazy whether or not I have a drink.'

'I noticed.' Beth nodded at a couple of locals before taking a seat at a round table. Playing with her super-short nails, she glanced at the fishing-themed paintings on the wall.

Banging the glasses on the table, Georgia edged into the curved bench seat. 'Kirsten told me there was some bad news on the lambing front, but it looked like you had loads.'

'We lost a couple in the storm the other week, but we're over halfway.'

Georgia tilted her head in commiseration. 'Sad, but you're doing well.'

Sipping the beer, Beth loosened up as the golden warmth flowed, relaxing her from the inside out. Chatting more about lambs and Georgia's art passed the time. Beth pursed her lips flat and looked over Georgia's shoulder at the ugly trout painting. 'You make me jealous.' She slid her finger around the rim of her glass.

'Why?'

'You're so creative. Your life seems idyllic.'

Georgia gave a wry smile. 'It is, except I have no money. But you shouldn't be jealous. You have amazing skills.'

'Such as looking after sheep?'

'Well, yes. And I know there's lots of paperwork you do. It's the hidden admin.'

'Tell me about it.' Beth took a deep swig.

'Why don't you do the woodcraft any more? Those carvings you made are incredible. I'm an artist and I don't know how you did them.'

'I never have the time these days. I'd like to, but stuff just gets in the way.'

'When the lambing is done, I'm sure things will even out. Look, I'll show you my latest paintings, see what you think. You're allowed to hate them. They might not be everyone's taste.' Georgia swiped through her phone and passed it to Beth. 'I'm thinking about doing an exhibition, maybe in the autumn. It's too hectic in the summer, but then I miss the high season, so I'm not sure.' She glanced towards the door, her gaze drifting. 'Uh oh, look who it is.'

Beth spun around. Her eyes widened. *Oh, no. Murray!* He was with Donald. Beth checked back at the pictures on the phone, fixated on them. Head firmly down. 'They're super.' Handing the phone back to Georgia, she grabbed her glass, but Georgia scanned over her shoulder.

'It's the hot, handsome and hunky Mr Henderson.' Georgia sucked her J2O through a straw, raising her eyebrows.

'You think so?' Beth sipped her drink, keeping her eyes forward. Her shoulders tensed with unease. She hated having her back to him.

'I do. He's lush, anyone can see it. Come on, even you. He is easily the best-looking guy on the island. Maybe even the country.'

'You sound like you're crazy about him.'

'Me?' Georgia said with a giggle. 'No, but I can't deny his looks. What about you? Are you and him still rubbing along?'

Beth rolled her eyes. 'No. He's a pain in the backside.' Ok, not completely honest. Georgia had described him to a T. Beth could add a lot more, but she wasn't going to.

'Look lively,' Georgia muttered through her teeth, 'he's coming over.'

Beth swore under her breath, freezing as a hand patted her shoulder. Even through her soft grey marl t-shirt, she felt the heat. Turning her head slowly, she glanced up at those twinkling grey eyes. Breathing was essential, but no, it wasn't happening. Did that mean she was already dead? Was this heaven?

Murray leaned down, drawing level to her face. 'Fancy meeting you here.' He was so close she could smell his minty breath. Her jaw tensed. When they'd met Georgia in the woods, Georgia had used that phrase, knowing it was a set-up. Maybe Murray supposed this was too. 'I didn't think you were due out for another hundred years.'

Instinct urged Beth to draw back, but she stared him out. The corners of his mouth curled up. The short hairs on his beard were so prominent. Her heart pounded like a mad thing. He smelt divine, all woody, citrusy and masculine. She hadn't been this close to a man for... well, ever. She whispered into his ear, 'Maybe it depends on the company.'

Laughing, he drew back, squeezing her shoulders before he let go.

Georgia's eyes almost popped from their sockets. Her wide red lips pressed together in a Cheshire cat grin, as she gave a little wave. She was the pretty one, the fun one. Why wasn't Murray giving her the attention? *Maybe he likes me.* Was that possible? A handsome man like him could take his pick. *Why would he choose me?* Beth raised her gaze fractionally to keep him just in her eyeline without turning around.

'Hi, Georgia. How are you?' Murray adjusted the button on his navy polo shirt.

'Very well.' Georgia tweaked the strap of her purple top, her grin still impossibly wide, eyes drifting between Murray and Beth.

'You stole my date,' said Murray.

'What's that supposed to mean?' Beth twisted to scowl at him. Heat bloomed in her face. 'We're not... she's a friend. And since when did you and I?'

'Just a joke.' He put up his hands. 'Don't murder me, please.'

'Then get lost,' she said, 'or I might.'

Georgia giggled and shook her head. Feeling stupid, Beth rubbed her neck.

'Point taken. But the next time you're out, it's on me, don't forget. There's a good dartboard over there.' He poked her shoulder before returning to Donald.

'I see exactly what kind of pain he is now.' Georgia sat back and examined her short red nails with the most irritating expression. 'He's just so very annoying.' She heaped on the sarcasm. 'And not in the least attractive.'

'Don't go getting any funny ideas.' Beth straightened the neck of her t-shirt.

'Like what?'

'He's a pushy flirt.' Beth gripped her drink, hoping she hadn't gone too red. 'He's always like that.'

'He is with you.'

'Look, can we not talk about this?'

Georgia grinned and waved, looking behind Beth. Who now? It was a relief when Robyn and Carl sat down. Beth used it as an excuse to move from her exposed seat to the curved bench, shuffling into a position where she could keep Murray in her sight. She didn't want him creeping up on her again. This seat came with perks. What a marvellous view of his lean backside perched on the barstool. She closed her eyes slowly. Seriously? What was going on in her head? Since when had lusting over blokes' derrières become a thing for Beth McGregor?

'So, how's everyone?' Carl beamed around, clutching Robyn's hand on the tabletop.

As Beth had been stuck with sheep for the last several weeks, there was plenty to catch up on. She didn't want to bore them with the lambs, so she contented herself with listening, surreptitiously ogling Murray as she sipped her beer, while he laughed and joked with Donald and some other locals at the bar. Taking Beth by surprise, Murray glimpsed over his shoulder and smiled. Her eyes flew back to the table. She almost dropped her glass. 'So, how's the new house?' she asked Robyn, trying to say something quickly. Georgia smirked into her food. Had she detected where Beth's eyes kept landing?

'Fantastic, thanks. We're staying at the cabin for the moment while we get some building work done. The house needs a lot of modernisation.'

'I'd love to see it,' said Beth. 'It sounds beautiful. And how are things with your mum?'

Robyn and her mother, Maureen, had known some troubles. Beth hoped she hadn't stuck her farmer's boots straight into the midst of a sensitive subject.

'Improving,' said Robyn. 'We're taking things easy, but she's a lot more understanding. I think we're both learning.'

'That's good.' Beth gave her a stoic pat. Robyn had previously confided in her, but she said nothing else; this wasn't the time or place. The smile on Robyn's face told Beth she was doing ok.

Sitting late, nobody wanted to move even though Beth had an early start. She'd drunk so much she was light-headed, and she needed the loo. On her way back, Murray spun around and gently caught her arm.

'Let me get you that drink.' He swivelled his knees to confront her. His eyes were level with her chest. Freeing her arm from him, she raised her hand to her shoulder in a bid to cover her lack of feminine curves.

Rubbing her collarbone, she said, 'Not now, Murray. I've already had a lot. I need to go. I have to get up at five tomorrow and that's in...' She checked the clock. 'Shit, six hours.'

'Ok, Beth.' His smile faded.

'I would do darts, but I'm a tad cross-eyed. I might end up hitting something I didn't mean to.' Her gaze travelled downwards.

'Or you might hit the jackpot.'

'You think?' Beth raised her eyebrows. 'And what's the prize?'

'I'm sure I could think of something.' Lifting his hand to her arm, his fingertips trailed down, softly brushing her skin. Goosebumps erupted all over.

'Ok, you do that.' She almost knocked over a chair in her rush to get back to the others. Picking up her jacket, she didn't sit back down. Georgia took the hint and pulled on her coat. They said farewell to Robyn and Carl and headed for the door.

Murray gave Beth a little wink as she passed. She paused, biting the inside of her lip, then taking a step back, she folded her arms. 'Don't wink at me.'

Donald and the other guys chortled and someone whistled. 'Watch out, she'll whip you silly,' sniggered one of them.

With a wolfish grin, Murray sized her up. 'I can't wait.'

'Oh, bugger off.' She pinged his shoulder. Looking away, he smirked into his drink, shrugging off the others' guffaws.

Georgia's enormous grin looked ready to overflow into a river of speculation. Beth was ready. Somehow, spectacularly, she directed the conversation onto how good Robyn looked and how happy she and Carl seemed. *I should get a medal for this,* she thought.

As Beth got out, back at the farm, Georgia said, 'It's a free country, Beth. If you like Murray, what's stopping you?'

'Murray? Don't be stupid. I don't like him. He's a puffed-up mainlander who loves himself. Why would you think that?'

Georgia raised her eyebrow. 'Everyone can see he likes you. He doesn't exactly hide it. And Beth, you couldn't take your eyes off him.'

'Now that's even more stupid. There's no way. We agreed to be friends, and that's all. How could there be anything else? Look at me. I'm a scruffy farm girl. Look at him and, well. You've got it wrong, really wrong.'

Georgia shook her head with exasperation. 'Why not just have some fun?'

'Oh, please. You don't know what you're talking about.'

'Ok, Beth. If you say so.' Georgia was still smiling as Beth slammed the door shut.

She watched the pink van's rear lights wind down the farm track, then squashed her warm cheeks. Perhaps she protested a little too much.

'Argh.' She stamped her foot in the mud. Murray! Murray! Murray! Why was he the only thing she could think about?

CHAPTER TWELVE

Murray

S pring sunlight split the gorgeous blue sky like a laser. Murray set off for his office without a jacket. Why bother on a day like this? His lightweight fleece and Timberland boots would do.

With a few things to catch up on, he was early, but the afternoon loomed in his mind. He'd received an email from a local estate owner. The name had resonated straight away, Archibald Crichton-Leith. Pretentious, yes, but that wasn't why. Murray's predecessor had tried and failed to secure a deal with Mr Crichton-Leith regarding the logging road. Murray tapped his keyboard and chewed his bottom lip. The email had asked for a meeting with him. What interest could Crichton-Leith have? It didn't affect the Ardnish Estate this time.

But after trampling over Beth's toes, Murray was on the back foot. He couldn't afford to upset anyone else and had agreed to meet with him. Now it was so close, impatience simmered.

Crichton-Leith's interest made no sense. Could it have anything to do with Beth? Was she friendly with his family and put him up to it? Maybe at the beginning, Murray would have believed it, but now she'd come round, it didn't seem to fit. Murray put his hands behind his head and leaned back, ignoring the chair's creak. Beth. It kept coming back to Beth. He deliberated on her more than was strictly necessary for a business acquaintance. Ha! Who was he kidding? Business be damned! No matter how hard he tried to ignore it, she kept coming back. Their flirty little chats brought a grin to his face, but he had to be professional. Another creak. Murray sat up. If he broke his neck, he'd be in no state for anything.

Just after two-thirty, a black SUV pulled up outside the village shop. Murray grabbed his fleece and headed down. A middle-aged man exited the driver's side, followed by a younger woman; short, with long black hair and huge sunglasses. She took them off and peered at Murray, giving him the once over, followed by the twice.

He rubbed his Adam's apple. The woman's black eyeliner was unnerving. As she continued her visual appraisal, Murray turned his attention to the man. 'Mr Crichton-Leith?'

'No, I'm Simon Jarvie, Mr Crichton-Leith's solicitor.'

'Oh, right. Murray Henderson.' He put out his hand to shake, but it caught him off balance. A solicitor? Why?

'And I'm Marcia Turnbull, I'm a representative of the family.'

Murray flinched as she rubbed her long-nailed thumb over his hand. He withdrew it quickly.

'We'd like to examine the logging road's proposed location,' Simon Jarvie said, frowning at the sky. Grey clouds lingered over the woody hilltop behind the village. 'There are many aspects we need to consider.'

Murray tucked his hair behind his ear. 'I can assure you, it goes nowhere near the Ardnish Estate. We're working closely with local landowners and farmers.'

'Nonetheless, Mr Crichton-Leith is an influential landowner and has many concerns regarding the project, these have been voiced frequently by his family during previous consultations. They're well documented.'

Murray's heart sank. 'Nothing will be carried out without appropriate surveys and consent.'

'Unfortunately, there's been an environmental complaint raised, which has reached the ear of Mr Crichton-Leith. He's deeply concerned.'

'What environmental complaint?' Murray drew his brows together. Nothing had come to him. He pulled out his phone, looking for a message from Anna Maxwell. Sometimes she sorted his mail, but he noticed nothing new.

'I have the details here. We can discuss that in due course.'

Murray folded his arms. Beth. Would she? She had the balls to do something like this, perhaps she'd made the complaint before their deal. Murray gritted his teeth. It was Naomi all over again. If she couldn't win or get her own way through merit, she dug up any old dirt and heaped it over him, or worse, fabricated something. Beth wouldn't stoop so low, would she? *Please, no.*

After discussing the plans for half an hour in the office, Simon Jarvie stood up. 'We'll take a drive to the site now.'

'Now?' said Murray. 'You haven't told me about the complaint yet.'

'Let's do the site first,' said Simon, 'before it starts to rain.'

A heavy weight fell into Murray's stomach as they drove to Beth's land. The weather turned in mockery of Simon's bright idea. Black clouds rolled in and rain battered down. Cursing, Murray raided his boot. No waterproof of any kind. How disorganised was he? His hair was already damp. He slammed the boot, forcing a deep breath.

'We need a brief site tour.' Simon Jarvie pushed up an umbrella.

'I'll contact the landowner,' Murray said, 'and let her know what we're doing.'

'No need,' Simon Jarvie said, 'there's a right to roam in Scotland.'

'That's hardly the point,' Murray muttered, following as Simon Jarvie stalked up the hill.

Marcia Turnbull didn't appear too impressed as they trudged into the muddy grassland. She had on leopard print Wellingtons that looked like they'd never been worn out of a neatly bordered garden. Carrying an iPad close to her chest, she wrestled with a brolly about twice her size.

Rain dripped down Murray's forehead. He flipped back his hair and unpeeled the fleece. The saturated sensation on his back was horrible.

'You can come under here,' Marcia offered, raising the brolly.

Murray arched an eyebrow. He was over a foot taller than her and he didn't fancy being hunched under there so close to her sharp teeth.

'Thanks. I'm ok.' He unstuck his arms.

Simon Jarvie stopped and made some notes. Murray pointed out the proposed route. Pulling out his phone, Simon took some photographs. Marcia banged her feet and looked around.

The rev of a quad bike sounded in the distance. Murray looked heavenward and held his breath before he turned to see Beth stopping by the road. She was going to explode. Even if she had something to do with it, she wouldn't want to miss this opportunity.

'Who's this?' Marcia asked, squinting from under the brolly, down the hill.

Clouds eclipsed what was usually a stunning sea view. Out of the gloom, Beth strode towards them, water dripping from her waxed jacket. From the little Murray could glimpse of her face beneath the hood, she looked furious.

Simon Jarvie glanced up.

'She's the landowner,' Murray said, *and she is going to kill me.* He pursed his lips as she reached them.

'What's going on here?' Beth asked.

Stepping forward, Simon Jarvie held out his hand. Beth barely touched it. 'I'm a solicitor working for Archibald Crichton-Leith, the owner of the Ardnish Estate. We're checking the proposed placement of the logging road with a view to carrying out a land survey.'

'Pardon?' Murray frowned. He hadn't mentioned a survey before.

Beth rested her hands on her hips, her left eyebrow raised. 'Why?'

'Mr Crichton-Leith has an interest.'

Beth glared at Murray. 'But it doesn't even affect Ardnish.'

'Not directly, but Mr Crichton-Leith is interested in local developments,' Simon Jarvie answered. 'And there's been a complaint.'

'What kind of complaint?' Beth said, her eyes still on Murray. He threw up his palms, trying to impart to Beth he knew no more than her. From her reaction, he assumed she was not the driving force behind this. A moment of respite lightened his chest,

Marcia Turnbull flicked a glance at Simon Jarvie, and he nodded. Opening her iPad, with difficulty under the huge brolly, Marcia read, 'Dear Mr Crichton-Leith, after reading about proposals for a new logging road on the Mull Community Woodland Group website, I am forced to contact you with some serious concerns regarding the environmental impact of this project.' She paused for a breather. 'Although the road does not specifically go over the Ardnish Estate, Creagach Farm backs onto it, as does the surrounding West Mull Woods. I understand no thorough marine and wildlife surveys have yet been carried out. As someone with a vested interest, I suggest your intervention before any preliminary work takes place. I have worked with the current manager before and he has been sloppy in the past regarding environmental issues.'

'I beg your pardon,' Murray snapped. 'I have never been anything of the sort. I would never carry out a project without consulting all relevant parties.'

Beth folded her arms and let out a cough.

Murray's jaw tightened. Yes, he'd overlooked consulting with Beth, but it was a genuine mistake. 'Who sent it?'

Marcia looked at Simon Jarvie. He gave her a brief nod and looked away. 'A Naomi Walsh from Forestry Land Trust, Perthshire,' she said.

'Oh for Christ's sake.' Murray's jaw set. He just restrained the urge to kick an enormous boulder. The meddling bitch. She still hadn't stopped. What a deceitful, spiteful cat. Was she still stalking him? On the website, looking at what he'd done, discovering the history. Did it stop here? Had she sent bogus complaints elsewhere? Furious, hot rage surged inside Murray. What did Naomi want? To ruin his life further because he wouldn't run back to her arms? Like this kind of thing would induce him to go anywhere near her!

'Mr Henderson,' said Simon Jarvie, 'don't take this as a personal slight on your character. We understand unique personalities see things in different ways. You should consider our involvement advantageous for all parties. An extra layer, so to speak. We've examined your credentials and have confidence you'll handle this sensitively.'

Murray felt about as sensitive as a cast-iron poker. He gritted his teeth.

Beth's eyes flashed red. 'I've only agreed to these plans in principle,' she said. 'And no surveys will be carried out on this land without my explicit consent. If I change my mind, there will be no road at all.'

Murray glared. *No Beth, no. Please don't do that. Not now. Don't be like all the others.* He'd just come round to the idea she was different. Naomi kicking him in the ribs was one thing, not Beth too.

'Well,' said Simon Jarvie, 'Mr Crichton-Leith wants to have all the current information.'

'Let's leave it for today,' Marcia said. 'It's too wet out here. Mr Henderson, if you fancy coming to the estate with Simon and me, we can give you a tour.' She smiled a red lipsticked grin at Murray.

'No thanks.' He balled his fists. 'I should get back to work.'

The two of them left. Murray and Beth watched as Marcia staggered down the hill, Simon helping her over the muddy bits. Rain dripped from every pore. Murray's raw hands chafed in his pockets. He studied Beth. 'None of that stuff was true, you know. And I will consult with—'

She put up her palm and twisted around to glare at him. 'Don't bother trying to explain. I should have known. It's typical of you.'

Murray pulled his hands from his pockets and flexed his fingers. Why did she always assume the worst? Why make it personal? He knew who was behind this, but how could he explain? It would sound like the most stupid thing that had ever left his lips. *My ex did it to annoy me.* He was soaked, cold and fed-up.

'Typical of *me*? That's rich,' Murray muttered, raking back his saturated hair. He needed to go home and dry out. He'd made one mistake, and Beth was going to hold it against him forever. She just couldn't get past it and Naomi's bloody letter had fuelled her fire.

'Meaning what?' Even with her stick-thin frame, Beth looked capable of wrestling a full-size walrus.

'You.' He confronted her, only the rain separated them, and it was no barrier. As soaked as him, Beth didn't appear fazed. Standing tall and poker-straight, her hazel eyes flickered as Murray glared. 'You come over as being so strong. A woman that runs a farm, keeps a cool head, always knows what she's doing.'

Beth folded her arms. Her brows snapped together like a stalking tigress. 'And that makes me typical?'

'No. That's what makes you special. And you know what, for a while there I believed you were special and impressive. But no. What's typical is you're just like everyone else. You're an indecisive, I'll-change-my-mind-whenever-I-fancy kind of girl. It's so last year, Beth. You really should ditch it. I thought you were better than that.'

She squinted through the rain; watery beads clung to her lashes. 'And I should care because?' She threw out her arms. 'After all, who is it dishing out the compliments? The arrogant, chauvinistic prat, Murray I'll-get-my-own-way-at-all-costs Henderson.'

'Yeah, whatever.'

'Don't you *whatever* me! You're so smarmy. And now you've been called out by someone else. Ugh!' Beth threw up her hands and stamped her foot in the mud. 'And how dare you consult with those solicitors like you own the place? Just because they work for some highfaluting estate owner. We normal, hard-working farmers don't matter. We don't have the money or the status. Oh, and I forgot, we're women. No point in consulting with us. Well, you sexist pig, take your new road and shove it where the sun doesn't shine. You can arrange with one of your fancy overlords to build it over their land instead. I'm sure you'll find them much more accommodating, just like the last person did. You're not the right man for the job and you never have been.'

She stormed back down the hill.

'Beth, stop.'

'Goodbye, Murray.' Her voice snapped like a pistol. She broke into a trot, covering the ground fast. He could catch her if he tried, but his energy had fizzled out. Sitting on a wet boulder, he watched her jump on the quad and speed off.

He covered his soaked face with his hands. This was a disaster. Why had he opened his big mouth? What a stupid thing to say. All the frustration with Naomi, he'd taken out on Beth. She riled him. He couldn't rein in his temper or keep control of himself. Every bloody time. Why?

Here he was, back at the bottom of the pile, thanks to his horror of an ex. And Beth was his worst enemy again. So much for their great progress. He supposed that drink was off the cards. For a very long time.

CHAPTER THIRTEEN

Beth

White-hot anger surged through Beth. She almost smashed the glass in the side door as she smacked it shut. Gillian spun in shock and stared over the kitchen island.

'Beth, what in the name—'

'Not now.' Beth stormed straight through the room, into the hall and up the stairs. She was cold, wet and furious, and she did not want to talk about it. Who did Murray think he was?

Turning on the bath taps, she felt like snapping the bamboo tray across her knee as the water trickled out in no great hurry. The joy of a private water supply. You'd think the rain would make it flow profusely, but no, it often had the opposite effect. Yet another job to add to the list. Unblock the tank. And for all that, what was she? A girl. A woman? A useless nobody who played at farming. That's what Murray believed. No longer bowing to the mighty Beth. Why did she ever trust a word that came out of those honey lips?

Was that what everybody thought? Did people just humour her? A trickle of peaty water formed a thin layer over the bottom of the bath. It looked as if someone had poured the dregs of a teapot into it. Putting her head in her hands, she tried to steady her breathing. This was her life, she had no alternative. And until a few weeks ago, she'd got on fine. No one had complained before. Then *he* came along. Her first impression was right. What a self-loving dick. Why had she kidded herself he was anything else? The little sparks he ignited in her were made of her own naïve stupidity. The flirting, the little looks, all part of his master plan to charm her into submission. Well, it wasn't going to happen. She would not lie down for Murray Henderson. Shivering in the arctic room, her teeth chattered.

He's nothing but an arrogant prick, she thought. *And I'm nothing but a silly girl.*

She checked the bath, barely an inch of water swirled over the bottom. Enough to drown her sorrows? Probably not. Dipping her toe in the puddle, she sighed. Great. Maybe a cold bath would wash away the stupid feelings crawling over her like a virus. At least Murray would never know. She'd given nothing away. Not that he'd care. No doubt, he was used to having girls fawning over his perfect abs and lithe body. One more wouldn't even register on his I'm-such-a-fit-babe-and-I-love-myself scale.

Sitting down, she hugged her knees; the water carried on dripping at her toes. She'd never given serious attention to relationships. They were things that happened to other people. But she was thirty. Time had taken on a whole new meaning. One day she wanted kids. She dropped her head. How would that ever work? She'd never find anyone in time, and if she found someone, how would she explain herself? It would have to be the world's most understanding man and a hideously awkward confession. A fool's hope that exact man was likely to be living on Mull right now. The farm was her legacy, but who was she keeping it going for? Some potential kids of Kirsten? Here sat Beth, the maiden aunt. Was that what all this was for?

The bedroom was cosy after the chill of the bath. Gillian had done the decorating, and it was probably too girly for Beth, or the image others had of her. She liked the oak dresser, and the white wrought iron bed, though the floral bedspread was twee. Jumping straight under the covers and warming up felt so inviting.

Her phone buzzed. With narrowing eyes, she saw Murray's name.

MURRAY: Hi, Beth. Really have to apologise. I had a terrible morning. Shouldn't have said those things. The heat of the moment got the better of me. I know I've done it again. I took out my frustration on you and I wish I hadn't. I hope we can still be cool. X

Be cool! What did that mean? So, he could rib her, toy with her, then betray her all over again? Not a game she wanted to play. And it changed nothing. The words were out, his true opinion vented. Why say them if he didn't mean them, or believe them on some level? And why did he keep ending his messages with a kiss? That was the last thing she wanted from him. Jellicle the cat peered at her from the bedspread as if reading her mind. Maybe he sensed the blatant lie she'd just told herself. But imagining Murray's lips kissing her while she lay in bed was too much. *Stop, just stop. Please.*

She didn't reply to the message that day or the next. The day after that she returned home from her rounds to find Gillian in the kitchen examining a gigantic bouquet. 'These were on the doorstep. There's a card.' Gillian peered at it, her glasses at the end of her nose. 'For you.' She looked at Beth.

A flush swept up Beth's neck. She guessed who they were from. Who else would make such a flamboyant gesture? After accusing her of being too much of a girl, he'd sent her a bunch of flowers. She rolled her eyes. What an idiot.

'Are you going to open it?' Gillian asked.

'What's the point?'

'It might be from an admirer.'

'Mum, are you living on the same planet?' She ripped open the card. 'They're from Murray, my number one fan.'

Gillian looked confused and curious, giving her an almost comical expression. 'Well, if he's sending you flowers. Who knows?'

'He did not send these out of the goodness of his heart. He's feeling guilty and paranoid. You know what you can do with these flowers? Shove them in the bin. I may be a pathetic woman, but I'm not pathetic enough to be won over by a bunch of flowers.'

Gillian frowned. 'What is going on? Has something happened?'

'No more than usual.'

'And are you going to tell me?'

'There's nothing else to tell.'

Gillian let out a sigh. 'He's very charming and handsome but looks can be deceiving. He's always a bit too smooth.'

'Oh yes. Smooth is his middle name.'

'If he's causing trouble, he'll get a piece of my mind, and I might just withdraw my signature.'

'He'll love that,' said Beth.

Gillian picked up the bunch of flowers. 'Shame to waste them. I'll split them up and put them into the holiday cottages.'

The first time anyone had ever sent Beth flowers, and she'd discarded them. *No wonder I'm single.*

Almost all the ewes had given birth and things were ticking along. As the afternoon drew to a close, Beth sat on her favourite hillock, legs stretched out, dogs at her feet, watching the serene sea at the hill foot. It was about a mile to walk to it and Beth felt like doing it, but before she could move, a flashy blue car pulled up. She threw back her head and groaned. What now? Their land was a wide-open hillside with scattered boulders and a few scrubby bushes, nothing to afford any cover. Nowhere to hide.

Jumping to her feet, she whistled the dogs. If she hurried, she could reach the woods. Surely he wouldn't follow her. The car door slammed, echoing below. Her pace quickened.

'Beth!'

She didn't turn. Even when he called again even louder.

'Beth, stop!'

The command made her tread even faster. How dare he think she would ever do what he wanted, especially if he spoke to her like that?

'Come on,' she muttered to the dogs. She broke into a run. Years ago, she'd been a proficient steeplechaser.

A tight grip caught her arm. She shrugged him off. 'Get off me.'

'Beth, please. I need you to listen.'

'Get lost, Murray.' She strode on, trying to ignore him, but he followed.

'Please. I've been a total knob. I know I have. Please, Beth. We need to talk.'

Why were his eyes so appealing? Not just his eyes. The absolute symmetry of his chiselled face broken only by an escaped strand of hair. Restraining the urge to touch it and thread it back into place, Beth clamped her teeth together and challenged him. 'No, we don't. You can talk all you like, but I heard you loud and clear the other day.'

'I know. I truly know that.' He held up his hands. 'It was stupid. Really stupid. The person who complained was... an old rival of mine, someone out to cause trouble. I was annoyed. I took it out on you, but, Beth, I shouldn't have. The worst thing is, some of it was spite.' He tapped his chest. 'My selfish spite and jealousy.'

'Jealousy? Ok, that's a good one. You're jealous of this?' Throwing out her arms, she gestured at the land, people and animals she was responsible for. 'If you are, on you go. Take over. Show me how a man would do it so much better than me.'

He shook his head and rubbed his brow, pushing away the strand of hair. 'I can't. That's my point. I can't even do the job I'm employed to. But look at you.'

'Yes, look at me.' She folded her arms. 'I'm Beth, the silly girl who plays farms all day long.'

'No, you're not. You're Beth the mighty, Beth the terrifying. You have power. And I couldn't handle it. It got on top of me, and I let rip in a stupid outburst. It was a low attempt to score a point. But it didn't. It's just made me look more stupid than ever.'

Beth's nose wrinkled; he'd said stuff like that before. How could she believe a word that came out of his mouth? 'Yes, Murray. You've got a habit of doing that around here. One of your many talents, like getting everybody's backs up, railroading everyone and having your head so far up your backside, you can see out your own mouth.'

Murray nodded at the ground, his shoulders low. 'I deserve whatever you throw at me. I've done a terrible job. This was meant to be my escape. Ha. I never really supposed things could be worse than... Well, another time. Listen, I just wanted to say I am truly, deeply sorry. Nothing I say or do will change that now, but really, I am.' He turned and strode away. 'And, Beth.' Glancing back, he gave a wry smile. 'You were right. I'm not the right man for the job.'

His pace quickened, and he was soon at his car. Beth watched but didn't follow. No way was she going after him. No way, but her heart sank. Would he resign? They might disagree, argue, fight, but she'd rather have him here doing that than not here at all. If Murray left... She closed her eyes and threw back her head. Going back to normal would be so dull. Murray's being around had added a new dimension to her life, and although she couldn't pinpoint the exact reason, she didn't want him to leave.

CHAPTER FOURTEEN

Murray

Murray sat with Donald, looking over the list in front of them. Notes were spread across Donald's kitchen table. Murray's eyes wound in and out of focus, blurring the colours on the lurid blind.

'Murray?'

Murray glanced up and loosened his collar. Donald had been talking, but Murray hadn't taken in a word. 'I'm sorry, Donald. I can't do this.' He pushed the papers away and leaned back in his seat. 'The more I think about it, the more I realise I'm not the right man for this job.'

Donald's brow creased, and he tapped the table. 'You've only been here a month. You can't be thinking of leaving already. Why?'

Murray sighed and looked away. The truth or an excuse? Or were they the same?

'Is it because of this complication with the Crichton-Leiths?'

'Partly.' It was in his mind, but he was used to Naomi pulling stunts. It was part of his normal. After the below-the-belt tactics she'd used to lose him his last job, she'd crawled back all devastated. When she'd discovered he'd got a new job somewhere she didn't want to follow, she'd tried everything to stop him going. This was just her latest scheme. No escape. Why didn't she get it? They were finished.

'Is there something else?' asked Donald.

'I had a run-in with Beth.'

'Again? I thought things were ok. She's agreed to the road, so what's the problem?'

'Just me,' Murray replied, rubbing his forehead. 'She was there when I met the solicitor and—' He got to his feet. 'We argued. I said some things. I shouldn't have, but I did. I've made a right mess-up so far.'

Dismay clouded Donald's eyes. Murray shared the sentiment. 'Listen, I've known many people come and go over the years. Mull is a tough place to live. It's beautiful, but man cannot live on beauty alone if you'll pardon my appalling parallel.'

Murray's lips curled up. 'Sure. It's not the island. I like it here. It's just...'

'Beth?'

He nodded.

'Well,' said Donald, 'I like Beth a lot. She's a hard worker and a good lass, but she's not always easy. She's very chummy with my lad, Will. Not so much these days, he's married, but at school, she was a bit of a riot. There were quite a few capers up on their farm. I never asked too many questions. She talks tough, but sometimes I wonder if there's a scared little girl in there. Someone who was thrown into responsibility at a young age and has had no guidance.'

'You think?' said Murray. 'I doubt she'd thank you for calling her a little girl. And she has a mother to guide her, she's not alone.'

'Gillian's not a farmer. Beth's learned it all herself. What I'm saying is just don't let her get to you. You're easily the best person for this job. Beth's tough, she doesn't give in. And neither do you. It's a personality clash. She probably sees you as the biggest threat to her territory she's ever had, and she doesn't know what to do about it.'

It was certainly a clash. Murray appreciated Donald's words, but he was trapped in the moment, like tyres spinning in the mud. So much to do, but it was impossible.

After leaving Donald's, he focused his brain forward. The first thing was to sort out Naomi, but how? If he acknowledged her part in this, it would only stoke her fire. She'd be thrilled he'd discovered it was her. Perhaps ignoring her was the best tack. He toyed with his phone. He could delete her contact details and un-friend her from everywhere. Would that work? If she was determined, she could find him. But why? Did she really believe he could care for her now? She needed mental help if she thought so. Maybe she needed it anyway.

Once she was sorted, he could deal with Beth. Just how, he wasn't sure. He needed a long run to figure it out. The weekend weather looked cracking. He pulled on his black and neon running gear and flattened his hair back into a band. As he squatted in the hall pulling on his trainers, a knock rattled the letterbox. Donald had said he'd pop by with documents. 'Come in, it's open,' Murray called, tying his lace.

The door swung forward, and he looked up. Beth. Not in her farmer's gear, but a powder blue t-shirt and jeans. Her light-brown, shoulder-length hair fell neatly around her face. Murray's eyes widened. Wow, she was trim. Hot. Beautiful. Jeez. Stop. His temperature rocketed, and he needed to swallow, but his mouth wouldn't close. Hand suspended over his shoe, he gaped.

'Hi.' She looked down and tucked her hair behind her ears.

'Hello.' He knotted his lace and sprang to his feet. Why was she here? He wasn't prepared. Her eyes roved over him. This outfit was great for running, but it was tight. 'I'm just heading out, but I'll hang fire if you want to talk. Come through,' he said. Anything to deflect her gaze. He felt naked and his body didn't always behave around her.

Fiddling with her ring finger, she looked around the living room as if checking for something. Her eyes lingered for a few seconds on his table where he'd been whittling some miniature animals from sticks. It was a pathetic effort compared to the sculptures he'd seen at her farm.

'Donald came round yesterday.' She chewed on a cuticle. 'He said you were talking about leaving.'

Murray gave a dry laugh. 'So, you came by to gloat?'

'Not really.' She crossed to his little window and looked out at the view. 'Are you aware of how difficult it was to get anyone to fill your post? You were the only applicant apart from, well, let's just say, someone who was never going to get the job. If you go now, there might be no one else.'

'And why would that bother you?'

'Because I'm part of this community.'

He folded his arms as she turned to confront him. 'Maybe you should have considered that before.'

She held up her hands. 'I'm not here to argue. I just don't want you to leave because of me.'

'Oh, Beth.' He rolled his head and rubbed his thigh. 'I don't want to leave, but you and I don't seem able to work together. If I stay, we have to. I don't want to hurt you or ruin your livelihood or anything like that, but my work will destroy part of your land. And I can't get around it. It hurts, we have to dig deep, but there's no gain without pain. I realise how precious you are about what belongs to you.' He nodded with wide eyes. 'And deep down, you don't want the road. I get that's why it's hard to commit. I'm the one you want to take it out on, but it can't be like that.' He shook his head. 'I messed up the other day because I didn't know what to do. I can't see the answer. I can't get what's best for the community without hurting you, which I don't want. And you can't do what's right for the community without making a personal sacrifice, which you don't want. And at the end of the day, it might be moot anyway, if this Crichton-Leith person runs roughshod through the entire thing with his bloody surveys and what-not.' Murray ruffled the hair at the front of his head and some strands fell free.

Beth rubbed her forehead and looked away. 'You're not as daft as you look,' she said.

'And how daft do I look?'

'With the man-bun and the Lycra? Pretty daft.' Even though she didn't turn round, he sensed a lightening in her tone. Ha! She was never one to shy away from a cheap point. Still, his ego was ready to take a hit if it meant they could get back on speaking terms.

'Charming,' he said. 'Look, can I show you something?'

'It depends.' She turned around and frowned.

'This probably seems lame but in my defence.' He took out his phone and flicked through the photos until he settled on one. It was an old picture now, his pre-beard days. In fact, Naomi was the reason he grew a beard, she hated any kind of stubble, preferring everything smooth. Well, he was done obliging her. He sighed at the screen; his short hair, Naomi like a super-model on his arm. Maybe Beth wouldn't appreciate this, but he'd started. 'You see this woman.'

Beth looked at the picture and screwed up her face, totally unimpressed. 'Your lover?'

'My ex.'

Beth's lips curved down, and she shrugged. 'Delightful, but so what? You want to leave so you can get back together?'

Murray gave a bitter snort of a laugh. 'No. The exact opposite. I came here to escape her. This is one place I knew she'd never come. We were on off for years. Life with her was one constant competition, but she didn't play fair. If I did something good, she'd ruin it. We planned once to move to America. I had an amazing job lined up with a house and everything. Then boom. She changed her mind. Just like that.' He snapped his fingers. 'I had to pull out. I turned down the job. Then she dumped me anyway. I'd already given my notice on my other job. So, I ended up out of work, taking temporary cover jobs all over the place, trying to get back in. Meanwhile, she came crawling back, and I went along with it. And it started over again. We worked together for a while. I got a great promotion, she got annoyed, so she dumped me and filed a harassment claim against me. It came to nothing, but it was there. No smoke without fire and all. I left and came here. But she's not done with me. She was the one who made the environmental complaint. That's why I got so mad.'

'And took it out on me.'

'Yes. And I regret it. Truly.' He cupped his hands in a plea. 'We've not been together for months, but she still hangs in there like a stalker, thinking I'll come back if she annoys me enough.'

Beth tilted her head and frowned. 'Why would that make you go back to her?'

'Precisely. It wouldn't. She's not worked that out yet. If she applied her intelligence to something worthwhile, she might actually make something of her life.'

'It sounds ridiculous to me,' said Beth.

Murray nodded. It was. 'I should never have dated her at all, but she was...'

'Very attractive. I can see.' Beth returned his phone and arched an eyebrow. 'You look better with a beard, though I'm still not sold on the man-bun.'

Taking the phone, Murray's grin flickered, but his pulse rate rocketed. She'd almost dished him a compliment. 'There's time yet.'

Beth eyeballed him. 'Well, you have a tough decision to make.'

'Do I?' Murray pocketed his phone in the flap on his upper arm. 'I'm not cutting my hair.'

'Not that.' She rolled her eyes. 'You have to decide who you'd rather come up against. Her or me?'

Murray raised his eyebrows and kept them up. Right now? No competition. His truthful answer would be totally inappropriate. *I'd love to come up against you any way you like.* He cleared his throat. 'You're right.'

'And?'

The corner of his mouth quirked up. 'You.'

She folded her arms. 'I'm the easy option, am I?'

'Hell no. But you're the nicer person.'

'Thanks.' Beth shook her head at the floor. 'Just as well it isn't a beauty contest.'

His eyes roamed over her. She'd win that, too. Should he say so? Did he dare? Beth had a natural perfection Naomi couldn't beat even with her layers of toner, primer, foundation, B-bloody-B and whatever other stuff she threw at her face every morning. He'd much prefer to look at Beth. And do so much more. But he was strapped into Lycra and unholy thoughts were risky in this outfit.

'Beth, you're a beautiful girl too.' Their eyes locked. Damn it, she was hard to read. Had he played this wrong? She looked ready to eat him for breakfast or knee him in the crotch.

'Oh, shut up, Murray. You say some stupid things, you really do.'

'Sorry.' He pushed back his stray hairs.

'Well, I'll head. Now we've got that out of the way.' She glanced at the table. 'What's this?' Her gaze landed on his pathetic attempt at a wooden owl. Ambling over, she picked it up.

'Oh that. It's nothing. Just something I was playing at. I enjoy woodcrafts. Put it down. It's embarrassing rubbish. I meant to ask you before, who did the carvings at your place? They're amazing. Was it someone local? I wouldn't mind getting some pointers.'

Beth's eyes slowly moved onto him, her cheeks glowed pink. 'It was me.'

'Seriously?' Murray's eyes widened. Beth's arms jumped across her chest, she bristled. 'No, no.' He thrust up his hands. 'I'm amazed and shocked, yeah, but not because you're a woman. Just because they're so damned good. Where did you learn to do that?'

Her shoulders relaxed and she half-smiled. 'I watched a YouTube video and gave it a go. If I do one a year, it's a bonus. The last one I did was over a year ago. I've been so busy.'

'Did you use a chainsaw?' His mouth fell open.

'I did. Another reason not to mess with me.' She winked.

Oh boy, he shook his head. She was a goddess, a chain-saw-wielding beauty causing all sorts of ructions below. He tugged his Lycra top as far as it would go and smiled, trying to compose himself. 'I won't, I swear.'

'Well,' she sighed, 'no rest for me. So back to work I go.'

'You know. Can I ask you? Why do you do it?'

'Do what?'

'The farm? You're good at it, but wouldn't you like to do anything else?'

She shrugged. 'There's no point in my thinking like that. I do what I do, and that's that. We can't afford to pay anyone to do it. We're diversifying with the holiday cottages, but it's not enough yet.' Her smile slipped, and she looked away. 'It might never be.'

He closed the short distance between them and put his hand on her shoulder. 'Hey.' She pulled back in surprise, but he didn't withdraw his hold.

'I'm not upset,' she said, with a feeble attempt to get her shoulder out from his grip. She could easily have snapped free if she wanted to. He knew she wasn't trying too hard.

'You're amazing.' The words tumbled out before he could reason. 'You should be proud of yourself.'

She blinked and attempted a smile. 'Don't get soft on me, Murray. I'm just a person doing a job.'

With a gentle tug, he pulled her close. She let out a little gasp, possibly a laugh, possibly a rasp of impatience, but either way, she returned his embrace. Her hands cupped where his scapula jutted out, while his fingers spread across her slender back. He was cheek to cheek with her. Her hair smelt beautiful. So natural, like spring blossom. The Lycra was far too tight around his groin now, tingles of electricity prickled all over, but he didn't let go. 'I am so sorry,' he whispered, closing his eyes, softly increasing the pressure on her back. 'I wish I'd never said any of those stupid things.'

Taking a deep breath, she let it out on his neck, across the little clump of hair too short to reach his band. He twitched, his skin suddenly hyper-sensitive. She pulled away, though he hadn't meant her to. She was welcome to stay there as long as she liked.

'Yeah. It's ok. We're good.' She clapped him on the arm, her cheeks very pink.

He walked her to the door. He'd planned to run three miles, now he needed at least ten. A flyer for an Easter Dance lay on top of his shoe rack in the hall, he'd put it there the day before and forgotten. 'Are you going to this?' He lifted the flyer. 'It looks fun.' And they could dance. Uh oh, make that a twenty-mile run. He blazed with adrenaline.

Beth looked at it. 'Maybe. I hadn't really thought about it.'

'Well, if you do. We'll have to dance. I can show you my moves for real.' He crossed his fists to the side and thrust out his hip in unison, forgetting the Lycra.

'Better watch you don't knock someone's eye out.' Her gaze fell below his waist, and she gave a little smirk.

'Funny.'

'You said it.' She flipped him a mock salute, still grinning, and made her way to the door. 'But I do not dance.'

'Oh, come on. You must have done some ceilidhs in your time.'

Beth opened the front door. 'I might have done the occasional "Strip the Willow", but that's it.'

'Then we'll do that. I'd Strip the Willow with you any day.'

She glanced heavenward. 'Murray, that is truly terrible.'

'Yeah, it was, but come on. One dance won't hurt.'

'Nope. No dancing for me.'

'Just one?' He tried to make his voice as appealing as possible.

Beth had taken a few strides when she turned around. 'No, Murray. No persuading. Remember, you don't like it when I change my mind.'

Fixing her in his gaze, he shook his head. What a cheeky and seductive grin. Beth jumped into the Land Rover, spun around and sped off down the track.

Murray watched her go. This time, yes, please god-dammit, change your mind. He sprinted in the tyre tracks. 'I will dance with you, Beth.' He told the wind. 'If it's the last thing I do on this island.'

Chapter Fifteen

Beth

Stepping back, Beth wiped her forehead, streaking it with mud. She let out a long sigh as she looked at the ewe licking the newborn lamb, coaxing it to its feet. That was it, the last one. And so early in April. Too good to be true. Finding a flat-topped boulder, a little way off, she sat down. Yes, things could still go wrong. She couldn't kick back and do nothing, but the brunt of it was done. Freeing her hair from its ponytail, she shook her head. Her shoulders lightened. For a few moments, she rested, enjoying the moment.

When she arrived home, Kirsten was leaning across the kitchen island talking to Gillian.

One glance at Kirsten was enough to tell Beth something was up. 'Everything ok?'

'Fine,' Kirsten muttered, her grip tightening around her mug.

'It's the Easter Dance,' said Gillian.

'Oh, that.' Beth took off her sweater. She hadn't forgotten Murray's plea, and as Gillian's friend, Maureen, at the Glen Lodge Hotel, was organising it, she couldn't avoid the subject cropping up and drip-feeding her reminders. She also hadn't forgotten her hug with Murray, that clinch which had brought her closer to him than she'd ever been to any man. His Lycra hadn't been enough of a barrier to block the feel of his body, and knowing her close presence had elicited such a virile reaction in him set her heart racing every time she thought about it. Something she was trying hard not to do.

'I'm helping Maureen set up. I just wondered if Kirsten was going. Think I've put my foot in it.' Gillian gave Beth a resigned look.

'Of course, I'm not going,' Kirsten said. 'I don't want to see Robyn fawning over Carl. Honestly, I'm sick of watching other people getting together. I'd rather stay at home.'

Beth fiddled with the cuffs on her checked shirt. She wasn't about to mention Robyn had texted her, asking her to come. The ideal opportunity for a chat. So far, after saying she'd like to meet up, she'd managed just once in the pub. *Nice try*. But not the real reason she was interested. She bit her lip as she hoisted herself onto a bar stool. Best to say nothing about it. 'Well, that's all the lambs.' She hoped to change the subject. 'I can't believe they're done.'

'Oh, wonderful,' said Gillian. 'What a relief. And you'll be free to go to the dance too.'

'Me?' A hot patch developed around Beth's neck. Catching up with Robyn was fine, but Murray. The phantom sensation of his barely concealed body pressed against her returned. Her heart quickened. Their flirty chats, his little looks, the hug. She couldn't shake the buzz he sent zipping through her and she knew for sure what she did to him. Despite the underlying panic, she craved more.

'Yes, you,' said Gillian, 'you're allowed to leave the house.'

'Maybe.'

'You should come too.' Beth looked at Kirsten. 'It'll do you good.'

'No thanks.'

Beth pulled a face at Gillian. With Kirsten in this mood, she didn't fancy a night in her company; she was worse than a wet fish, but Beth didn't want to go on her own. The other option was Georgia, but she was a chatterbox, a gossip and incorrigible nosey-parker. She'd be on the lookout. The imperative to behave would be ever-present, and Beth wasn't sure if she could. Palpitations fluttered at the notion. If Murray liked her too. What might he want to do? She steadied her hand as she cut herself some bread. All sorts of things might come out. How would he take it? Could she bear to tell him? Was there any hiding it?

It turned out Georgia wasn't just a busybody; she was also a miracle worker. Somehow, she persuaded Kirsten to go. The three of them piled into Georgia's van clad in their finery, or in Beth's case, the same black dress she'd dragged out for every formal occasion for the last ten years.

'Well, Kirsten, you might get lucky, a party of hiking hunks might be in for the weekend.' Georgia grinned. They were like a troop of Cinderellas in their pink pumpkin coach.

'It's not as if I'm going to date some random tourist,' Kirsten insisted, her cheeks going slightly pink.

Beth made no comment, looking out of the window as a glorious evening rushed by. Kirsten had done it in the past if Will Laird's gossip was to be believed. He'd told Beth he'd seen Kirsten sneak into a hotel with a man, but Beth had never pressed her and now wasn't the time to rake it up.

'Why not?' Georgia smiled. 'You might miss a chance. What if it's Mr Right? You might end up going off with him and living happily ever after.'

Kirsten shook her head. 'You live in Lalaland.'

Georgia giggled. 'You're so right. I really do.'

Beth let her mind wander to Murray. Perhaps he wouldn't go. And that was better, yes? No. She wanted to see him. Didn't she?

Georgia pulled up in the busy car park. Beth saw no sign of a blue Audi, but people were good at car sharing. He could easily have got a lift. Beth fiddled with her straps. The uncertainty was driving her mad.

'This looks great.' Beth looked around as they headed up the steps to the entrance to the Glen Lodge Hotel. 'Amazing view.' The sea provided a stunning backdrop behind the rolling green lawn. Beth hadn't seen it since she'd helped move furniture a few months ago. They strolled through the foyer, into the dining room, where round tables were set at the edge of the newly installed dance floor. Colourful spring blooms contrasted with the pristine white tablecloths. The low hum of chatter filled the room, punctuated with an occasional shrill laugh and the clink of glasses. At a table near the wall-to-wall window, Gillian leaned over, talking to someone. She'd gone early to help Maureen. Glancing up, she gave them a wave.

Beth smoothed her black dress. She was in control. Complete and utter control. If Murray showed up... Hell, she'd need a drink. A large one.

Not long after they took their seats, Carl joined them. Beth sipped her beer as she watched Kirsten withdraw to the back of her chair and fold her arms, not looking at him. Even when he spoke to her, she answered curtly and showed more interest in her drink than his face. The man she used to worship. How quickly things could swing if it all collapsed. Beth gulped her drink. If she'd misread Murray, even slightly, she could open herself to all kinds of trouble.

Carl excused himself. Beth tipped her glass and raised an eyebrow. Hopefully, it summed up her apology for Kirsten's glum mood.

'At least you've been spared a lifetime of looking at that back-side,' Georgia said, her eyes trailing Carl across the room.

'And how is that bad?' said Kirsten.

'Because it gets tighter every time I see it and, honestly, who likes a tight arse?'

Beth smirked into her drink, and the corners of Kirsten's lips flicked up. 'Oh, haha,' she said. Beth waved to Robyn, who hovered close to Carl, obviously not wanting to come over. Kirsten's face fell again. 'You're not going to talk to her?'

'Yes, I am,' said Beth. 'She's nice.' She got up and patted Kirsten on the shoulder. Not looking back, she crossed to Robyn and Carl, very grateful Robyn wasn't a huggy-type either. Beth greeted her with a smile.

'I'm glad you made it,' said Robyn.

'Well, the lambs are all born, so I've got a bit more free time. Everything's looking good here.' She scanned the room, landing on the door. People were still arriving. 'You two did a great job.'

'Yes, business has picked up. Now we can focus on us.' Robyn's eyes skimmed over Kirsten. *Awkward.* 'How's your sister?'

'She's...' Beth wasn't sure *fine* was the right word. 'You know.'

Carl ran his hands through his golden curls. 'It's all my fault. I feel guilty, but I never led her on or anything, we just didn't click.'

'I know.' Beth sipped her beer. 'She does too, deep down. She's just lonely, she gets down on herself. It's hard to meet people here, the island isn't exactly crawling with young singles.'

Bang on cue, Murray strolled into the room, adjusting his cuffs. Beth grabbed the bar as her knees failed. Holy crap. He looked too amazing to be allowed. His crisp white shirt fitted neatly around all the places it should and fell open just enough. He corrected the belt atop his navy trousers, so it was dead centre. Beth almost sloshed her drink down her front. Tottering back, she tried to hide behind Carl's broad shoulders. Murray had noticed the table with Georgia and Kirsten. He made a beeline for it, running his fingers through his loose hair.

'Could this be a man for Kirsten?' Carl asked as Murray sat at the table. 'I'm not looking for a bromance, but if I were a girl, I'd find him hot.'

Robyn shook her head and smiled.

'I don't think Kirsten knows him. In fact, I don't think they've ever met.' A note of concern strummed in Beth's ears. How would it be if Murray shifted his attention to Kirsten? He'd turned on the charm. She recognised that look. The one that gave her goosebumps. Kirsten was beaming and laughing. So was Georgia.

'It would be nice for her,' said Robyn, 'and us.' She clutched Carl's hand as they watched.

A million scenarios played out. What if both women took a shine to Murray? How would it be watching Murray with Kirsten? Seeing him leaving the bothy of a morning, slightly dishevelled with a smile from ear to ear. Beth turned to the bar and ordered another beer, still fantasising.

If Murray preferred Georgia to Kirsten, Kirsten's heart might be broken again. They might fall out and cause a rift. Beth swigged back her beer. Georgia was pretty and fun. People loved her smile and her humour. What a gorgeous couple she and Murray would make. Beth's heart died a little death.

'Did you get the road thing sorted out,' Carl asked. 'I heard stuff about it, mostly second-hand from Georgia. She told me you and he had some kind of altercation.'

'Yeah. We sorted it. There was a conflict of interests, but it's ok now.' She hoped it was. More scenarios burst into her head. If Murray and Kirsten became a thing, how would that affect the road? Would he consider himself family, give himself rights, try to dominate, butt in on family decisions?

Murray swivelled in his seat, draping his arm along the back-rest. With a slight double-take, he spotted Beth. She swallowed a large gulp of beer, unable to get behind Carl quick enough. Not that he would have completely hidden her, despite his broad shoulders. If anything, she was slightly taller than him. Terribly exposed in her short black dress, she clenched her long legs together. Sure, they were useful for striding around the hills, chasing errant sheep, but just now they dangled like two useless bean poles, ungainly and a little too white despite her outdoor lifestyle. At least she'd shaved them. Tights would have been advantageous, but she didn't have any.

With a little twitch of his lips, Murray's gaze travelled from her face downwards and back. As it returned to her eyes, he gave her a tiny wink. She froze, not sure what to do. His smile broadened. He looked back at the table. What did that look mean? An invitation? Taking the mickey? Her fingertips lingered on her V-neck. She had no cleavage. She still wore the same bra-cup size she had at twelve. Not the most flattering shape. Perhaps Murray was sniggering at how flat her dress looked. Pivoting around again, he lifted his chin slightly, willing her to come hither. Even she couldn't summon the power to refuse. 'I'll catch you again later.' This was it, she was going in.

Murray's grey eyes sparkled as he raised them to her. Beth gave him the smallest of smiles, concentrating hard on containing the butterflies trying to escape her chest. She sat, smoothing the dress, her knees jutting out.

'Fancy meeting you here.' Murray beamed, zeroing in on her.

'Indeed.' Beth placed her bottle on the table. 'And I haven't changed my mind.'

Those eyes. Why did he have to stare? And the smile. Thank goodness she was sitting, her knees had given way. If Murray wanted her to change her mind all he had to do was ask. She was under his spell. Where had the gooey, girly Beth come from? She was ready to melt.

He leaned back in his chair, closer to her. 'We'll see.' He arched his eyebrows.

'I'm sure Georgia will oblige,' Beth said. *Why am I encouraging him to dance with my friend? Just seize the bloody day for Christ's sake.* Fiancé Frank would give her a dressing down if he found out she'd let a moment like this slip. If Beth had his confidence, she'd be right in there.

'What am I to do?' said Georgia.

'Dance with Murray,' said Beth.

Murray quirked his lips with a playful pout. Georgia smiled and looked between the two of them. 'No problem, but it's not dancing time yet. Food first.'

'Yes, Beth, food first,' Murray said quietly. 'I don't know about you, but I'm hungry. Very hungry,' he added in a wolfish whisper. 'And I know what I want.'

Beth shuddered involuntarily, contemplating every millimetre of honed masculine perfection from the well-groomed hair to the shiny shoes. 'Then shove one of those in your mouth.' She pushed a bowl of olives towards him.

He grinned, holding her gaze as he popped one in his mouth. 'It'll do for starters.'

A smile tweaked Beth's lips, and she looked away, shaking her head towards the middle distance.

Georgia sparkled at keeping the chat rolling along through the meal. Beth chipped in when needed, but it was impossible to stop her gaze straying to Murray as he feasted on lean steak and homestyle chips. Even more disconcerting when every time she looked, she found him smiling back.

Stopping mid-story, Georgia leapt to get her phone from her bag. 'I have to show you this,' she said. 'I don't really like phones at the table, but this is hilarious.' She whipped it out and scrolled down the screen. Kirsten huddled over, and they giggled.

Aware the others' attention was diverted, Beth's eyes drifted to Murray again. He laid down his napkin, leaned towards her and whispered, 'You look so beautiful.'

Unable to speak, she gaped. He really thought that? Not just his charm? Maybe it was. Or too much drink. Though he'd said he was driving and seemed to be knocking back nothing more potent than ginger beer.

Georgia glanced over. Murray smiled innocently, but it obviously didn't fool her. Had she heard or guessed what he'd said? Heat flushed in Beth's cheeks. Georgia passed the phone to Murray to watch the humorous clip. He leaned over to share with Beth and Georgia's smile grew. The distraction of his aftershave, the seductive woody scent with a citrusy hint, made Beth heady. Focusing on the silly clip was impossible with Murray's cheek so close. She could kiss it. How would it feel? Smooth, with just the slightest rough edge where his beard started. Forcing her eyes to the screen, she watched the ridiculous slideshow of bizarre lookalikes, including a man with a haircut resembling Super Noodles. Funny, yes, but the proximity of Murray set every nerve in Beth's body tingling. She couldn't concentrate.

'That last one was awful.' Murray returned the phone to Georgia.

She put it in her bag and carried on talking, but Beth caught her glancing at them, curiosity etched into her face. Beyond the large window wall, the sun had set, blocking the sea view. The inky blackness was dotted with stars. Lights in the room dimmed and, on the stage, the ceilidh band sprang into action.

'Dance time,' said Georgia. 'So, Murray, you still want to dance?'

He fiddled with a button on his chest, smiled and stood up obligingly. Georgia winked at Beth and followed Murray onto the dance floor. Beth sipped her drink, wishing his hand didn't look so at home on Georgia's back.

'Earth to Beth.'

Beth heard Kirsten's voice and bumped back to the table. 'Sorry, what?'

'What's going on with you and him?'

'How do you mean?'

'The road thing. Is it all ok? I didn't know what to say in case I put my foot in it. Mum said he's a bit of a slippery character and to be careful what we said to him.'

'It's fine.' Very fine, her eyes settled on his hips as they swayed to the music. He was heavenly and a slick dancer. She swigged her drink. Of course he was. 'Everything's sorted.' Well, road-wise. What about other matters? Their dance, for instance. If she just bent a little, it could be her up there dancing with him, but she was a terrible dancer, she'd look ridiculous. He looked like he'd practised in clubs all over the place with his glamorous ex. Beth's experience was limited to getting the occasional turned ankle at a barn dance. *I'm just not in his league.* Georgia was a mainland girl too. She knew all the moves and looked in her element, shimmying with her hands above her head.

'Do you fancy him?' Kirsten asked.

'What?'

'Well, you keep ogling him.'

'I don't.' With a wrench, Beth turned to Kirsten. 'How can Georgia talk and dance at the same time? What are they talking about?'

'You, probably,' Kirsten muttered. 'That's all he talked about before. That's why I thought he was trying to get one over on you. It seemed he wanted us to dish the dirt.'

'But I haven't got any dirt.' Technically, she had plenty back at the farm, but none of the interesting kind. The last bars of music extended, and everybody clapped.

Georgia sank back into her seat. 'Murray's getting more drinks.' She fanned herself. 'Wow, he's a bit of a hottie, isn't he?'

'You were getting right in there.' Beth tapped her middle finger on the table.

Georgia grinned broadly. 'He's not for me.'

Beth gaped. 'No?'

Checking he was safely at the bar, Georgia said, 'He's attractive, I'm not denying it, but I'm happy on my own and I'm pretty certain he's got his eye on someone else.'

'Who?' Beth blurted out.

'Beth, stop being dense. You. Obviously!'

Ok. Her face had to cool down, heat burned her cheeks. She rubbed her exposed shoulder and frowned. 'I don't, he...' Whatever she was trying to say didn't want to come out.

'Eh, duh?' Kirsten smacked her forehead, totally over-egging her reaction. Georgia giggled, shaking her head at what was clearly an amusing but very private joke. Beth sure didn't get it.

The band leader announced the next dance. 'Let's get some sets together for "Strip the Willow".'

'Aye, aye,' Georgia said with a smile, 'look lively, Beth. He's got the business face.'

Before Beth could do anything but let out a whispered curse, Murray reappeared behind her. He set a tray of drinks on the table.

'Come on.' He placed his hand on her bare shoulder, his thumb slid over her dress strap. Beth nearly died. 'This is the one you can't refuse. It's your dance.'

'What? No.' She pulled her shoulder free, almost sending the tray of drinks flying. 'I don't dance.'

'Oh, go on,' said Georgia. Kirsten said something similar at the same time. 'This dance doesn't require any skill.' Georgia continued, 'It's more like hammer-throwing, only with people. You'll be fine. Go on, break a leg.'

'She probably will,' Kirsten muttered. 'Or she might break his.'

Beth swayed. Her hand was in Murray's. How? Was her palm sweaty? He clung so tightly, she couldn't get it out to check.

Lining up opposite, she faced him in the set. 'You better watch out,' she warned him. 'This dance can get rough.'

'Then give me what you've got.' He smiled and almost imperceptibly licked his lower lip. 'I can't wait.'

Drawing her gaze from him was hopeless. If he could read minds, what a vision he'd be receiving. His eyebrow raised a little and the corner of his lip followed suit. Oh god! He knew what she was imagining. His smile broadened. Was he thinking the same? Was Murray, the most handsome man in the universe, thinking about *her*? His eyes locked on hers for what seemed like forever, then strayed to her lips. She followed suit. What she wouldn't give for a taste. The first taste.

The music leapt into action. Whatever she'd been pondering before whirled away. Spun here, then there. Her hair flew around, flicking free from the updo Kirsten had styled for her. Beth caught glimpses of Murray's grin, felt his grip on her arm. Thank goodness for flat shoes and a strappy dress. It kept her cool as it floated around, but not enough. An exhilarated blood-rush shot through her.

No longer the skinny teen who'd done this dance with the local minister and ended up bruised down her left arm, Beth was more than a match for Murray. He laughed as she spun him off his feet. This was just the beginning. Beth's mind and heartbeat raced in tandem. Murray was a man of experience and she was, well, untried, untested, and thirty. The embarrassment threatened to eat her from the inside out.

At the end of the dance, she threw back her head. She'd got through it. Phew. Murray's breath whispered on her neck. He was on her. Her pulse raced so fast she almost keeled over. Panic. A convulsion. Heat.

'Let's get some air,' he said. 'Come with me?' It was a question, but he put his arm around her shoulder and led her. Heart pounding, she didn't look at anyone, her eyes trained forward. They left the room in a bustle of couples congregating for the next dance, crossed the dazzlingly lit main foyer and out into the cool velvet evening. It might have been cold, but Beth's boiling blood was better than central heating.

Gravel crunched under her feet; Murray guided her around a corner where the extension jutted out from the old building. Without thinking, Beth veered into the alcove. Murray coiled his arms around her waist and held her tight. 'I want to kiss you so badly,' he said. 'Can I?'

Yes, not another second longer. This was it. Sliding her arm around his neck, Beth pulled him in. He met her lips with hunger. A swooning sensation filled her stomach. She wanted to discover everything about his mouth, returning his pace with zeal. Instinctively, she melded with him, craving more and more. Murray's powerful arms gripped her and sucked her in. Still maintaining contact with his lips, she pressed against him, coupling her hands behind his neck. Utter heavenly bliss. She let out a moan, tilting her head, intensifying the kiss.

With a deep groan, Murray clenched her tight. His tongue gently grazed her lips. With tongues involved, she could hardly breathe. It was all happening, new and insane. Murray's hand slid down her back, resting low on her waist. Other-worldly sensations overwhelmed her. And, oh god, the feel of him. Her flimsy dress was no barrier. He was sizzling hot, firm in all the right places, so damned seductive and knowing she was responsible for his arousal made her pulse rocket. Every nerve in her body yearned for him. Teasing her with short kisses, he gripped hard, drawing back to catch a breath, but only for a second before leaning in again. He cupped her cheek, heightening contact. Slowly, deeply. She was ready to pass out. Dazed and intoxicated, her breathing was all over the place.

'Oh, Beth,' he groaned, still on her lips. 'You're amazing. What a kiss.'

She strained to get air. 'Murray.'

'Shh,' he whispered. It was almost another kiss. His eyes fixed on her. 'Let's not stop.' He tasted of ginger beer and black pepper. Beth's insides contracted as he nipped her lips, in and out, tormenting her. He threaded his fingers through her hair. 'I want you so damned much. Together, we can make fireworks. I'm so hot for you. Why don't you come home with me?' The words were a wolfish growl.

Beth froze. She swallowed, staring at him, trying to focus on those beautiful eyes. He trailed his hand out from her hair and traced his thumb down her cheek. A tingling erupted at his touch. Why had they stopped the incredible, gorgeous kiss? Blinking, she tried to find some sense in her befuddled head. Go home with him? He wanted to make fireworks with her. Bloody hell. A spasm of tension twitched in her shoulders. She couldn't. Parts of her body wanted to, but if he found out the truth, he'd laugh her out of the house. 'I... I can't Murray.'

'Why? What's wrong?' He released her, flexing his neck. A slight frown broke out on his brow. 'We'll be safe, don't worry. I've got so much to give you, Beth.'

'People would talk.' Beth swayed back, narrowly avoiding tripping over a plant pot.

'About what?'

'If I left with you. It would be obvious.' She tapped her face and quickly tidied her hair behind her ears. Yes, just that, not the ridiculous truth. The blatant reality she'd never done this before. The shivers in her body were part lust, part terror.

He shrugged and ruffled his hair. 'And does it matter if people know? I'm not ashamed. We're consenting adults and I like you... A lot.'

'This is Mull, not a big city. My mum's in there, my sister, my friends. I can't just go running off with you.' She blinked several times and fiddled with her neckline. What was she doing? This was a chance, and she was killing it. She had to. It wasn't real. He was caught up in the moment. In the cold light of day, he'd drop her. It wasn't meant to be like this. She hadn't waited all these years for a one-night stand with someone who'd been round all the blocks already. 'I'm not like that. I don't want to be a notch on your bedpost.' It was out before she could stop it. Of all the stupid things to say.

Murray frowned and stepped back, breathing very deliberately. 'Wow, ok. Is that what you think? You've got every right to say no, and I get the small-place mentality, but seriously, Beth, you've got me all wrong. I'm not a bedpost-notching kind of guy, but hey, there you go.' He turned away and raked his hair.

'Murray, I didn't mean anything by it. I just can't do this. This whole thing.' Beth looked around. 'There are things you don't know.'

'It's cool.' He tugged at his shirt sleeve. 'I respect your decision. I'm just sorry that's your opinion of me.'

Biting her lip, Beth struggled to find air. 'Can we just forget about it? Let's go back inside.'

Murray furrowed his brow. 'Forget? Wow, sure. You know. I think I'll just go.' For a second, he scanned her face, then he leaned in and placed a kiss on her cheek. 'Take care.'

Pulling his keys from his pocket, his car flashed in the distance and Beth watched him head directly for it. He didn't look back. She remained rooted to the spot, rubbing her hands up and down her arms, suddenly cold. Alone. What had she done?

CHAPTER SIXTEEN

Murray

Running was Murray's answer to everything. He solved all his problems on runs. And they worked off the pheromone hangover. His feet ached as he threw himself in the door after an eight-mile gut buster. He'd pushed himself harder than ever to try and eradicate the memory of how monumentally he'd screwed things up with Beth. Things had moved so fast, he hadn't stopped to consider. His mind had been elsewhere. 'Ugh.' Allowing anything below his waistline to rule his brain was never likely to end well. He slapped his forehead. *Why did I come on so strong?* Because of what she did to him. She drove him crazy in all the right – and the wrong – ways. Shit! How insensitive he'd been. If the tables were turned and *his* mother and sister had been inside, he wouldn't have wanted to be so blatant either. Especially in a place this small. Jeez. What a boor. Beth had laudable reasons not to do something they might regret, though how she'd kept her wits about her during that kiss was anyone's guess.

But the notch on the bedpost comment stung. Never had he ever done that. *You'd have been happy with that result though, wouldn't you?* A voice niggled in the back of his head. It sounded like Naomi. During their many separations, she taunted him with stories about the men she was seeing, but if he'd dared see anyone else, she'd have branded him a cad, a cheat, and an adulterer. So, he'd remained faithful while she did as she pleased.

His phone flashed on the coffee table. Please be Beth. His eyes rolled heavenwards. Why had he thought about Naomi? *Careful what you wish for.* Her little round picture had popped up. *Delete her, you idiot.*

NAOMI WALSH: Hey, Babes, why don't you answer? Missing you. I might come and see you. I was chatting with your mum, she's coming over for a visit. I might come with her. We can have some fun on the beach, handsome. How's your new job? All well with the road? Wish you'd come back. That would be amazing. Love you, gorgeous & I miss us.

He launched the phone across the room with a tirade of swearing. It hit the carpet with a thud. 'You are not coming here under any circumstances!' he yelled. No. Not to his retreat. He wouldn't let her anywhere close. Her poisonous words sickened him. Love? *She loves me!* Ha, if that was love, he wanted none of it. Standing over the phone, he resisted the urge to stamp on it. Seething, he un-friended her on every social media site. He wouldn't even grace her with a reply, though nothing short of a restraining order seemed secure enough.

And his mother! How could she? She fawned over Naomi. Well, people did. Naomi was beautiful and charming, but she was also an ego-centric, self-loving bitch with stalker-like tendencies.

Phone in hand, Murray hit call before he was aware he'd done it. The ring tone jarred in his eardrum. 'Mum,' he said before she'd got any words out. 'Are you planning on visiting me?'

'Oh, hello, Murray. Bruce! Murray's on the phone!' Murray held the phone away from his ear as Janet Henderson relayed this information to her husband and the rest of the street. 'Yes, darling. I most certainly am coming to visit.'

'Well, don't.' He almost slammed the phone down.

'Oh, Murray. How terribly unkind.'

He screwed up his face. 'I know. I'm sorry. I didn't mean that. You and Dad can come, that's fine, but don't bring Naomi. I don't want her here. Do you understand? I don't care what she says, we aren't together anymore.'

'Naomi? I haven't spoken to her for a long time,' said Janet. 'Why would I be bringing her?'

He balled his fists. Another of Naomi's lies. 'Good.' His breathing calmed.

'And how is the island, darling?'

'Beautiful. I'm in love.'

'Oh, Murray, you've met someone?'

'No, Mum.' He frowned. 'With the island.' But his heart tingled. Love? Jeez. There was a thing. He'd just read Naomi's version of love. They'd been together on and off for eight years. Yeah, he knew exactly what "love" felt like. He wasn't going down that road again unless he was absolutely certain.

'I thought you'd maybe met a pleasant island girl.'

I have. He kept the words firmly inside his head. *But she doesn't want a guy like me. She needs a useful guy who can help her around the farm. Definitely not me.* He'd seen the scorn in Beth's eyes at what she considered his "mainland ways". 'I've met lots of friendly people, Mum.'

'I'm so glad. You always were a sociable boy. You've been so popular ever since nursery school.' Even though Janet could be borderline insane at times, she was still his mum and something about her words soothed the turmoil taking place inside him.

Murray stroked his fingers through his hair and let her chirrup on. So, no Naomi. She was gone, really gone. A weird, empty, helpless sensation slid up his arms. Nothing left to prove. If things fell flat, so what? She'd never know.

'That's for when you get married.'

'What?' Murray realised his mum was still talking, and he hadn't listened to any of it. Getting married? Even after eight years with Naomi, the concept hadn't occurred to him. 'I am not getting married.'

'I know. Weren't you listening? I was reminding you of my grandmother's wedding ring.'

'Right, yes.' Though Murray didn't know what she was talking about. 'Well, I should go. I have things to do.' He put the phone down and dropped his head into his hands, his hair draped around. Ridding himself of Naomi was a great distraction, but all he wanted to think about was Beth. He'd pushed too soon. Was anything salvageable? Was there any point? Maybe she was right. He'd got so caught up in the heat, he hadn't considered the bigger picture. Well, she'd chucked a bucket of icy water over his head. If he shifted his focus, he could get back on track. See her as Beth, the farmer, once more. Or Beth, the friend. A niggle of doubt picked away at him like a crow on a birdfeeder. Was it possible to forget and move on? Why did he think not? The Beth effect. Where the hell did he go from here?

CHAPTER SEVENTEEN

Beth

I nside a dusty chest in the barn, Beth found her chainsaw equipment. Pulling out the mask and gloves, she wiped them down. It had been a long time, but the lambing's early conclusion had left her oddly bereft. During the gruelling period of its duration, she wished for it to end so she could get some peace, but now it had, she wasn't sure what to do with the extra time.

Gillian was cleaning the guest bothy at the track end, next to the one she'd handed over to Kirsten. They'd had guests over the Easter weekend and as April moved on, the tourist season picked up. Kirsten had taken a group on a tour and would be away all day. Beth was alone with time on her hands. Clanking about inside the barn getting the equipment ready, she didn't register a car pulling up. As she clicked open the chainsaw box, she glanced outside. Across the courtyard, someone was at the farmhouse door. During the season, that wasn't unusual, people often came knocking for bed and breakfast, or guests from the bothy appeared needing plasters, cooking oil and all the other things they'd forgotten to pack.

Dusting off her hands, Beth stepped out of the dim barn. She squinted, the bright spring sunlight shone in her eyes before she clocked who it was. Even from behind it was obvious. Aside from being the most attractive derrière this side of Tobermory, there was only one man-bun that slick on the island.

Beth pulled back. She'd tried hard not to think about him. With no success. Kirsten and Georgia suspected all sorts of things after the dance, but the truth was worse than all of it. Beth was the mistress of fobbing people off, she'd held off the questions and chat with her curt answers. But what now? She swallowed and flattened her lips. In all her scenarios, she hadn't worked out what the hell she'd say to Murray when they next met. She'd had him on a plate. It made her cringe. What must he think of her? Wiping her hand across the saw's dusty handle, she drew in a deep breath. Where was her courage? Her sense of adventure? Maybe she didn't have any. She was made to grind with the guys, not have fun with them. Not in the way Murray wanted.

He turned to walk away from the door, and she emerged, forgetting how she must look with her heavy gloves and her face-shield tilted up, not to mention the chainsaw.

Murray's brows raised, sitting high on his forehead. He put up his palms. 'Ok, that's scary. I'm here in peace, I swear.' The little quirk at the side of his mouth was unbearably gorgeous.

'Well, good.' Words lodged in her throat. Looking at him was a struggle.

'I've got some excavators and people working in the woods today. They shouldn't disturb you, but in case you see or hear them and wonder what they're doing, it's just routine, ok?' He ran his hand through his hair, his eyes didn't settle. He seemed distracted.

'Sure, fine.'

He gave her a flat-lipped smile. 'Ok, I better head. I'll leave you to the massacre.'

'Very funny,' she muttered. As he got into his car, she flipped down the mask and powered up the chainsaw. What better way to channel her pent-up energy than to blast it into a sculpture? So that was where they were now. Polite? Friendly? Meek? She channelled into the wood, letting the frustration flow into the vibrations, shaking her arms. Well, at least she'd managed a kiss with Murray. The thirty-year-old's first kiss. And what a fantastic, mind-blowing kiss it was.

Something was emerging from the wood; she rolled the saw over it. Sometimes things started abstract and gained form as she went, other times she planned them carefully. Sometimes they were just trash she threw on the fire. She wasn't an artist, she just messed about with it until she got something she liked.

After cutting a round shape, she examined it. A plaque? No, a pile of rubbish. She was so out of practice. If she planed it down, maybe Georgia could paint something on it, or not. It reminded her of an old-fashioned pocket watch, but on a grand scale. Perhaps it was nature's reminder of her biological clock.

How had she got here? Since her dad had died, year after year had merged into one long farming calendar. His death had suspended her appetite for anything else. She missed his guidance, his stories, his laugh. Pressing her lips together, she glanced up to stay a tear. She'd planned to work in engineering, completing her degree by Open University while still at home so she could help with the farm work, but she'd never finished it. Dad had died shortly before her final exams. Grief had taken over and working out how to run a farm became a constant, full-time occupation.

It was too late now, for everything. Before Murray had shown up, she'd been fine with it. Mostly. His arrival had awakened something she wasn't sure how to put back to sleep. Why did he have to be so perfect? Far too perfect for her.

Throwing off her mask and gloves, she stared at the ludicrous bumpy wooden circle. No one in their right mind would want anything like that. Marching towards the burning-pile, she went to throw it in as a man and woman came striding up the drive. Serious hikers, middle-aged, with up-to-date clothes and shiny walking poles.

'Oh, that's marvellous.' The woman stared at the ugly carving. 'Did you just make that?' She glanced behind Beth to her makeshift workshop.

'I did.' Beth lifted her visor, screwing up her face at the would-be plaque. How could anyone consider it marvellous?

'Wow. We were admiring the sculptures on the way up the path. Did you make them too?'

Beth nodded.

'Gracious,' the woman put her hand to her chest, 'so refreshing. In this day and age, there's still too much male domination for my liking.'

Her husband arched his eyebrow from his place of safety under her thumb.

'You can keep this if you like.' Beth handed her the plaque. 'I was just practising.'

'Thank you very much,' the woman said. 'I'll try transferring a photo of the view onto it, that would be a lovely souvenir and I've seen a way to do it on Pinterest.'

Beth smiled. If her talents ran to giving people simple pleasures, she could at least take some joy from that.

'Beautiful spot here,' the woman went on. 'We've been in the woods and we met...' She pointed randomly behind her head. 'I can't remember his name, anyway, I think he lives here, your husband, perhaps? He told us about the new logging road and how, in future years, we'll be able to use that instead of trekking across fields. Sounds like an exciting time.'

Beth lost the thread. Her husband? Seriously? He was that cocky, he'd given them the idea he owned the place? Waiting until they'd gone on their way, Beth pulled off the mask and gloves. She dashed inside, changed into clean jeans and a short sleeve check shirt, and emerged, flexing her fingers. Moments later, she was on the quad racing over the field. Bleats from the ewes and new lambs echoed as they frolicked around.

Mac and Rab sat behind Beth, their coats flapping as she powered up the hill. An engine rumbled not far off. This might be routine, but the location of the tree cutting was interesting. Just beyond the boundary fence, a log excavator smashed at a tree in exactly the place the proposed track was meant to come in.

Hopping off the quad, Beth strode up and vaulted the fence. The dogs followed at a trot. The noise from the excavator was so loud Murray was wearing ear defenders. Staring at an iPad, he made notes on it, frowning. Beth marched up behind him and tapped him on the shoulder. His expression rolled from one surprise to the next.

Yes, it's me, Beth's feigned smile told him as he pulled off the ear defenders. 'Fancy meeting you here,' she shouted. 'Can we talk?'

He pointed to the path beyond, where presumably he thought it would be quieter. She strode ahead, across the path and into a copse on the other side that muffled the sound enough for her ears to relax. The dogs roamed about, sniffing, and disturbing piles of beech leaves.

'What do you want to talk about?' Murray clung to his iPad.

Now she was here, she wasn't entirely sure. Why was she so angry? If some woman had mistaken him for someone else, so what? It wasn't his fault. The urge to see him had lured her. Any flimsy excuse. Why not the truth? What was that exactly?

Tugging at her collar, she looked around. 'Why are you cutting the trees so close to the boundary? It looks suspiciously like you're preparing the way for a road. The road you don't actually have formal permission for.'

Murray's jaw set and he looked away. 'This again? I thought you understood the position here?'

She folded her arms. Murray looked annoyed, but Beth couldn't stop even though she wanted to. The words rolled out. 'I do, but the excavators.'

'I told you about them this morning.' His voice was higher pitched than usual. 'We're cutting trees on our side of the boundary. It doesn't affect you in the slightest.'

'But you're acting like it's going ahead.'

'And it is. We agreed.' He looked heavenward and raked his hair. Beth rolled her lips. She was digging herself a hole. He was right. She was being deliberately antagonistic, she couldn't help it. Stuck on the back foot, she wanted to regain the upper hand, but how? Everything she said made her look more and more stupid.

'Why are you really here?' Murray looked at her and a muscle in his jaw twitched.

'I...um.' Her certainty failed. Why, indeed? She'd come all this way to argue about something that wasn't even a point any more. Pathetic. 'I just wanted to see...' *You!* The word lodged, and she swallowed. 'How things were.'

He held up his palms and gestured around. 'Take a look. I'm not hiding anything.'

She poked her tongue into her cheek and glanced around. 'And you haven't consulted any surveyors or anything?' Why? She shoved her hands in her pockets. Why couldn't she say what was on her mind? The words spouting out weren't even close.

Murray frowned. 'I've spoken to several surveyors and consultants. I've taken advice on many points, including, but not limited to: structure, conservation, agricultural mitigation and drainage.' He ticked them off on his fingers. 'None of these has led to any further action regarding your land.'

Beth could imagine him in a suit saying these words to a table of businesspeople.

'It would have been courtesy to tell me you'd spoken to all these people.'

'Good god.' Murray rubbed his forehead. Even when he was irked, he was gorgeous. *Bloody hormones*. Maybe if she went for it, out here in the woods. Perhaps if her desires were satisfied, she could back down. 'This is my job. You've been busy doing yours, I've done mine. I don't need to fill you in on every conversation I have. Why don't you just trust me? You're so uptight.'

'Pardon?' She stiffened. That cut seriously close to the mark. Was it so obvious? Maybe to a man like him it was. Mac lay down at her feet.

'Just chill out a bit, Beth. I'll do nothing on your land without consultation and express permission from you.' Murray tilted his head and his eyes flickered with a gentle gaze, setting goosebumps erupting across her shoulders. 'I know what you think of me. I got your message loud and clear, but can we at least keep it professional? I've agreed to keep you in the loop, and I will.'

She drew back into a tree. Uncertain. Afraid. What message had she given him? Did he imagine she disliked him? That wasn't true. It was embarrassment, terror. She couldn't see the way out of the woods.

He checked his iPad. 'I'm on a tight schedule today. Is there anything else you want?' He looked her over. She held her breath, but before she could reply, he said, 'Nope, thought not. So goodbye.' Marching down the track, he bypassed the area near the excavator where she needed to go to get back to the farm.

Beth kicked a pile of sticks. Mac bounded after one. Putting her head down, her fists balled. None of that had been necessary. All she'd wanted was to be with Murray. Back at the quad, she slumped on it and put her face in her hands. Rab poked his nose under her elbow. She'd thrown away a chance. An incredible chance.

But a chance of what? Breaking her duck? Stupid phrase. Shaking her head, she absently stroked Rab's nose. She wanted to break more than a duck. But if she gave into temptation, she'd satisfy an urge for a day or two, and what then? They didn't have a future together. They had a spark, but it wasn't going anywhere. Being with Murray in the long term was a fantasy. With low shoulders, she returned to the house.

Monday arrived with a 'surprise!' Literally. Gillian and Kirsten jumped out as Beth came in for breakfast.

'Happy birthday!' said Gillian.

Thirty-one today. What an achievement. As Kirsten had a tour later and Gillian had a changeover at the bothy, Beth had no reason to expect anything exciting for the big day, other than getting to eat cake for every meal. She wasn't too bothered. Getting on the wrong side of thirty wasn't much call for celebration.

'How was your date?' Gillian asked Kirsten.

Beth looked up from her chocolate breakfast, crunching on a mini egg cake. She was out of the loop again. She wasn't aware Kirsten had a date. She covered a moment of anxiety by gulping her tea. What if it was Murray? Would he stoop that low? If he couldn't have one sister, he'd take the other. As the conversation played out, Beth realised it wasn't him.

'It wasn't a date. My oh-so-charming boss would kill me if he thought I was dating someone from a tour.' Kirsten sighed into her cereal. 'He was just a nice guy, and we went for a coffee. He wasn't even that interested in me, he just wanted to know about some people he thought he might be related to.'

'Well.' Gillian took a sip of coffee. 'You'll find someone. You're only twenty-seven. I just hope it's soon. I can't wait for grandchildren.'

Kirsten reddened and looked at her feet.

Beth carried on with her cake. This exchange wasn't unusual. She was a bystander. Neither her mother nor sister deemed it necessary to include her. Which suited her. Mostly. What could she contribute? Still, it irked. 'What about me?' It was a surprise the words came out aloud. Must be the sugar rush.

'In what way?' Gillian frowned over her cup and sat down.

'I might have your grandchildren first.'

Gillian swallowed her coffee slowly with a humouring, placating smile, but Kirsten looked up. 'So it's true.'

'About what?' Beth frowned.

'About you and Murray? Are you pregnant?'

'Wait? What?' Half Beth's cake fell on the floor.

Gillian dropped her cup, spilling coffee all over the table. 'I beg your pardon.'

'No, of course not,' Beth snapped. 'Murray? Are you having a laugh?'

Kirsten didn't answer but tipped her head and gave Beth a "yeah, right" look. Kirsten had seen them sneak off together at the dance and been there when Beth returned alone, flushed, in a daze, not realising her hair was messed up. Somehow, she'd fobbed off the questions, but she knew Kirsten and Georgia had been speculating ever since.

Gillian furrowed her brow.

'Well, what do you want me to say?' Beth widened her eyes, looking between the two of them, trying to look innocent.

'We saw you dancing,' Kirsten said. 'And then you disappeared with him.'

'Beth?' Gillian frowned. 'Is everything all right?'

'Yes, fine.' Now she was red and very hot. 'He was leaving, he had something to give me. I went outside to get it. Then he left. That was it.' She loosened her collar. Seriously? Her choice of words. Things weren't improving.

'You were away for ages.'

'We were talking. About the road.' Beth countered.

Kirsten looked sceptical, but Gillian relaxed. 'Well, that's good.'

'Yup, just great,' said Beth.

Kirsten's suspicious face stuck throughout breakfast. Even as she left for her tour, she had a gleam in her eye that said she didn't believe a word Beth had said. Gillian flapped around, drying dishes. Beth grew aware her mother was watching her. She peered over her third mini egg cake. 'What? It's my birthday, I can eat as much cake as I want.'

'Yes, of course.' Gillian stepped back and folded the dishcloth. With a very deliberate action, she placed it beside the sink. 'It will all come right in the end, I'm sure. And I will always be here for you, my lovely girl.'

Trotting forward, she kissed Beth on the cheek. Beth almost fell off the stool. 'What? Mum. Thanks, but...' Beth's phone buzzed. Glad of the excuse to escape Gillian's clutches, she picked it up and opened the message.

FIANCÉ FRANK: Hey, my dearest betrothed one. Happy birthday!! Now you're officially too old for me again, but I haven't forgotten our deal. Coming home next week. Roll out the carpets, raise the flags and start planning the royal wedding. Can't wait, my darling! Love U XXX

With a smirk, Beth laid down the phone.

Gillian lifted her glasses, resting them on top of her head. Her brow creased, and she half-opened her mouth, closed it again, then shook her head before saying, 'I need to go clean the bothy. You enjoy your cakes.' Placing a pat on Beth's back, she left with a frown.

Beth stared after her. Had Gillian just read that message over her shoulder? Maybe she imagined her prayers had been answered and Prince Charming was on his way to rescue Beth. Well, if she did, she was in for a shock.

Georgia called in later in the morning with a present. Beth smiled at her, but she wasn't looking forward to another grilling. 'Are you ok?' Georgia asked.

'Yeah. Why shouldn't I be?' She was getting edgy. Why did people keep asking her that?

'No reason.' Georgia smiled. 'Sometimes birthdays make people wistful. It's my thirtieth this December, and I'm dreading it. I thought you were having a moment, that's all.'

Beth ran her fingers through her hair. It was getting long. 'Maybe I am. Listen, would you walk with me? I need to get some air.'

As Beth spent most of her days outside, this wasn't exactly true, but she was restless. They proceeded towards the woods; the dogs scampering around delighted to be running free. Georgia was full of her usual chitchat about everything and nothing, but when they got halfway up the hill she said. 'You looked upset back at the house. Has something happened to one of the lambs?'

'No.' Beth shook her head, she almost laughed. A short bark lodged in her throat.

'What is it?' Georgia smiled at her with her wide lips and even teeth. Such a pretty smile that invited confidences.

'Why do people always assume if I'm bothered about something it must be the sheep, or the cows or the dogs? Like I have nothing to do with people.'

Georgia laid her palm gently on Beth's upper arm. 'I didn't mean any harm by it. You're a dedicated farmer, that's all. I know how important it is to you, but is there something else?'

'No. That's just it. There's nothing else. This is me.' She looked around. 'My past, my present, my future.'

'Oh, Beth.' Georgia's forehead creased with concern. 'If you want a change, you need to do it.'

'How can I? If I leave, the place falls apart. And I don't know if I want to leave. It's not as if I can do anything else and this farm has been in our family for centuries. I'd hate it to collapse on my watch. I just don't like the idea this is all I'm going to have, forever. Everyone else will move on. Life will change, as it does, but I'll still be here when I'm old and grey, on my own.'

Georgia took hold of Beth on both arms. She was considerably shorter, but her grip was firm. 'You have a right to be happy. If you want to do something, do it. It's not easy, but one bridge at a time. You don't have to be a martyr to this place. Everyone knows your dedication.'

Beth scanned around the countryside as Georgia spoke. Yup, she was astute. The words gave Beth hope. She just had to find the courage to do something about it.

CHAPTER EIGHTEEN

Murray

'Dad said you were having some problems with the Mc-Gregors.'

Sitting in the Harbour restaurant in Tobermory for a relaxed committee meeting and a pleasant Monday lunch, Murray rubbed his forehead and focused on Will Laird. 'You could say that. We're ok now. On the road front.'

'Well, Beth's a character,' Will said. 'She and I go way back, we've been friends forever.'

'Yeah, she's got spirit, all right.' Murray opened his notes. Too much spirit for me.

'Not half. She's drunk me under the table several times.' Will adjusted his tie. 'Mum and Dad really like her. I think they hoped we'd get together, but she's one of the guys. You don't cross that line with Beth. I wouldn't have dared, she's a good-looking girl, but she's a foot taller than me and she runs roughshod over me at everything. Maybe I've got an inferiority complex.' Will chortled into his panini.

'She definitely likes to be in control.'

'Just wait until Frank gets back. Then we'll have trouble.'

'Who's Frank?'

'Beth's bestie. When the two of them get together, I hide.' Will lowered his voice and leaned away from his father. 'I once fell down the middle of a haybale stack and almost got stuck, thanks to the two of them. All just nonsense, Beth got me out, but they're a right pair.'

Murray furrowed his brow. 'She's a strong, stubborn woman, I know that much.' He didn't have time to dwell. Donald looked around Will, checking if Murray was ready. Murray tapped his agenda on the table and said, 'I've had several emails from Simon Jarvie, the solicitor for the estate at Ardnish. He believes the logging road presents a danger to the ecology and biodiversity of the area. Can I ask, off-record, why the owner of Ardnish is so against this project?' He looked around at the faces at the table.

Anna Maxwell, the secretary, steepled her fingers. 'Your predecessor wanted the road to go across the Ardnish Estate, the Crichton-Leiths objected, and things got nasty.'

'Yes, it was an unpleasant business,' said Donald. 'Your predecessor didn't get on with the Crichton-Leiths. That was why he left. This Archibald Crichton-Leith has newly inherited the estate, but the family are historically stubborn. They have an unpleasant reputation on the island. They've always been very touchy about land use. He seems to be following in the footsteps of his ancestors.'

'But he won't be able to stop this development, will he?' said Anna. 'Because there aren't any ecological problems, are there?'

Murray flattened his lips and shrugged. 'I guess that remains to be seen. He's talking about having all sorts of surveys performed.' Just another spanner in the roadworks. Murray sat back and tented his hands on the table. As the meeting rolled on, he couldn't help wondering if the road was cursed.

After the meeting's conclusion, he took a stroll along the promenade of the quaint seaside village, past the multi-coloured facades, heading for the supermarket. His mind fluttered over the problems with the road, but landed once again on Beth. Beth and Frank. Who was Frank? She'd never mentioned him, but then when did she ever talk about things like that? Her walls were thick, shutters pulled tight. Maybe he just hadn't asked the right questions. But the idea of her having some man as her best friend unsettled him. Why? He wasn't sure. Head in a daze, he almost ran into Georgia Rose.

'Hello.' She waved her fingers.

Murray dropped back to earth. 'Oh, hi. How are you?'

'Very good, thanks. I was just at Creagach Farm. It's Beth's birthday. We went for a walk, it's made me late for everything I planned to do, but hey, it was a birthday, and now I'm procrastinating a bit more.'

'It's Beth's birthday, is it?' Murray smiled and rubbed his neck. 'Can you tell me something about her?' It was out of his mouth before he could get it back.

Georgia arched an eyebrow, opened her mouth and closed it again. He watched her expression turn thoughtful. 'What exactly?'

'Well, is she? I don't know.' He mussed up his hair and looked over the marina. 'What goes on in her head?'

'I'm not sure what you mean.'

'I don't know myself.' He rubbed his chin. 'Who's she into? What kind of guy does she like?'

'I'm not entirely sure. Why? Are you interested?'

'Maybe.'

Georgia eyed him, furrowing her brow. 'I haven't known her that long. She's easy to get on with, but she isn't easy to get anything out of. She doesn't really talk about guys. Or anything personal.'

'I've noticed.'

'Like what happened with you, for instance.' Georgia's eyes sparkled with curiosity.

'Nice try.' Murray adjusted the collar of his shirt. 'But you won't get it out of me either.'

With an enormous grin, Georgia lifted her brows and batted her eyelids in an unconvincing gesture of innocence. 'Can't blame a girl for trying. Especially with all the intrigue flying around.'

'Still, my lips are sealed.'

'Have it your way.' She looked anything but satisfied.

'Listen, without saying too much.' He tapped his foot. 'I made a mistake. I went in too strong.' He pressed his lips together. 'She rebuffed me, and it upsets me. It's her choice, but...' He flattened his hair on top of his head. 'I don't know what to do.'

'Yeah, guys don't appreciate being rejected.'

'It's not that.'

Georgia gave him a knowing look.

'Ok, it's partly that,' he qualified, 'but I like her. I really do. I didn't think she was my type, but she is. I guess I'm just not hers.' Where was all this coming from? And it was so true. She was more than he'd ever dreamed of.

'Aw, that's sweet.' Georgia smiled, she had a cute little dimple that made Murray grin too. When had he become such a sap? 'As I said, she's hard to read, but my gut tells me she likes you too. She's been single for a while, so she's had a long time to deliberate on what she wants.'

Murray shook his head and sighed. 'No pressure then.' And what exactly did the magnificent Beth want? He needed to find out. And wow, if it was someone for the long haul, maybe he could still be that guy. Why settle for a few hours with Beth if he could have so much more?

Chapter Nineteen

Beth

Having her birthday in the lambing season was a cruel twist of fate, but with the early births that year she'd at least enjoyed some of it, mostly the cake. Still, she had to do her evening rounds. She drove the quad down, instantly noticing the blue flashy car at the bend in the road. She almost turned the bike. Not a birthday battle. How could she trust herself not to say something stupid?

Murray leapt out and waved, making turning back impossible without looking very rude. She approached. Why was he dressed like that? In his crisp blue shirt and smart trousers, he looked like he was on his way out somewhere.

'Fancy meeting you here.' He strolled towards her with his hands behind his back. His eyes ignited with a provocative glint, and the corners of his mouth curled up.

'What are you doing here?' Beth looked around, trying not to keep eye contact. His gaze was burning through her.

'A little birdie told me it was your birthday. Surprise!' With a flourish, he pulled a shiny gift bag from behind his back and proffered it to her.

'Is this bribery?'

'Absolutely.' He beamed with a seductive smile. 'And maybe a token.'

'Of what?'

'Friendship?' He nudged the bag in her direction.

She looked away, grinning. This chivalrous Murray was possibly more alarming than the cheeky, flirtatious one. He edged closer and slipped the bag into her hand. The touch made her flinch. Goo was about to erupt from her heart again, clogging her brain and making her irrational. The hair, the beard, his heady man-scent, his chest, the heat. And what was he doing?

He rubbed his thumb down her arm. She froze. 'Beth, I'm sorry about the dance, well, not the actual dance but the aftermath. I got carried away. You kind of have that effect on me.' He pursed his lips and looked into her eyes. She blinked as he continued. 'I didn't mean to be so pushy. It wasn't like me. I shouldn't have invited you home. I apologise.'

Beth frowned, what? His soft voice was unnerving. 'You. What? Hang on.' She fiddled with her neckline, unsure where to look. What to say? 'Rewind a second. What effect do I have on you?'

'I think you know.' He gave her a meaningful look. 'You're a very attractive woman. Stunning, in fact.'

'Good god, Murray. Get a grip.' She bit her lip. What was this? Murray raised his eyebrows. 'I mean it.'

'Thing is...' She didn't know what the thing was at all. Everything about this conversation sounded terrifying. Her foot twitched and tapped.

'It's ok.' Murray smiled again, running his fingers through his perfectly styled hair. Beth inhaled a waft of his gorgeous woody scent. Was that a hint of vanilla? 'I understand,' he continued, 'I know that... Well...'

Heat rushed to Beth's cheeks. What did he understand? Was it *that* obvious? Did everyone know? This was exactly what she was afraid of. Murray had experience oozing from every pore. Being a pathetic loser just wasn't her, but that was exactly what she was. 'Listen, I need to go.'

'Beth, please. I don't mind. It's—' He took her fingers in his.

She pulled them out straight away. 'What? An honour? You think I've been saving my body for you?'

'What? No, of course not.' He screwed up his face. 'People don't get to our age without baggage, I'm cool with that. I've got plenty of it myself.'

Heat spread over her neck like the plague. Murray's eyes surveyed her, puzzled and questioning. 'Are you ok?'

'Sure. I agree. Everyone's got baggage. I just don't think your baggage is compatible with mine.' Her heart rate increased six-fold. Had she done enough to cover?

'Right. Ok. I get it.' He glanced at his feet, then seaward, like he was steeling himself to say more.

Whatever it was, Beth couldn't deal with it. His idea of her was so far from the truth. Jumping on the quad, she started the engine.

'Beth.' He caught up with her. 'Look, I don't want to fall out. You're friends with a lot of guys. Why not me? Let's keep things cool. It's better when we're friends. Can we at least be that?'

'Sure. Welcome to the gang. And thanks for the birthday present. I can't hang about.'

Hiding the present under her jacket when she got home, she crept into the kitchen. She didn't want Gillian interrogating her. Up in her room, she opened the bag and stared at a box of handmade artisan chocolates from the chocolatier in Tobermory and four truckles of cheese from the island dairy. He'd remembered. It must have knocked him back a fair bit. The chocolates looked exquisite, she'd never had such an indulgent gift. Checking out the different varieties of cheese, she came to the card. Her eyes popped out when she read the words.

For the Beautiful Beth

Love, Murray

Love? No, no, no. She flopped back on her pillow and started picking off the chocolates, one by one. They were divine. Just like him. If only it was him. But she'd just successfully friend-zoned him. All to cover her stupid failings. Why was she such a fool? What else could she do? It had almost come out. And the look on his face. Well, she wasn't ready for that kind of humiliation.

Opening the card again, she stared at the words. *Love,* Murray? It was just a word people wrote. He always signed his texts with a kiss, but this felt like more. Lack of experience talking. Again. She'd never been in love. Even her crushes had been stupid. Guys who were friends never looked at her sideways. Not when she took great pleasure at beating them in races, drinking games and even ploughing competitions. She'd condemned Murray to that pile too.

'Arghh!' She threw her head onto the pillow and yelled at the ceiling, 'Why is this such a mess?'

CHAPTER TWENTY

Murray

A call came late on Monday night. Murray had hoped all day to hear from Beth. Maybe she hadn't appreciated her gift. Or his words. Yes, he'd used the *L-word* on the card. Crossed the invisible line Beth drew round herself to keep out the men. The friends-only zone. Had anyone ever broken through that barrier? Surely someone. How the hell had they done it? But the call wasn't from Beth. It was his mother.

'You're what?' Murray asked.

'Coming to stay on Thursday, and Alison and the kids are coming too.' Murray gaped at the phone. His mother, father, sister, niece and nephew? In three days' time?

'I live in a one-bedroom cottage,' he said. 'And you can't day trip here from Dumfries. You'll have to find accommodation, but it'll be impossible, it's the holidays.'

Janet Henderson wasn't a woman to be put off. Murray knew he'd inherited some of her stubbornness. 'I'm sure you can ask around. You must have made some connections.'

Murray groaned. If he didn't try to find something, he could see them turning up at his door on Thursday evening anyway. The obvious person was Beth. At least two outbuildings at her farm were converted into holiday lets, plus they had guest rooms in the annex. But would she even want to talk to him? Her mum might help, even though she was quite terrifying herself and would Beth hate him for going behind her back. The following morning, he called their landline. Gillian answered.

'Well, I have one of the bothies free this week, it was a late cancellation, but it won't fit five. I could get three in at a push if I give them a camp bed. We're full otherwise.'

'Oh no,' Murray groaned.

'The only other thing would be your parents stay in Kirsten's old room. It's not exactly a guest room, but I can tell it's an emergency.'

'Seriously? You would do that?'

'We like to help our neighbours.' Her tone was clipped.

'I will be eternally grateful. Thank you so much.' If she'd been in the room, he would have kissed her and braved the consequences.

A flurry of calls and texts followed as he acquainted everyone with the arrangements, including Beth. He deemed it best, though he wouldn't have minded an early morning call to berate him. It was some hours later when he received her reply.

BETH: Lucky for you, I have such a generous mother.

He read her irritation and sarcasm in every word, but he let it go. He had to because a loud knock on his door startled him. For a second, he thought it was her. That was her kind of joke, sending him an irritated text then appearing at the door before he could reply. But it wasn't her. A man about the same height as him, dressed in an expensive tweed jacket stood on the doorstep. He offered his hand to Murray.

'I'm Archibald Crichton-Leith. Are you Murray Henderson?' His voice was deep and refined.

Why was *he* here? He didn't look at all like Murray had imagined. Somehow an image of a stuffy old man played around his head when he heard the name, but this man looked no more than late thirties.

'I am. How can I help you?'

'My family owns the Ardnish Estate.'

'I know.' Murray's jaw stiffened.

'And I believe you're the new Community Woodland Group manager.'

Murray nodded and folded his arms.

'Excellent. Well, I thought, we should meet in person. I expect you're annoyed at my interference, but I have some viable concerns. I've organised a meeting with some people and I wonder if you'd like to come along, as a courtesy.'

'Sure. When is it?'

Archibald Crichton-Leith checked his Rolex. 'In about half an hour. We're meeting at the proposed development site.'

'What?' Murray glowered. 'And the landowners are aware?'

'Perhaps you can contact anyone you think should be in attendance,' said Archibald Crichton-Leith. 'I'll meet you there.'

Murray dashed to put on his shoes. He wanted to be there because knowing his luck, Beth would spot Archibald Crichton-Leith, put two and two together and get sixty-seven and a half. But at the risk of doing something else she didn't like, he sent her a quick text to say what was happening.

MURRAY: Urgent! On way to show landowner new road, be there 30 mins. Meet me if you can x

Damn! The kiss again. He couldn't help himself. Desperate not to let Archibald Crichton-Leith do anything without him, Murray followed the beige Jaguar towards the road site. A black Freelander had parked already, and as Archibald Crichton-Leith got out a silver saloon pulled up. This was quite a party, but no Beth.

Archibald Crichton-Leith shook hands with a wiry little man that got out of the silver saloon. They huddled together, whispering in a suspect and rude manner. Murray thrust his hands in his pockets and glowered. A very tall, thin man got out of the Freelander. Archibald Crichton-Leith shook his hand and beckoned Murray. Adjusting his collar, Murray scanned around and took his time going over. What a nerve, summoning him like that.

'This is John Colton, an environmental expert.' Archibald Crichton-Leith introduced the wiry man, Murray shook his hand. John Colton's face reminded Murray of a gerbil. 'And Richard Linden, a consultant in marine ecology.'

Murray shook the taller man's hand. Richard Linden made minimal eye contact and shuffled his feet, looking uneasy. Murray couldn't blame him, it seemed somewhat excessive bringing in a marine ecologist. The sea was a mile down the hill. It provided an impressive backdrop, but making a road in a field could hardly have any impact on marine life, surely?

'These experts will carry out investigations into the negative impact this road will have on the environment. Now, Mr Henderson.' Murray pulled a fake smile as Archibald Crichton-Leith spouted forth. 'I'm not doing this out of wickedness or to hinder progress. I'm doing it because I love this island and I value its future.'

'Sure.'

Archibald strutted up the hill. John Colton scampered along at his side.

'Is there likely to be any danger to marine life?' Murray jogged to catch Richard Linden.

Richard rubbed the back of his neck. 'There's a possibility the building work could be invasive and cause damage to habitats only found this close to the sea.'

Murray looked at him, unable to hide his scepticism.

'But probably not,' he conceded. 'I'm not sure what he expects me to find.'

'If he's paying you to do this, do you have to give him the result he wants?' Murray couldn't help voicing his fears.

Richard frowned gravely ahead. 'He might want that, but I don't fake results. I'll give him the truth. I won't tip the balance. Personally, I think he's looking for something that isn't here.'

'Agreed.'

They'd gone a bit further when a sharp tap landed on Murray's shoulder. He turned to see Beth and almost hugged her. 'Thank god you're here,' he said. 'And Georgia.' He noticed her just in time.

'Hi.' Georgia waved.

'I'll explain in a bit,' Murray muttered. The urge to pull Beth close and hold her was unbearably strong. He contented the impulse by brushing his shoulder against hers.

Archibald Crichton-Leith perceived their arrival and scanned around. With a shrewd smile, he strolled back and introduced himself and the others.

Beth shook his hand. Pouting, she looked him up and down. Murray grinned at his feet. Archibald Crichton-Leith had the air of country chic, but he was obviously too dapper for Beth. Murray knew the feeling. How often she'd assessed him in the same way.

'Your family is highly respected in the area,' Archibald Crichton-Leith said.

'I should think so,' she muttered. Archibald's eyes roamed over Georgia.

Giving a brief wave, she said, 'I'm just a nosey friend.'

Archibald turned immediately to business. 'Once we have the findings, we'll report them to everyone at a meeting next Friday.'

'And none of these surveys will damage the land?' asked Beth.

'They won't cause the least inconvenience, I assure you.' Archibald beamed with an air of condescension. He marched onward, talking to the two other men.

'Listen,' said Georgia, 'I can't hang about. I've got a shoot at three, I have to get back. See you guys later.' She leapt down the hill towards the road, waving.

Murray looked at Beth. Her cheeks were pink, and she rubbed her arms. 'Will you come to that meeting with me, please? I need you.' Murray's hand touched the small of her back. She stared at him.

'What?'

He leaned in close. 'Please, just come. You're so much better at this kind of thing than me. You get this island and its crazy ways.'

'*You* want *me* to help you? And defend this road.'

'Exactly.'

Beth cast him an ironic look.

'Is this where you propose to join to the woodland?' Archibald called from above.

Murray gave Beth a brief pat on the arm and followed. After much discussion and a lot of bluster from Archibald, he and his ecologists left. Beth and Murray remained in awkward limbo, watching the cars pulling away one by one.

'Well,' Murray adjusted the cuffs of his jacket, 'I'll arrange that meeting for next week. I need to get my family's visit out of the way first. Thanks for helping me out there.'

'You can thank my mum.'

'I will, though she won't thank me. You'll see why in a day or two.' He smiled at her and their eyes met. She looked away quickly, obviously not wanting to talk. 'You want a lift back up the road?'

'No, I'll walk, but Murray...'

He edged closer. 'Yes.'

'I just. Oh, nothing. I'll see you.'

Watching her stride along the road, he sighed. Keeping her as just a friend was going to be very, very hard because that wasn't what he wanted at all.

CHAPTER TWENTY-ONE

Beth

B eth heard footsteps on the landing and gathered the guests had gone to their room. The guests she dreaded meeting – Murray's parents. Trapped in her room, she waited until the coast was clear. Peering out, she checked the upstairs hall was empty before nipping downstairs. Gillian stood in the kitchen, slapping a rolling pin off her palm.

'Is it safe?' Beth asked.

'Not for long,' Gillian said through gritted teeth. 'If I'd agreed to my own public flogging, I might enjoy it more than this. They've gone to unpack.'

It wasn't like Gillian to look so angry. She could be short-tempered at times, but, for guests, she usually turned on the charm. 'Are they awful?' Beth asked in a quiet voice.

Gillian drew in a long breath and looked to the ceiling. 'This is going to be a very long weekend, let's just say that.'

An oil drum clattered outside, resonating around the courtyard. Both Gillian and Beth glanced out of the window where Murray's niece and nephew were trashing the yard.

'What are they doing?' asked Beth. 'Are their parents here?'

'Their mother. She's gone to the bothy.' Gillian grimaced out the window. 'Call Murray. I can't deal with this. I don't know what he can do, but this is beyond a joke.'

Beth pressed the phone to her ear and waited. 'Your parents are here,' she told Murray as soon as he answered. 'My mother wants you here, sharpish.'

'I'm in the middle of—'

'You better move otherwise you'll be an orphan. My mother isn't in a charitable mood.' Ending the call, she fixed herself a strong coffee and joined Gillian at the window.

Gillian's forehead creased as she watched the scene of carnage unfold. 'If they were mine, they'd be for it.'

'I hope I was never that bad.' Beth shook her head as the boy raced into the barn shrieking.

'You had your moments as a teenager, but I never would have let you get that far.'

The boy came out dragging her chainsaw box. 'Right, I've had enough.' Beth dumped her mug and proceeded outside. The little girl looked up and froze. 'What are you doing?' Beth asked the boy.

'What's in here?' he asked.

'Something dangerous. Now, let's put it away, we don't want anyone to lose fingers. Barns aren't suitable places for kids to play.'

'Why? What is that?'

'A chainsaw. Now, let me have it.'

'Uncle Murray!' The boy shrieked. Beth spun around to see him charging towards the approaching blue Audi. She cringed as the car emergency stopped. That was close. Unperturbed, the boy bolted onwards. Murray jumped out and lifted him high above his head.

'Hey, Jack, how's it going?' Murray put him down and bent towards the girl. 'And Lucy, you've grown.'

'I'm not as big as you.'

'That's true, not yet,' he said.

'Girls don't get *that* big,' she said as though he was a giant.

'I did,' Beth muttered, shoving the chainsaw box back into the barn as Murray continued to chat to the kids. She turned back to see the porch door open and a short, plump woman emerge. A blue floral top bulged around her huge bosom, joining her middle with no noticeable divide. She pushed onto tiptoes and dragged Murray into an engulfing hug, holding him firm with her heavily freckled arms. 'Ah, Murray. It's good to see you.'

She didn't let go of his neck, even when Murray gasped for air and tried to prise her off. Beth backed into the barn to observe, not wanting to intrude on the family reunion. Murray's father followed his wife and son into the courtyard as Murray pointed into the distance where the sea was visible. Like Murray, his father had an angular jaw and chiselled cheekbones, and he was slim, the opposite of his wife. Beth hadn't considered what Murray's parents might look like, but they seemed too ordinary. How had two normal people spawned a hunk of godlike perfection? As they spoke, Jack jumped onto a bale and started pelting them with loose bits of straw.

'Jack, get down.' Murray's sister strode up the path. She had a strong family resemblance with her brother, but the angles on her face gave her a harsh, don't-mess-with-me look, rather than the effortless beauty they bestowed on Murray.

Murray lifted Jack by the waistband, resulting in loud shrieks of laughter. They moved towards the front garden and Beth saw her chance to nip inside.

'I don't think we should let them in here,' Gillian said as Beth returned to the kitchen. 'Maybe we should make them use the guest lounge.'

'You shouldn't have let them through this way. Maybe we could lock the door and force them to come in the front.' It was where the guests for the annex came in. It made sense.

The outside door burst open and plump Mrs Henderson barged in, steering little Lucy in front of her. 'Where's the bathroom?

'In there.' Gillian pointed to the understairs cloakroom through the open door.

'In you get, Lucy, quick. She's desperate, I hope she doesn't have an accident.'

The girl charged through the room, tripped over the strip between the kitchen and the corridor and sent a vase of flowers crashing from the side table. The ensuing shrieks could have woken the dead. Gillian closed her eyes, clearly hoping when she opened them, everyone would be gone. Beth peered through, pressing her fingertips to her temple, not sure what to do. Murray and his sister came running in.

'Oh my god, what happened?'

Mrs Henderson explained as she comforted her granddaughter.

'That's Alison, my sister,' Murray said, but Beth didn't have a chance to say anything.

'Stupid place to put a bunch of flowers.' Alison bundled up her daughter and stroked her back. It was loud enough for everyone to hear. Murray adjusted his collar.

'Well, it seems to me just a minor oversight,' Mrs Henderson said. 'If you're not used to children about. Wait until you have grandchildren,' she told Gillian. 'It all comes back. Valuables safely hidden away.'

'Let's get you to the toilet and check you're not hurt.' Alison lifted Lucy out of sight. Mrs Henderson was mopping up the mess with a towel she'd snatched from the front of the range cooker.

'Leave that, Janet,' said Gillian, 'I'll get it.'

Janet heaved her giant body upright before she spotted the doorstopper. 'This ought to be moved as well.' She laboured back down, picked it up and thrust it unceremoniously behind the sofa, in the lounge area. 'That'll make it a bit more child friendly.'

'She shouldn't have been running,' Murray said.

'Hmpff.' Janet struggled across to the sofa and slumped into it. 'Oh gosh, these cushions are a bit lumpy.' She hauled one out from behind her back and lobbed it to the other end. Aghast, Beth stood like a statue. What could she say?

'We have a guest lounge,' Gillian said as she swept the broken glass into the shovel. Her honey-sweet voice barely disguised an eruption Beth knew was simmering not far from the surface. She'd never heard her mother lose it with a guest. This might be a first.

'Oh no, this will have to do,' said Janet. 'I've just sat down. I'm not getting back up again.' She stretched her arm back and split the blinds with her fingers. 'I see Jack's giving his granddad a run for his money. Bruce will be exhausted. I'm not sure all this running about is healthy at his age.'

Beth's gaze flickered over Murray as he moved to the window and opened the blinds. Outside Jack shrieked, charging along the gravelled path, across the lawn and over the daffodils.

'Jack misses his dad. He works on the rigs,' Janet told the room at large. 'He's away for his three-week stint offshore. Shame his off-weeks didn't correspond with the holidays.'

'Hmm.' Murray replied on everybody's behalf.

'So, this is a working farm. Is your husband the farmer?' Janet ran her heavily ringed fingers through her short auburn curls, observing Beth.

'Me? No. I don't have a husband.'

'Oh.' Her nose crinkled. 'Sorry, who are you then?'

'She's my daughter,' Gillian said, the edge to her voice very clear.

Alison re-entered with Lucy. She carted her into the lounge area and sat down, checking her knees and her hands.

'I see,' said Janet.

Though Beth was sure she didn't. Now the cogs in her mind were ticking round, wondering where old Mr McGregor was.

'Beth runs the farm, Mum,' Murray said, turning from the window. 'I told you on the phone.'

'Who's Beth?'

'I am.'

Janet raised a flabby eyebrow. 'I don't remember you telling me anything about it, Murray. I've heard things like that before. Modern farms have secretaries and things. So, you help your father?'

'No, my father died seven years ago. I'm not a secretary. I'm the farmer.' It wasn't a boast. God, no. It was more like confessing to a prison sentence.

Alison pouted and looked Beth up and down. As soon as she realised Beth had seen her, she dropped her gaze and started to put Lucy's socks back on.

'Dear, dear,' Janet muttered, placing a pudgy hand on her giant bosom. 'That's no job for a lady.'

Beth rolled her eyes with a sigh and walked behind the kitchen island.

'Mum,' Murray sat at the other end of the sofa from his mother, 'Beth's not a lady.'

'Well, thank you, Murray.' Beth folded her arms and leant on the kitchen island.

'Oh, me and my mouth.' He threw his head back and smacked his brow. 'Of course, you're a lady. Yes, Mum, Beth is a lady. That's not what I meant. She's a farmer first, then a lady.'

'I'm not sure that's very flattering either.' Beth shared a disgruntled look with her mother. Gillian shook her head as she filled the kettle.

'She's an excellent farmer.' Murray looked up and smiled at her. She pretended not to notice. 'And an extremely beautiful lady.'

'Murray!' She gritted her teeth, still determinately not noticing him, hoping she hadn't gone too red.

'Oh, Murray,' said his mother. 'Stop being so rude.'

'What's rude about that? It's a compliment.'

'It's only a compliment if you're being serious. The poor girl can see you're taking the mickey. Now leave her alone.'

'I am not taking the mickey,' he said defiantly. His mother ignored him.

Alison looked askance. 'Run out and play with Granddad.' She sent Lucy off. Beth got to the door and opened it before the little girl ran headlong into anything else.

'You really shouldn't joke, Murray.' Alison's voice was a stage whisper. Beth felt like saying, *do you think I can't hear you?* Instead she started helping Gillian. She didn't want to get involved. It was embarrassing enough. 'She looks like she might knock you out,' Alison continued in her low voice.

'I might,' Beth said, making Alison jump. 'But I'll have to forego that pleasure for another time. I have to check on the lambs.'

Murray smirked, keeping his eyes on his feet. He looked ready to burst out laughing. 'Actually, why don't we all go?' He clapped his hands. 'The kids will love the lambs. And it's a pleasant afternoon for a walk.'

Beth glared at him. Knocking him out now seemed an excellent plan.

'I'm not going anywhere,' said Janet. 'I need a rest after the drive. It's such a long time to sit.'

Beth and Gillian exchanged another glance. She was going to take a break from sitting... by sitting? Alison trooped out to tell the children and her father.

Murray approached Beth as she hovered in limbo. He edged his head around, forcing her to look at him. 'Ready?' He grinned.

'Tell you what,' she said into his ear. He was right on her. She was conscious of both their mothers. 'Why don't you take them up the woods, show them your road plans. I'll go see the lambs.'

He tipped his head. 'Oh, come on. Where's your sense of adventure? We can always play hide and seek and lose them.'

That part couldn't come soon enough, especially when Beth got landed with Alison as they walked the steep downward path towards the shore.

'So, you're a farmer?' Alison said, treading through the ferns covering the path.

'Yup,' Beth said, looking away and rolling her eyes at the distant silhouettes of the small isles across the western sea.

'And you've always lived on this island. How do you stand it? I'm nearly thirty-seven and I've lived in three different countries.'

'Have you? Wow.' Beth hoped she sounded enthusiastic. She didn't feel it.

'And really, not being funny, but what do you do for entertainment?'

'The usual things,' Beth said, though she wasn't sure that was true. Her entertainment was a night out at the pub every couple of months, usually with Will and Donald Laird, occasionally Georgia or Carl.

'So, are there nightclubs and cinemas?'

'Not really, but there are pubs and dances and film nights. It's a different lifestyle.'

'Wow.' Alison blew out a breath. 'I thought Murray was mad signing up for two years. How have you survived here for what? Twenty-eight, twenty-nine years?'

'Thirty-one. And I just get on with it. This is what I do.'

Beth frowned. She knew Murray's contract was only for two years. It vindicated her actions. He wouldn't be around long term.

'So, do you have a partner?'

'Me?' Beth said, wanting to delay her response. This was her least favourite subject. 'Nope.'

'It must be hard meeting people,' said Alison, 'and I guess speed dating and the internet are out. Your nearest matches could be over the sea.' Looking at Beth, Alison flicked her reddish-brown hair over her shoulder and gave a brief laugh. 'There must be a lot of redundant women on the islands.'

'Excuse me?' Beth stopped and glared at her.

'I meant no offence.' She lifted her hand to her mouth. The corners were still turned up, as though she'd said something very witty.

'Well, actually,' Beth ploughed ahead, 'I am a little offended.'

'Really, I meant nothing by it.'

'But you wouldn't say it about a man, would you?'

'Sorry, truly,' Alison backpedalled.

Heavy footfalls. Beth sensed Murray but didn't turn around.

'What's going on?' Murray asked. Beth glanced behind. He was half a head taller than his sister. Alison threw out her palms.

'Your sister thinks I'm a redundant woman,' said Beth.

'Whoa,' Murray said. Alison glared at Beth.

'It was just a silly comment. I didn't mean anything by it. God knows, I'm the last person to be sexist.' Alison looked away before adding quietly, 'I seem to have touched a nerve.'

'It was a pretty stupid thing to say,' said Murray. Beth put some distance between them, but his voice was so clear, she heard every word. 'You should see what Beth does. You couldn't even contemplate it. She's hardly had a day off in years. I can understand why she'd be offended by being called redundant. I'm offended by it.'

'Yeah, well, I said sorry. And I mean it.' Alison jogged to catch up. 'I apologise. I meant no offence. You mistook my meaning.'

Beth glowered. 'I know what the term means.'

Alison gave an apologetic shrug, then stopped and waited for her father, who was behind with the children.

'Beth, I'm sorry.' The back of Murray's hand touched hers as he spoke. She breathed in his woody scent with a slight quiver. 'She and my mother sometimes don't stop to reason before they speak.' Beth threw him a look. 'Ok, and sometimes I'm the same.'

'Well, she's probably right.' Beth hopped off the path and leapt down an embankment onto the beach below. Murray followed, vaulting on to the shingle from the edge. 'Please, leave me alone,' she said.

'Sure.' He turned to walk away.

'Listen, Murray.'

'What?' His piercing grey eyes caught hers.

'Some of the stuff I said. I didn't mean.' Her voice came out as a whisper. She looked around desperately.

'Hey.' Murray stepped up and gently wrapped his arm around her waist, pulling her in tight. 'It's ok.' His finger trailed down her cheek.

Closing her eyes, Beth leaned in.

'Beth.' Her name was little more than a breath on his lips. 'I still want you. I can't stop the urge. It's unbearable. Please, can I... Just one kiss.'

'Ok.' She locked eyes with him as he dipped in and the touch of his lips filled the aching gap in her stomach. The world stopped. Starting soft, he moved in deeper, long and needy. She threaded her fingers in his hair and held on; she needed him so badly. Desperately.

'I want you, Beth, I really want you.'

'I know, but...' She made to pull back.

'What's wrong?' he asked.

'You don't know me, Murray. Not really. You think you do, but...'

'Then tell me. I'm listening.' Shouts from above. Murray ignored them, focusing on Beth. Could she send a message telepathically into those penetrating grey eyes?

Holding off the moment of confession, answering the call of her body instead of her brain, Beth kissed him again. He pushed her back into cold stone. Placing his palms flat against the rock-face behind, caging her, holding onto the kiss as long as they dared. The shouts got louder.

'Murray. This is insane. Your family.'

'That's what you do to me.' His low voice was hungry and wolfish. He tugged her t-shirt up at the back and slid his palms over her bare skin. The deep urges inside her throbbed like crazy at the contact. 'Even the idea is driving me wild.'

Seriously? Why now? She was ready to throw caution to the wind. This was it. How could she resist any longer? He was so hot-blooded and tempting. The shouts were almost upon them. She pushed him off. 'They're looking for you.'

He groaned and raked his hand through his hair. 'I'm here.' His raspy voice echoed upwards, and he waved.

Beth leaned back against the rock, pulled her t-shirt back into place and closed her eyes. At some point, she'd have to open them and face the big bad world, but for now, she just wanted to savour the taste of Murray while his scent still lingered on her neck. It was perfect, almost.

CHAPTER TWENTY-TWO

Murray

Leaving Beth was the last thing Murray wanted to do. If only they could run off together. He was so close to cracking the wall, but something didn't sit right. What was she holding back? Sure, he'd not known her long, but what was so dreadful she couldn't just tell him? His emotional baggage could fill the turntable at Heathrow Terminal Five. Nothing she had could be worse, could it?

Gillian looked like she'd stuck her finger in a socket when they returned from the walk. Her iron-grey hair, usually so neat, was all over the place, her glasses perched askew atop her head. She chopped a courgette at manic speed. Her frazzled expression seemed to correspond to a lazily smug look on Janet's face. Murray was aware his mother could be gruelling company. She'd probably sent Gillian jumping through hoops, abusing her guest privileges, and being thoroughly lazy. Murray sighed. Part of his obsession with keeping fit came from a fervent desire to never be as indolent as her. Her struggles with diabetes and high blood pressure were a niggling worry for all of them.

Motivated by a desire to keep everyone alive, he said, 'Maybe we should go out for dinner tonight.' Getting them out of Gillian's hair looked imperative. She seemed ready to take someone out with her vegetable knife. 'I'd like to try Am Bàta, I pass it so often and it looks great.'

'Oh no, Murray,' said Janet, 'I can't go out tonight. I'm far too tired.'

'I'll call the restaurant. You'll love it,' said Gillian. 'I know the owner.'

'I insist, Mum. Go and get ready.'

Before Janet could utter another word, Gillian was on the phone. Cool air hit Murray's cheek. He turned to observe Beth sidling in, possibly attempting a sneaky disappearance, but he blocked her. No matter how tough she tried to look, she was still stunning. The fact she lifted straw bales, sheared sheep, birthed lambs and drove a tractor just made her even more attractive. Craving her touch, he wanted to draw her close again. *Everyone's watching*, he reminded himself. Did that matter? He would tell the world right there and then how much he wanted her, but she'd be mortified. They weren't there yet. Close, but he didn't want to blow it again.

'Come with us,' he said with a smile.

Slipping her thumbs into the belt loops on her jeans, Beth gaped at him. The utter incredulity in her eyes made him laugh.

'Yeah, I get your reaction. I don't want to either.' He whispered the last part in her ear, taking in the fruity scent of her conditioner. His eyelids shut for a second as he inhaled it.

'Murray, for god's sake,' she muttered, drawing back. 'And yeah, I'll stay here, thanks.'

With his fist, he gave her a playful cuff on the elbow. 'Enjoy the peace.'

'I will.' She landed a punch on his arm that almost dislocated his shoulder.

Am Bàta was a modern restaurant in a wooden building resembling a boat. Its name meant boat in Gaelic; Donald had informed him. Murray passed on the information as he and his family trooped through the shiny glass doors.

'And do the owners speak Gaelic?' asked Janet. 'I won't know what to order, I'm half-English. I don't understand things some Scottish people say, never mind Gaelic.'

'If they do, I'm sure they'll speak English too. I don't think anyone these days only speaks Gaelic.'

'Why bother with all these silly names then? No one can pronounce them.' Janet squeezed her clutch bag against her broad hip, casting an examining eye around the pine interior.

'I can, Granny, it's easy,' said eight-year-old Jack, rattling the Wait to be Seated sign.

Bruce ruffled his grandson's fuzzy head. 'Smarty-pants.'

Murray placed his hands on his back, nodding at a group seated near the window, the only other people there. Good. He couldn't imagine his niece and nephew sitting quietly for two hours, not if the afternoon performance was anything to go on.

A smartly dressed server led them to a table near the back at another window looking out over a well-tended kitchen garden. Murray cringed as his mother squeezed herself into the corner, almost toppling the oval table. 'These modern places,' she moaned, 'always try to squash in too many tables. It's all about the money, never the comfort.'

Sometimes her mouth was a live cannon. And god forbid anyone mention her weight. It was everyone's fault from her children to the government, never her own. Murray kept his eyes off the server standing patiently beside them with the menus tucked under her arm.

'Do you have dairy-free options? Lucy doesn't get dairy, she's allergic,' said Alison.

'Of course,' said the server. 'You'll find it all marked on the menu.'

'Good.' Alison swept back her hair as she sat.

Murray wanted to lick his finger and chalk up a point to the restaurant. His family were so disapproving. His life was commonly the source, he'd never reached the giddy heights they'd planned. And at thirty-four, he still hadn't provided a big wedding and grandchildren. *Was that day getting closer?* Seriously?

He was contemplating marrying Beth now? Startled by the idea, he rubbed his forehead, hoping no one had seen any physical signs of his mental aberration.

Unable to decide which menu option was most suitable, Janet held them up with her deliberating and indecision. Lucy and Jack started kicking each other under the table, and Alison hissed at them. Murray wished he'd accepted a lift. He needed a drink. Even if it meant walking the few miles from Creagach back to his cottage in the dark. Resigned to being sensible, he downed a pint of ginger beer. The taste reminded him of the Easter Dance, Beth, and their beautiful kiss.

'I'm not sure what to make of the McGregors,' Janet said, knocking the table. 'Rather an unconventional set-up.'

Grappled away from his pleasant musings, Murray blinked. 'Is it?'

Janet pulled an "obviously" face. She loved moaning and even if he'd set her up in the smartest hotel on the island, she'd have had some complaint.

'Gillian seems nice,' said Alison, 'but Beth.' She turned her lips down to indicate her distaste.

Murray stroked his beard and looked out the window. If they dared insult her. Glancing back at the table, he smiled at little Lucy. She walloped Jack over the head with the menu.

'Oh, the *farmer?*' His mother's tone was mocking.

'Not nice, Mum,' Murray muttered, removing the menu from Lucy and shaking his head with a wink. 'Best not,' he told her.

'Might mess up Jack's hair.' Leaning his hand over Lucy, he ruffled Jack's head, making him giggle.

'She got quite aggressive with me.' Alison rested her fingers on her chest. 'I made a silly remark, and she got very touchy.'

'It was considerably more than a silly remark.' Murray placed the menu back in the holder on the table and confronted his sister.

Alison arched her eyebrow. 'You've got the hots for her, haven't you?'

'Hush.' Bruce cocked his head at his grandchildren, who weren't listening, being now involved in messing up each other's hair.

Murray wasn't going to deny it. He kept his expression impassive and looked at his fingers.

'Well, I should hope not,' said Janet.

'Why?' Murray glanced up. 'She's a smart, independent woman. Why would it be so dreadful to find her attractive?'

Bruce coughed into the back of his hand. Apparently, this conversation wasn't to his liking. The arrival of food spared him, but Murray knew Janet wasn't done. Plastered across her face was a broad smile, like she was sitting on a golden egg about to hatch.

As soon as everyone had their plate, she said, 'You're wasting your time, Murray, if you're hoping for anything from Beth.'

'I don't follow.' Murray smoothed his napkin across his thighs.

'Well, she's engaged to someone already.' His mother leaned across the table for the salt.

Murray's eyes rose slowly to challenge her. Honestly, the levels she'd stoop to were mind-blowing. Why would she say something so ridiculous? 'No, she isn't. She would have told me.' *And she wouldn't have kissed me. Would she?*

'Curious.' Alison arched her eyebrow.

'No, she wouldn't have told you,' Janet said with finality. 'It's an unusual set-up, so Gillian informed me. We had a jolly good discussion. Beth's very dedicated to the farm but there's a man she's known a long time, they've been engaged for years. He's gone off to travel, but he's coming home soon to settle. Beth keeps it hush-hush. It can't be easy with him away for so long.'

'I know how that feels with Colin being away on the rigs,' said Alison. 'But this guy has been away for years, you say? Sounds fishy to me.'

'This is nonsense,' said Murray. It had to be. Didn't it? Fragments of things Beth had said floated into his consciousness. *Your baggage isn't compatible with mine. You don't really know me.* Was this what she'd been holding back? Was it possible she liked him, but all the while she was bound to someone else? Honourable Beth wouldn't break her promise. No matter how she felt.

'It's all true, I assure you. He phoned while I was talking to Gillian. He said he's coming home soon. He can't wait to see her. I'm curious, I wonder what sort of man she'd go for.'

'You and me both,' Murray muttered, shaking his head. This was unbearable. If he couldn't have Beth, how could he stand seeing her with someone else? His insides twisted uncomfortably. The exquisitely presented poached salmon and asparagus now looked inedible. He glowered at the plate. A lead weight pressed on his chest, forcing an aching lump towards his throat. Just ten minutes ago a wonderful dream had been heading to a climax, now it lay dead by the wayside. What had he done? Pushed his way in, not stopping to consider. If only Beth had told him. Why hadn't she trusted him? Or did she share his feelings, knowing she couldn't act, so teased him instead? Running his hand across his face, he said, 'This is ridiculous.' Meant only for himself, but it came out louder than he intended,

'What is?' Janet nodded. 'Oh, honestly, Murray, you're not smarting about Beth, are you? There are plenty of girls out there a lot better suited to you than her.'

'Yes, thank you,' said Murray. 'I'll decide for myself if you don't mind.'

Alison watched him. She waited until after she'd eaten, then leaned over. 'You are smitten, aren't you?'

He pulled away from her, squinting. 'And what if I am?'

Alison shook her head. 'Oh, Murray. You never learn.'

'What do you mean by that?' Why did she always assume she knew everything?

'You always choose the most unsuitable women.'

Incensed, Murray put up his hand. 'I don't get why you'd consider Beth unsuitable.' Apart from her being engaged elsewhere, while indulging in flirting, cuddling, kissing and leading him a merry dance.

'It's not her. It's why you want her. You enjoy the competition. You've picked some tough girl farmer and made it your mission to have her.' Alison smirked. 'There's a real living person in there, a heart you'll break as soon as you've got what you want. You can't force her into breaking a promise to someone else, just for some lusty five minutes, and have her regretting it the rest of her life.'

'Can we talk about something else?' Murray slammed his glass on the table. Was this the impression everyone had of him? That he was a bed-hopper. It was so far from the truth it was laughable, but his capacity for humour had ebbed to ground zero.

Alison sat back, looking pleased she'd scored a point. She'd got one thing right. In his thirty-four years of life, he still hadn't found the right woman. He'd chosen wrong every time. Beth was the latest in a lifetime of failures.

The memory of her kisses still lingered inside him. They'd been real, hadn't they? But she'd stopped every time. Murray flexed his fists. It wasn't right. He couldn't force her to change. If he let go now, he could salvage some of his self-esteem. Maybe.

'What happened with Naomi?' Janet blinked serenely, clasping her hands. 'I got a bit lost. Are you and her still seeing each other? Non-exclusively, of course. Is that the term?'

'No. I'm not like that. We're finished. I don't do non-exclusive. This is Mull, not "Love Island".'

'Oh, I don't watch that rubbish.'

Bruce choked into his soup. Janet thumped his back and Murray switched off as Janet tried to explain she'd only once watched "Love Island" by accident. Murray reclined in his chair and sighed. Beth. She was still the only thing he could focus on. Was she seriously messed up? Maybe she locked herself up every night and cried. He couldn't bring himself to believe she'd deceived him out of spite. No. She was closed and hard to crack, but when they'd kissed, the response and connection between them had been so powerful. She couldn't fake that. Could she? Or had it been lust, pure and simple? Could he ask her to break the promise? Was that fair? Maybe she truly loved the man but missed human contact. *Am I just an outlet she doesn't care much for at all?* His shoulders slumped, and he rubbed his brow. Had the time come to hold his head high and walk away?

CHAPTER TWENTY-THREE

Beth

Both Beth and Gillian shot up from the TV screen when they heard the car in the driveway. Beth's eyes widened in surprise, she'd been sure Gillian had fallen asleep in the chair. Her radar was obviously on high alert.

'I'm going upstairs. I don't care if Janet thinks I'm a sad bumpkin who goes to my bed at eight-thirty,' said Gillian. 'I can't stand another second talking to her. She gave me such a grilling. I said anything to shut her up. Which reminds me.' She flapped away a yawn. 'I forgot, I was so tired, but there was a call for you earlier. It was from Frank. He said he'd tried your mobile. No reception, I suppose. He, erm, seemed eager to speak to you. And he's coming back on Sunday.'

'Oh, yes, right. I'll message him.' Beth glanced at Gillian. Her mother had a slight frown. She rubbed her fingers, her mouth doing a goldfish impression like she had something further to add but couldn't find the words.

'Beth. Is he? I remember when you were younger, and you used to joke, but—'

Car doors slammed.

'Quick, upstairs,' said Beth. 'I don't want to talk to any of them.'

Beth bid Gillian goodnight as she reached her bedroom, nursing an urge to lift her dresser and barricade the door. Lured by the appeal of Murray, she twitched back a floral curtain. Her room looked over the front garden so she couldn't fully see the courtyard, but no need. At the track end, rear lights turned out and accelerated down the road. He'd left. Downstairs, voices carried from the kitchen. The fridge door opened several times and cupboards banged open and shut. What a liberty! They'd just been out for dinner. Janet Henderson looked capable of eating a whole cow, and here they were back two seconds and raiding the fridge.

Lying reading a book she'd taken from Gillian's pile about a handsome city boss falling for a country girl masquerading as his secretary (images of Murray in a suit had supplied her imagination with enough material to keep going), Beth was still awake when Janet and Bruce came up to bed sometime later. She hoped they had plans for the next day that didn't involve her or her mother. Turfing the book and closing her eyes, she lay back, hoping sleep would come quickly.

Beth made sure she was up and about long before anyone else. She hadn't slept well, but she didn't care. A long morning making small talk was not on her list of things to do today. No way.

It was almost seven-thirty, and she was high on the field when she glanced at the blue flash of a car pulling up. She stared through the cool, damp morning mist. This had to be a joke, right? Panic darted up her legs, making them shudder as he got out of the car. Yesterday on the beach had left unfinished business. Why was he here? To finish the business? Fifteen hours ago, she'd wished he would pick his moments better. And here he was. No one else about for miles. They were alone.

Waving, he headed towards her. His usual smart, confident air was evident in his brisk strides, but something was different. Hands slumped in the pockets of his burgundy gilet, his smile looked pained, his grey eyes ice cold.

'Fancy meeting you here.' Beth placed her fists on her hips, a gesture of bravado because she was actually a blabbering piece of jelly. Murray's genuine smile flickered for a second. 'What brings you here so early? Are you taking your family somewhere nice?'

'Yeah, we're going to Iona.' He mussed up his hair, freeing a thick strand from his band. 'It has to be done. Scotland's most famous island and all that.'

'Sure does. It's a super day for it.' She frowned, something was odd about him. He looked like he was working up to saying something. Oh god, he wasn't going to ask her to go too? 'I can't come with you,' she said. 'If that's what you're thinking. I have the lambs.'

'I know, Beth.' He stepped forward, rubbing his hand over his honey-trimmed beard. Frown lines covered his face and his eyes looked strained. What was going on? 'Listen, we need to talk. It's... important.'

'About what?' Her brain trawled through a mash of crazy ideas, trying to work out what it could be. Heart pounding nineteen to the dozen, she guessed it wasn't business. And if not...

'I really like you, Beth. Really. In so many ways. I admire so much about you.'

This was scary. Her pulse raced so fast, it throbbed in her ears and her fingertips. Frozen, she took deep breaths. *Hear him out.* Maybe it was time to confess. Would he understand? All her muddled emotions were slotting together. She wanted to trust him, to believe he was the real deal.

Inching closer, he rubbed his thumb down her upper arm. Struggling to breathe, Beth parted her lips, her eyebrows pinched together. He continued, 'You deserve to be happy. You really do, and I wanted to be that guy, but I realise now, I got it all wrong. Whatever you do is your choice. I respect that. You're a special girl. You always will be.' He leaned in and kissed her cheek, lingering just long enough for the bristles above his lip to send tingles racing through her skin.

'Murray, I don't—'

'It's ok.' He put his hand on her shoulder, pressing it gently. Warmth and comfort dispersed through her veins. She craved his touch so much, but his words were all wrong. 'I hope you're happy, Beth. I won't bother you any more. Take care.'

'But...' What?

He was gone. Still trying to fathom his meaning, she watched him speed off. Why couldn't he be the guy any more? Why couldn't he make her happy? Because she'd pushed him away! Double fist-palming her forehead, she cursed everything in sight. He'd given up on her. She'd done everything to ignore the feelings kicking about inside. Jeez, she hadn't even thanked him for the world's best birthday present. Could she blame him for bailing out? Why had it taken her so long to work out how she really felt?

Further up the hill, the early sun hit the grass. She strolled out of the shade and sat on a sun-kissed patch of green, her head awash with emotion. About half an hour later a convoy of vehicles passed, taking Murray and his family southwards. The Murray-shaped gash in Beth's chest twanged with pain. She wanted him back. Dazed and disillusioned by everything that had happened in the past couple of months, she got in the Land Rover and drove. Where? She didn't know. She needed space. If she'd dared to follow her heart and not let the other stuff get in the way, she could have had Murray already. Should she follow him to Iona? Too far, she couldn't leave the lambs that long. And what would she say? If he rejected her in front of his entire family, how could she bear it? Beth reached the village of Salen and was going to carry on through the village when she remembered Georgia lived there. Mindless chitchat might ease her brain. As she rang the doorbell, panic prickled in her fingertips. Would Georgia try to draw something out of her? Beth hated talking about herself. It was easier to hide, but she wanted to make sense of things.

'Hi, Beth.' Georgia opened the door and Beth slumped inside. 'What's up? You look terrible.'

'Do I? What's wrong with me?' The words toppled out. 'Too tall? Too ugly?'

Georgia's eyes opened wide, then she frowned. 'What are you talking about? I mean terrible as in exhausted, worn out. You're not ugly, Beth. You're a beautiful woman, and there's nothing wrong with being tall.'

'Isn't there? I'm built like a guy, I dress like a guy, I work like a guy. Is that why guys don't actually like me?' Beth flopped onto the sofa.

'Oh, Beth. Of course, guys like you. Maybe you just don't see them in the right light. They're not all made to be just friends.' Georgia sat opposite. 'And you're no way built like a guy; you have a cracking figure. What's brought this on?'

'Murray,' Beth said through gritted teeth, focusing on the bizarre chandelier made from driftwood and wine glasses hanging from Georgia's ceiling.

'Beth, he really likes you. I met him in Tobermory on your birthday, and he told me so. What's holding you back? He's out there waiting on a plate, for heaven's sake, take him.'

Beth covered her face. The idea of saying the words sickened her.

'Whatever it is, Murray will understand.'

'Will he? You have no idea how embarrassing it is. I'm not even going to say.'

Georgia patted her on the knee. 'You are you. Murray admires you for that reason alone. If you've got hang-ups about something, you can bet he has too. He's been around a bit, he'll get that.'

'That's exactly the point.' Beth threw back her head. 'He's been around all these blocks people keep going on about and I haven't been around any.'

'So what? You've done plenty of other stuff he hasn't. Go and tell him.'

Beth gaped. 'Tell him! Are you mad? Just like that?'

'Beth. You are the toughest girl I know. If a herd of highland cows escaped, I'd call you. If you can deal with that, you can deal with this. Find Murray, talk to him. Tell him. And I don't mean just tell him what's held you back. Tell him how you feel, that's what matters.'

'I don't even know how I feel.'

Georgia peered down her pert little nose. 'Yes, Beth, I think you do.'

'But how can I say it?'

'Beth, you can drive a tractor. You've helped about a million sheep give birth.'

'So?'

'That's a hell of a lot scarier than saying three little words.'

Maybe in Georgia's world, but in hers, she'd happily take the tractor, the sheep and an entire herd of highland cows.

CHAPTER TWENTY-FOUR

Murray

On Saturday morning, Gillian McGregor had packed an enormous picnic basket for lunch. Murray was grateful, but he suspected she'd filled it so full in the hope they would stay out all day again, as they had done the previous day on Iona. Spending a day there was always special, but try as he might to change the broken gramophone record in his head, Murray had spent his time reflecting on Beth. Realising more and more how stupid he'd been. Barely two months had passed since they met. How could he think he knew her at all? He could put the powerful connection he had with her down to lust. Clawing at his heart, deeper emotions battled to get out, but Murray had no intention of letting them. Devoting time to his family was today's priority, and he intended to do it.

'You're a marvel.' Janet clapped Gillian on the back as she bent over to lift two extra bags full of snacks and drinks.

After almost losing balance, she stood up straight. 'Thank you.'

Murray waited, hands sunk in the back pocket of his jeans, while his family made their last-minute preparations, the ones that always took hours longer than necessary. 'I'll get them.' He jumped forward and took the bags from Gillian.

'Well, you can't have a simple life,' said Janet. 'Lord knows, I couldn't live here in the long term.' What a blessing. Much as Murray loved his mother, he didn't want her living so close. 'I'd miss the shops. I think Murray will be glad when his two years are up, and he can get back to normality.'

'I'm in the room, Mum. You don't need to talk about me like I'm not here.' Though he was distracted. Beth clumped across the courtyard to the barn as he stood at the porch door, ready to leave.

'Well, you miss Tesco, don't you?'

Murray furrowed his brow. 'Seriously, Mum? There's more to life than the supermarket.' His eyes strayed to the window. Beth was busy in the barn and deliberately keeping her distance. This was torture. Trapped so close and not able to be with her.

'Your contract might not be renewed,' said Janet. 'So, you should stick with the two-year plan.' She lowered her voice and added to Gillian. 'He does miss it.'

'If I leave, I might miss here more.'

The sceptical look on his mother's face told him she didn't believe it. He glanced around and caught Gillian's eye; she looked thoughtful, and a little confused.

They drove the few miles to Calgary Bay and its huge sandy beach, and Murray discovered the distractions of building enormous sandcastles and swimming in the sea. Jack and Lucy hadn't noticed the temperature was barely above thirteen degrees and were treating it like a midsummer's day. Murray was content to go along with it, and even donned his swimming shorts, while Alison and his parents huddled on fold-up chairs wrapped in their coats with their backs to the wind and their hoods up.

Random ideas of how Beth might look in a bikini drifted into his mind. She hid in comfy outdoor clothes, but when he'd seen her in that dress, and touched her under her t-shirt, she was svelte. Why couldn't he get her out of his head? Could they be "just friends"? Have a good spar over various disagreements? It wouldn't be the same, not with another man on the scene. How could he watch them together? Ending his contract suddenly seemed the preferable option. Maybe Janet was right. He had to avoid the agonising hell of seeing Beth in the arms of someone else.

She wasn't around when they got back. Murray strained his neck, checking for her. Gillian had made an evening meal for them but had set it up in the bothy. Only Janet complained as she didn't fancy the walk back to the house afterwards.

'I'll give you a lift if it's that bad,' Murray said, knowing full well she'd scoff.

He helped Gillian lift the trays down the path. It struck him as odd Beth wasn't doing it.

'Is Beth ok?' he asked.

Gillian gave a little cough. 'Yes, I think so.' Her cheeks were pink and flushed.

'Has something happened?'

'No, not really. She's in her room getting some things ready. A close, a very close, friend of hers is coming home tomorrow.'

'Tomorrow?' Murray ceased pushing the bothy door with his elbow and stared. 'Is it her fiancé?'

Gillian raised her eyebrows. 'Goodness, she even told you. How odd. Let's get this stuff inside.'

Murray held the door and let Gillian enter. As she passed, he rested his head on the door. He didn't want to be anywhere near here tomorrow. He couldn't stand it.

Sunday morning came round too quickly. Murray had almost got used to the chaos of his family's company when it was time for them to leave. He kissed his mother goodbye. As he did so, a car pulled up the drive. A young man with a surfer-like tan and bleached blond hair got out. Beth sidled out of the house to watch the Hendersons depart. Yelling from some way off, the blond man whooped at the sight of her, 'Beth! Beth, darling. I'm home!' Running to her, he grabbed her around the waist. Murray wanted to avert his eyes, but a dismal intrigue held his gaze. Beth was taller than the man. She returned his hug with a smile and an almost desperate expression. The man laid his head on Beth's shoulder, looking sickeningly at home.

'So, that's the man,' Janet said with raised eyebrows. 'Well, well. He looks about fifteen. And couples where the woman is taller always look strange to me.'

Beth flung her arm across the man's shoulder and led him into the house. As the door closed, a crushing blow struck Murray in the chest. He didn't dare imagine what was going on in there.

Back home, reality struck. This was it. Whatever thread of a dream Murray had clung to had unravelled beyond his control. After all his failed relationships and poor choices, he'd finally found someone he loved. Yes, his eyes blurred, he loved Beth. Not just lust. Love. His heart threatened to burst with it. He'd only known her a brief time, but she was the one, the only one. No one else had come close.

He put his face in his hands. Life was unbearably cruel. And he had the bloody meeting with Archibald Crichton-Leith that Friday. He needed to prepare, but getting his head in gear was not happening.

He'd invited everyone on the committee and opened it to interested parties, including Beth. Would she come? What if she brought the man with her? How could he bear it? Would they hold hands, kiss at the table? Oh, god. He may as well throw in the towel and let Archibald Crichton-Leith do whatever he wanted. His race was run, and he had no desire to keep going. If it finished here, that was just fine.

CHAPTER TWENTY-FIVE

Beth

The pub was busy, which suited Beth; she and Frank could blend in and hide. He spent a long while playing catch-up with several locals, giving Beth a bit too much time to dwell on Murray.

'Are you all right, darling?' Frank returned to the table with two drinks. 'You look far away.'

'Just thinking. Thanks.' Beth took her drink, chilling her hands around the cool glass. Her eyes flicked around, hopeful, apprehensive. She'd once met Murray here. Would he be here tonight? His parting piece had left her in such an awkward limbo, she didn't know what to do. Frank sat opposite, grinning as he creamed off the top of his lager.

'I thought you had a boyfriend,' said Beth. 'Where is he?'

'I do, darling. And wait until you see him. He's gorgeous, but he won't be here until next week.'

'Typical. Even you manage to get a boyfriend before me.'

'Aw, no, darling. You're too beautiful for that. You've always been my most beautiful girl. You can't fall by the wayside unnoticed, like a flower trampled by the hoof of a highland beast.'

'Stop talking crap, Frank.'

He knocked back his drink, chuckling. 'I thought it was quite poetic. Speaking of poetry and hot men, did you see the holidaymaker at your place? Just as I arrived. When you were making my coffee, I peeked out and my word, I saw this man in the courtyard. Never have I ever seen the like. If he's available, I'll ditch Enzo straight away.'

'Do you mean Murray?'

'I don't know. Do I? Is this magnificent specimen a friend? He had a dapper little beard and his hair. Oh, his hair. It was beautiful.'

'That's Murray. And yeah.' Beth sipped half her beer in one. 'He's all those things. And then some. Only he's not gay, so butt out.'

'Enzo will be pleased. But do tell.'

'What exactly?'

'Come on, my betrothed, out with it. You agree he's hot totty, so what's the story?'

'Guess.' Heat rose in Beth's neck, swelling her cheeks. 'I can't say it.'

'You're in love?' Frank's blue eyes burst wide.

'Yup.'

'Oh, my god! My betrothed.' His hand leapt across the table and held Beth's. 'You're actually in love. And does this paragon share your love?'

'No. Well, not any more. I thought he did. Everything was just fine, and I blew it.'

'Really? Have you and him?' He winked towards the door.

'No. Well, we kissed. Things got heated. But I'm. You know. There aren't a lot of men around here. And he's, well, you see what he's like.'

'I most certainly do.' Frank stroked her hand. The ache in Beth's chest lightened. 'Why not tell him your fears, darling? If he doesn't accept you, he's not worth it. If you're really in love with him, then who better to start with. And if he turns out to be a rotten egg, he'll have your fiancé to deal with.'

Beth almost cried into her glass. 'Thanks.'

The meeting on Friday afternoon was jotted on the calendar, but Beth wasn't sure what to do. Should she even go? After a week of indecision spent entertaining Frank, when Friday came, she paced about the upper field, edgy and uncertain. What to do? She'd half expected a call or a reminder, but Murray had gone deadly silent. She didn't dare message him. What would she say? She'd turned him down once too often, and he hated indecision. If she told him now, would he be mad? Was he over her? A pain in her chest prickled away. Was this a broken heart? It felt like a gash nothing could fix except Murray. But if she really wanted him, she had truths to confess, sickening, embarrassing truths.

When she returned home for lunch, Gillian was unloading shopping bags. She closed the fridge door and frowned. 'That Janet Henderson has a lot to answer for. She ate me out of house and home. That's me finally got to the shops to restock.'

'Hmm.' Beth stared out the window as she scrubbed her hands.

'Beth, you might think I'm a clueless old woman, but I'm not that daft. Something's going on. I know it is hard for you running the farm, and how difficult it's been, and Kirsten and I are of very little help, but this is more. I hoped you'd tell me in your own time, but I feel totally in the dark. So, will you please tell me what is going on with you and Frank?'

Beth's forehead creased. 'What?' Not the name she'd expected. Or the question. 'Frank?'

'Yes, Frank! The man you've been at the pub with almost every night this week. The one who rang up asking to talk to his betrothed, saying it was your fiancé. I remember when you were younger you had all sorts of silly plans. I never suspected any of them were true. Until I, well, I know I shouldn't have, but I noticed the message he sent you on your birthday. I couldn't believe it. Kirsten said she thought it was a joke, so I left it, but after the phone call, it set me wondering again. Even Murray knew about the engagement. When were you going to tell me?'

Glaring, Beth slapped the tabletop. 'Murray? Murray thinks I'm engaged to Frank?'

'Well, are you? What the devil *is* going on?'

'Of course not. Frank's gay.'

'Yes, I noticed. I suspected when he was younger, but when he called saying those things, I wasn't sure. People swing both ways. Now, that I see him again, it's obvious and I don't want you to get hurt.'

Rubbing her forehead, Beth gritted her teeth. 'Why would I get hurt? It's not real. He calls me names like that all the time, they're silly nicknames we used to call each other at school. How could you really think that?'

'Well, you don't talk about things like that. How was I to know?'

Beth pinched the bridge of her nose. 'Seriously? And Murray? How did he find out?'

'I assumed you told him. It hurt me a bit, you'd told him, and not me.'

'I didn't tell anyone because there was nothing to tell. Have you told anyone else?'

Putting her hand to her chest, Gillian pulled out the corner of her mouth. 'Oh, Beth. Don't be mad. I told Janet Henderson. She was here when I got the call, I was confused. She was all over me, questioning me about you and Murray. I wasn't sure what to say. She seemed to think you and he were somehow involved.

Well, it just came out about Frank. She latched onto it straight away and I just let her because it kept her busy.'

Slowly, Beth closed her eyes and opened them again.

'It's ok.' Gillian stretched her hand across the table and placed it over Beth's. Beth snatched it away.

'No, it isn't.' She wanted to stamp her feet and scream. 'Don't you get it?' She swore and fisted her forehead.

'Please, calm down.'

'Calm down? Murray thinks I'm engaged. Oh, my god!' Shaking her head, she tried to knock sense into it. Was this why he'd gone cold?

Gillian furrowed her brow. 'What is all this about Murray? Why is it such a big deal?'

Jumping to her feet, Beth drew in a huge breath. 'I need to go and talk to him.'

He'd be at the meeting soon. Beth dashed to her room and threw on some make-up. Kirsten was busy, so she did it herself. Leaning towards the mirror, she moved her head from side to side. Not too bad. She wasn't a model, but she'd pass as respectable. Her hand shook as she finished her mascara. The nerves weren't about the meeting. She couldn't care less about it. If some landowner persuaded Murray to hold off on the road, it would be more than she'd managed. No. She needed to catch him. If he believed she was engaged, he might do something crazy. Like leave. She didn't want that. If she were there, she could keep her eye on him, catch him at the end. Talk to him. Her heart pounded. She needed to get him somewhere quiet. Somehow, she had to get the words out. The right ones.

It mattered. He mattered. It was real, and she had to do something about it even if she made a fool of herself. Before she left, she waited in the kitchen for Gillian to come in from feeding the hens.

As Gillian stepped inside, she sized up Beth. 'You look nice. Are you all right?'

'Yes, stop asking me that.'

'I have to because you don't talk to me.' Gillian kicked off her boots and looked up. 'Not about anything important.'

'If you really want to know, I'm off to find Murray,' Beth said the words deliberately, staring at her mother. 'And tell him…' She swallowed. 'That I.' Why were her eyes misting over?

'Oh, Beth.' Gillian marched forward and hugged her. 'Save the words for him. I know what you mean. Go find him and tell him. You're so strong, you've held this place together for years. You deserve to be happy.'

Beth entered the Dervaig Hall with searching eyes. No Murray. She hadn't even noticed his car. Joyce Paterson sat near the back wall with an empty seat beside her, Beth bagged it.

'Oh, hello.' Joyce looked up and smiled. 'Long time no see. I haven't seen you since the last meeting.'

'I've had so much going on with the lambing and everything.'

'Well, I've heard something very interesting on the grapevine.'

Beth dreaded what was coming next.

'Murray Henderson may be on his way out.'

Beth furrowed her brow. 'He's leaving?'

'Well.' Joyce turned round in her seat and faced Beth, obviously pleased she had something new. 'I ran into Donald earlier. He'd just spoken to Murray. I don't know what Mr Crichton-Leith is going to say, but whatever it is, Murray's got jumpy. He told Donald he wants to cut his contract short. His family were over last weekend and it's brought things home.'

Beth rubbed her forehead. Just as she thought. How could she tell him in time? What if he'd already given his notice? Like he'd done with his other job when his ex had changed her mind. She'd done the same thing, he'd never forgive her. Ever. Scraping back her seat, she decided she had to find him. But before she could move, the door opened. Murray came in with Archibald Crichton-Leith. Both men were stony-faced and grim. Murray glanced at Beth but looked away so quickly she didn't have time to acknowledge him. After adjusting his tie, he placed his iPhone on the table and flexed his long fingers. He was in a slick suit and... *Oh man*. Beth gaped. He was just gorgeous.

Fixed on his beautiful eyes, she listened as he welcomed them and introduced Archibald Crichton-Leith. Murray didn't look anywhere near her. 'As the owner of the Ardnish Estate that backs directly onto the West Mull Woods, Mr Crichton-Leith has some information to share, so I'll hand over to him.'

'Yes, thank you.' Archibald Crichton-Leith flicked the auburn tinged hair at his brow.

Joyce smirked at Beth. 'He's a bit of posh totty, isn't he?' she whispered. 'It's nice having a bit of eye-candy, between him and Murray, it's quite a treat.'

Beth only had eyes for Murray. No one came close in her book. Even as Archibald spoke, she couldn't stop staring at Murray. Did he sense it? He fingered his collar, still resolutely looking elsewhere.

'Although I don't live permanently at Ardnish, it's my duty to keep up with local developments.'

Beth snorted but passed it off as a cough. Finally, Murray glanced at her. His face twitched, and he looked away quickly.

'I've commissioned several land, marine, and ecology surveys regarding the new logging road's proposed location. We have discovered some considerably rare orchids. I believe the destruction of this area to create a path would be devastating for the area if it incurred the loss of any rare species, and therefore not in keeping with the group's aims.'

Murray sat impassively, his hands tented at the table, his jaw set. Only his thumbs moved, tapping together. 'Thank you,' he said as Archibald concluded. 'Because of these findings, the road plans will be put on hold until we find a more suitable solution.

I might add nothing would have gone ahead without our own land surveys.'

Poor Murray. He looked crestfallen. His baby lay by the wayside with no certainty of being picked up again. He checked his phone. Perhaps he was expecting some last-minute reprieve from the ecologist. The orchids were not there after all. Whatever, it didn't come; he looked away with a sigh.

A debate started, and a few people questioned Archibald. 'What was the point of a marine survey?' Neil Paterson asked.

'I wanted to be thorough. Although the road doesn't go directly to the sea, we have many coastal plants and wildlife species nearby.'

Beth wrestled her phone from her pocket. Keeping it low, she hashed out a text.

BETH: I am NOT engaged. Fiancé Frank is a nickname. Frank's my best mate, that's all.

Her heart pumped too fast. She pushed send and waited, holding her breath.

Seconds later, Murray looked at his phone. His brow furrowed, and he glanced up, straight into her eyes. She folded her arms and peered back at him, her eyebrow slightly raised. He opened his mouth like he was about to say something, remembered where he was and closed it again. Clinging to her phone, Beth's thumbs moved across the screen like lightning.

BETH: I have a confession. I feel really stupid about it, but I've never been with anyone, ever. You were my first kiss, and that's as far as I've got. I feel totally inadequate. Sorry. x

With a deep intake of breath, Beth hit send and waited with her lips pressed together, barely able to force her eyes upward. What would he think?

Glancing down, Murray's brows furrowed. He half shook his head. His mouth opened and closed, he swallowed, his Adam's apple pulsed. Beth fixated on the layer of barely-there stubble covering it, her heart hammering. The flush of heat in her cheeks burned like being up against a naked flame.

'What do you think?' Archibald Crichton-Leith fired at Murray.

Murray stared at his phone. 'I, eh.'

'It seems to me,' Neil Paterson said, on the other side of his wife, 'that you've lost the plot, Mr Henderson. We had high expectations from you, but so far there haven't been many actions. There's a lot of fancy stuff on the website, but it hasn't translated into action.'

Murray's face hardened, but his eyes sank back to the message. Beth bristled. She had an urge to hurt Neil Paterson and her fists balled.

'It might look like that,' Murray defended, 'but some of our plans are long-term aims.'

'What about the toilets?' Neil countered. 'Still nothing on them?'

Beth felt only a tiny flicker of amusement as Joyce smirked at her.

'I believe a team has been booked to install them in a couple of weeks.'

'You believe?' Neil said, incredulous.

Archibald Crichton-Leith sat up straight. 'Please,' he said, 'my findings were not meant to discredit Mr Henderson.'

Rolling his eyes, Murray gritted his teeth. He looked ready to stand up, fling the folder of papers across the table and leave, possibly lamping Archibald Crichton-Leith on his way to the door. 'All right,' said Murray. 'This is just an emergency meeting to discuss this particular hitch. I can assure you all the other work that was agreed is coming along fine. At our next scheduled meeting, all updates will be presented. Perhaps we can keep our grievances until then.'

'Why?' Neil asked. 'When else do we get to have our say?'

'You're welcome to discuss anything at any time.' Murray fingered his iPhone. 'I'd just like to stick to the agenda here.'

'And what about the gala day?' asked another woman. 'It's in May and I've heard nothing about it. Usually, we have the whole thing planned by now. It's only a couple of weeks away.'

'Yes, everything for the gala day is ready.' Murray looked towards Anna Maxwell, the secretary. 'You've sent all the emails?'

'Eh, it's on my to-do list.'

'So, the emails will go out to you this week,' said Murray.

A hoard of voices started up again. Murray's face glazed over like he was listening but not hearing a thing. His eyes strayed to his phone before he raised them to Beth.

Her heart hammered. It was so loud in her ears maybe everyone could hear it too. What had he made of the messages? It was too late to take them back. He looked broken, like his hard work had led to nothing. Everyone wanted to rip a shred of flesh from his back.

Beth coughed. 'Listen up,' she said, surprised at how loud her words were. Everyone looked at her. Fever fired into her cheeks. 'I think it's time for everyone to back down and shut up. This isn't the time or place to air your petty gripes. If you haven't had an email about the gala day, so what. Is it really going to change your life? If Murray says it's coming next week, then expect it next week. And as for you.' She glared at Archibald Crichton-Leith. 'You better have some bloody impressive evidence about the existence of these orchids because it sounds like a load of pompous tripe to me. Murray fully intends to have his own surveys carried out, and if these refute your evidence, it's going to make you look very dodgy.'

'Listen, Ms McGregor—' Archibald said.

'Don't you Ms me. Just make sure all the information you have is accurate.'

'All I want to do is what's right for the community.'

'Then butt out and let us get on with it. You don't even live here most of the time. It's my land the surveys refer to. I'm sure there's a way to get this road without affecting any native species.'

'That may be so.' Archibald loosened his collar. 'And I would be quite happy with that. If you'll keep me informed on the progress.'

'I'm sure Murray's secretary won't mind doing that.' Beth swallowed and glanced at Anna, aware of Joyce's bulging eyes gaping.

'I, I, yes, I will,' Anna said.

Murray frowned, mouthing at Beth. His fingers stroked the screen of his phone.

'Good. Well, that's all. Now, excuse me.' Face redder than a tomato, Beth stormed to the door, looking at no one. In the corridor she flopped against the wall, heart still pounding, digging her fingers into her cheeks. The heat was unbearable. She needed to get out before Murray digested the message. Why had she sent it? He hadn't made any kind of reaction that suggested his feelings. Or anything. Maybe she'd got it all wrong.

The door banged open, and she jumped. 'Beth.' Peering around, she watched Murray emerge. Her heart walloped, trying to break free. Shaking his head, Murray held up his hands and whispered, 'Please, wait here. I wanted to make sure you didn't leave. I need to sort that lot out.' He corrected his tie and tweaked his lapels. 'Then we need to talk.'

That was it? Talk? How ominous did that sound? Hiding in the disabled toilet, Beth waited, listening to Murray thanking everyone and dodging questions. A scraping of seats from within, twittering voices and footsteps in the corridor all eventually died away. What now? With shaky limbs, she listened.

'Where are you?' Murray's voice spoke from outside the door. She opened it a crack. Murray frowned as she emerged. 'Beth, I don't know what to say.'

'Then don't, I already look like I've been out in the midday sun for too long. I shouldn't have said anything. Why do you want to talk to me?'

'Isn't it obvious?'

Shrugging, she glanced around, ready for the humiliation. 'I guess. My message.'

He furrowed his brow and shook his head a fraction. 'Well, yes, and no. Let's go outside, it's a beautiful day.' Turning off the lights, he held out his arm for Beth to pass. They made their way outside into the fresh, cloudless afternoon. Murray loosened his tie.

'Just get it over with. Say what you have to say.'

Cocking his head to the side, he smiled. 'Beth, all I really want to say is... I love you.'

'What?'

He nodded, pulling up his left shoulder a fraction. 'Just that. I love you.'

Biting her lip, Beth stared. He moved forward, leaned in, and captured her mouth so deeply, she almost fainted. Grabbing his tie, she held him close. Could she hold the moment forever? The taste of his lips, the woody scent, the strength in his body, the way his starched collar grazed her neck. She arched into him, slipping her hand inside his charcoal suit jacket, and anchoring her fingers around his belt, his lips glued to hers.

Pulling back, she trailed her hand down his cheek, across the bristles of his immaculate beard. 'You understood my message, right?'

'Sure, but don't sweat it. Just think of the catch up we get to play.'

'It doesn't bother you?' She searched his eyes.

'Why would it? A person isn't defined by one experience. I love the girl in here.' He almost crushed her against him. 'And it's not like you're a blushing novice, you're full of passion. Just because you haven't taken that one step, doesn't mean you're a failure.'

'I just feel stupid about it.'

'Well, don't. Your spirit and determination are what make you so special. I think I've been a little bit in love with you, ever since I saw you wrestling a highland cow. Possibly the weirdest thing I've ever found attractive.'

She let out a little laugh and smirked. 'Honestly, that's the easy part of my life.' Beth tugged at the neck of her top as Murray slipped off his jacket; the sight was causing her a cardiac arrest. 'I wanted you to know that. Well, that I...'

'It's ok, Beth. You don't have to say it.' He slid his hand around her waist. The jacket slung over his arm pressed into her back as he pulled her in, kissing her again.

She melted as he held her so tight she was part of him. Her fingers rested on his broad chest, stroking the shirt fabric. 'Stop.'

He tucked a strand of her hair behind her ear, holding the connection between their eyes with such force, Beth could hardly bring herself to speak, but she had to.

'What's wrong?' he asked.

'I do have to say it. And I will. I can do it.' She took a deep breath. 'Murray, I love you.'

Murray grinned, then broke into a laugh. It dazzled her more than the blue sky. If this wasn't a moment for celebrating, what was?

'That's great to hear.' He beamed.

'How about we go for that drink then?' She ran her gaze over him, took hold of the end of his tie and drew him forward. 'I can beat you at darts, and later on, you can show me your moves for real.'

'You bet.' Thrusting his arm around her, Murray held her close. 'We might even get to "Strip the Willow".'

Beth rubbed her cheek over his warm shoulder until she couldn't resist kissing him again. Inhaling the warmth of his breath, she relaxed, pulling back and arching her eyebrow. 'That's still the world's worst pick-up line, Murray.'

'Yeah, it is. But, hey. Worked, didn't it? I'm the guy walking off with the most amazing girl on the island.'

If he believed so, who was she to disagree? Even if she missed the bullseye every time that afternoon in the pub, she was the one heading home with the prize.

EPILOGUE

Beth

At the Easter dance, Murray had predicted he and Beth would make fireworks. As she straddled him in bed, letting new and exciting sensations rock her world, she knew he'd been oh so right.

'God, Beth,' he groaned, lying beneath her, his hands fixed on her hips, his normally immaculate hair spread wide on the soft white pillow as he gazed at her with his wolfish grin. 'You're incredible.'

Beth leaned forward, bracing herself on his shoulders as pleasure built fast and hot. She couldn't stop what was coming and she didn't try. Any embarrassment she thought she'd feel had been swept away over the last fortnight. Now she couldn't get enough of Murray and visits to the Westview Cottages had become a regular part of her schedule. He'd re-routed her world and had a way of making her feel like a goddess. Whatever hang-ups she'd harboured were well and truly put to bed.

Her body took on a life of its own. Moaning and grinding against him, she fell over the edge of desire. Seconds later, he groaned in pleasure. As the tremors died, her body sagged, and she flopped onto his chest. He held her tight, stroking her hair and pressing a dreamy kiss on her forehead. 'I love you so much,' he whispered.

'I love you too, but we can't hang about. We've got the fair to sort out. I need to get to the hall.'

Murray rolled her over, resting on top of her. 'You do, but if we're ten minutes late, who'll notice?'

'Um... Everyone.'

He kissed her through his laugh. 'Ok. Let's get up then.'

Showered and dressed, they made their way to the village hall. Beth got stuck in lifting boxes of decorations, while Murray spoke to some people from the committee.

'So, what's the goss?' Georgia giggled, unpacking a box of spring decorations.

'What do you mean?' Beth hauled another box from under the stage and dumped it beside Georgia.

'Any details on the new and exciting lurve life?'

'Like I'm going to tell you that. Sod off, you nosey-parker.'

Georgia grinned at Kirsten. Beth saw them and ignored it. Whatever they were fishing for, she wasn't going to tell.

'I just can't believe it,' Kirsten said, holding the end of a string of bunting to the wall, reaching on tiptoes to a spot just out of her arm's length.

'Tell me about it.' How stoic farmer Beth had landed the stud that was Murray would end up the stuff of legends. Beth took the string's end from her sister and placed it half a metre further up. Kirsten scowled, but Beth lifted her eyebrow. 'It's not my fault I'm taller than you.'

'I love it,' Georgia said. 'I had a fimbling-feeling it would end well. And Murray is so gorgeous, you lucky thing.'

'Should I be jealous?' Beth hung the bunting's other end to the far side of the hall.

'No.' Georgia smiled. 'He's all yours.'

'How did you manage to find someone before me?' said Kirsten. 'When you weren't even looking?'

'Life likes to throw you a curveball every now and then.' Beth grinned. *And I waited for a long time.*

'I wish it would throw me one. Speaking of which, what is Mum like? Can you believe she thought you were engaged to Frank? How funny is that?'

'Not that funny,' Beth said. 'Just as well Frank's not staying, he fancies Murray more than his boyfriend, I think.'

'Well, Murray only has eyes for you,' said Kirsten. 'And you've leapt from zero interest to can't get enough in thirty days.'

Beth smiled as she looked around at the finished room. 'It was a bit longer than that. I guess no one tickled my fancy before.'

'I bet that's not all he's tickled.' Georgia grinned.

Beth's cheeks reddened, but she didn't reply. Murray's moves didn't disappoint.

'Hey.' Murray poked his head around the door. 'It's looking great in here. Thanks, girls.' Approaching Beth, he slid his arm around the small of her back. 'And you're looking especially gorgeous,' he whispered, pulling her in for a kiss. She melted, not even caring the others were watching. He was irresistible.

'Get a room,' Kirsten muttered.

'Sorry.' Murray smirked, sharing a look with Beth.

'So, what's to do outside?' she asked, rubbing her forehead on his.

'I need your help with the stage, no one seems to know how to build it.'

Rolling her eyes, she followed him out. 'That's what happens when you leave a group of guys in charge.'

After figuring out how to fix up the stage, Beth looked up to see Kirsten and Georgia chatting at one of the stalls.

'I feel bad for them,' she said aside to Murray. 'They'd both love to find somebody, and I've snuck under the wire and robbed them.'

'Not of me. They're nice girls, but I wouldn't have dated either of them. You're the only one.' Murray beamed. 'And don't worry about them, they're both young. Someone will come along. Look at us.' He wrapped his arms around her waist from behind, kissing the back of her neck. 'When I arrived here two months ago, I'd never have believed this.'

With the gala day in full flow, Murray headed off to check the games stall and Beth helped Gillian carry trays of home baking into the hall. Gillian flapped around, manically organising her stall, but something about her gave Beth a prickle of anxiety. Gillian seemed a bit too obsessively preoccupied with the tiny details of her table and the positioning of plates, avoiding Beth's eyes. Anything to prevent talking to her.

'Are you ok, Mum?'

Stopping dead, Gillian stared at the trays balanced behind her stall before turning to face her. 'Oh, Beth. I'm fine.'

'Come on, Mum. Tell me. I can see something's up. And don't say it's the stress, you do things like this with your eyes shut.'

'I don't want to say anything to upset you.' Her eyes misted over.

'Mum, what's wrong? Have I done something? Is it Murray?'

'No, well, yes.'

A chill of anguish flooded Beth. It was possible to love Murray without Gillian's approval, but it would be so much better with it.

'I'm delighted for you, Beth. I truly am. I like Murray. I thought he was a slippery fish when we first met, but I was wrong. He's helpful and charming. It's just...'

'Well, what?'

'I worry about the future. So many things. He only has a two-year contract. What will happen after that? Will he leave? Will you go with him? I can't see how things will work. Most of all, I want you to be happy, but I feel so uncertain.'

'Listen, Mum.' Beth pulled her in and hugged her, she was so tall, Gillian barely reached her shoulder. 'It might not even get that far. Everything's new just now. I can't see the future.'

'I'm sorry, I shouldn't have said anything. Maybe seeing you so happy has made me a bit lonely.' Gillian recovered herself, straightened up and smoothed off her apron. 'But it doesn't change how pleased I am for you.'

'I miss Dad too.' Beth bit her lip.

'Yes, we all do.' Gillian reached up and stroked her cheek. 'We've been blessed to have you. We'd have lost everything if it weren't for you. Now, please, don't worry about things. You get out and enjoy yourself. Enjoy that lovely man and the rush of young love. Go on, off you go. Forget what I said, it was just a silly moment.'

Beth strolled out, looking for another job to do, or Murray, whichever she found first. Gillian's words drifted around her head and, try as she might, Beth couldn't simply forget. Because the same ideas plagued her too. Negative thoughts threatened to penetrate the fluffy cushion of happiness. Would they still be together in two years? Or two months? She wanted him so badly. It wrenched her gut to even consider ending it, but she had no certainty this wasn't just a passing thing. Her heart wanted so much but could she be sure Murray did?

'Hey.' Beth felt Murray's hand tug hers as she wandered around, her brow furrowed as she stared at him. 'Are you ok? You look stressed.'

'I'm fine,' she said.

A microphone screeched, and Carl Hansen got onto the makeshift stage with his guitar. Murray turned to watch. Beth lowered her head. Could she bear to condemn the bright spring nights, the bliss of waking on Murray's chest, and the sound of his heartbeat to memory, when it had only just started?

'Beth, I know that face. What's up?' Murray said.

'Nothing.'

Carl tapped the mic. 'I'd like to sing this for my girlfriend, Robyn.' He strummed a few notes before beginning the song, "You're Beautiful".

Murray wrapped his arm around Beth's waist. 'That's cute,' he said, 'but don't expect me to do that. I really can't sing.'

'Yeah, please don't. I'd die of embarrassment.'

'But you are beautiful,' he whispered in her ear.

Beth's eyes landed on Kirsten. She was close to the stage but moved away as soon as Carl began his song. Standing alone, a little up a hill, she watched, hugging herself. Carl was the man Kirsten had dreamed of. As his song ended, she sidled away towards the hall.

'Maybe I should go to her,' said Beth.

'I expect she wants to be alone,' Murray said, joining in the applause with his arms still around her. Beth rested her head on his shoulder. His grip on her waist tightened. 'Let's go for a walk.'

With a glance towards the hall door, she held Murray's hand as he led them onto the road and down the hill, past the pub towards the shore.

'Where are we going?'

'Let's sit for a bit,' he said. They got to the low marshy area near the water's edge and Murray dropped onto a flat boulder, patting it for Beth to join him. He put his arm around her, and she mirrored his move. The sea lapped the shore a few metres from their feet, on the grassy inlet. 'I know what's up, Beth, because the same things are bothering me.'

'What things?' Beth stiffened; his voice sounded grave.

'I only have a contract for two years. I don't know if it'll be renewed after that or not. It depends on lots of things.'

'Yeah.' Beth looked at her knees. The rug was set to be pulled from beneath her feet. This too-short dream was ending already. And she wasn't nearly done. They'd barely started. 'Murray, I know, but—'

'The thing is…' He traced his finger down her cheek. She melted in its wake. 'I don't want to go after two years. I want to stay here. I want to cuddle up, make lots of babies, and grow old and grey with you.'

'Murray.' Beth's eyes teared up. She bit her lip, not sure if she wanted to laugh or cry. Was this for real?

'And, Beth, I'd like to learn the farm ways. Even if it's paperwork, being your labourer, or bringing you as much cheese and chocolate as you can eat, whatever, I'll do it. Then I can help you and make it my life too.'

He was serious? Someone wanted this life? To help her? 'So...'

'So, is that something that sounds ok to you?'

Beth's face relaxed, her body followed. 'Well, I never decided what I wanted in return for letting the road go ahead. This might be acceptable. Especially the cheese and chocolate.' She winked. 'Though you'll need to get used to mucky clothes.' Closing her eyes, she allowed the warmth of what he'd said to penetrate every vein.

Before she could open them, a soft kiss landed on her lips. 'I'll try.'

'Just don't ditch the suits forever. You've no idea how many fantasies you wearing them has fulfilled for me in the past couple of weeks.'

Murray's cheeks split with a laugh. 'I'm so glad. And likewise, you keep wielding that chainsaw and we'll be fine.' He watched her for a few seconds. 'Beth. Seriously, I'm in it for the long haul.' His smile was wide. He was so handsome, Beth almost nipped herself. How had she landed someone this incredible? A stray hair fell over his right eye. Beth reached for it and threaded it back into place.

'Me too, Murray.'

He slid his arm around her shoulder and kissed her again. 'You've driven me crazy since the moment I clapped eyes on you. Now, we can drive each other crazy for the rest of our days.'

Beth traced her finger down his bearded cheek and rubbed noses with him. 'There's an offer I can't refuse.'

They locked eyes, smiling. Beth couldn't wait to start the rest of her life with Murray, but right now, she just wanted to gaze into those pools of grey, knowing he was all hers.

The End

MORE BOOKS BY MARGARET AMATT

Scottish Island Escapes

A Winter Haven

A Spring Retreat

A Summer Sanctuary

An Autumn Hideaway

A Christmas Bluff

A Flight of Fancy

A Hidden Gem

A Striking Result

A Perfect Discovery

A Festive Surprise

The Glenbriar Series

New Beginnings in Glenbriar

(A free short story to introduce the series)

Stolen Kisses at the Loch View Hotel
Just Friends at Thistle Lodge
Pitching up at Heather Glen
Two's Company at the Forest Light Show
Highland Fling on the Whisky Trail

Free Hugs & Old-Fashioned Kisses

A short story only available to Newsletter Subscribers

ACKNOWLEDGMENTS

Thanks goes to my adorable husband for supporting my dreams and putting up with my writing talk 24/7. Also to my son, whose interest in my writing always makes me smile. It's precious to know I've passed the bug to him – he's currently writing his own fantasy novel and instruction books on how to build Lego!

Throughout the writing process, I have gleaned help from many sources and met some fabulous people. I'd like to give a special mention to Stéphanie Ronckier, my beta reader extraordinaire. Stéphanie's continued support with my writing is invaluable and I love the fact that I need someone French to correct my grammar! Stéphanie, you rock. To my lovely friend, Lyn Williamson, thank you for your continued support and encouragement with all my projects. And to my fellow authors, Evie Alexander and Lyndsey Gallagher – you girls are the best! I love it that you always have my back and are there to help when I need you.

Also, a huge thanks to my editor, Aimee Walker, for her excellent work on my novels and for answering all my mad questions. Thank you so much, Aimee!

ABOUT THE AUTHOR

Margaret Amatt

Margaret has told and written stories for as long as she can remember. During her formative years, she spent time on long walks inventing characters and stories to pass the time.

Writing books is Margaret's passion and when she's not doing that, she's often found eating chocolate, walking and taking photographs in the hills around Highland Perthshire. Those long walks still frequently bring inspiration!

It's Margaret's pleasure to bring you the Scottish Island Escapes series and The Glenbriar Series. These books are linked (even the two series have crossovers!) for those who enjoy inhabiting Margaret's world of stories but each can be read as a standalone if you'd rather dip in and out with individual books.

You can find more information about Margaret on her website or by signing up for her newsletter.

www.margaretamatt.com

MAP OF MULL

*The Isle of Mull where the Scottish Island
Escapes series is set*

Ingram Content Group UK Ltd.
Milton Keynes UK
UKHW040849090523
421432UK00005B/41

9 781914 575723